THE OFFICE WAS A MESS.

Papers and a few books were scattered about the floor. Latham's desk chair was lying on its back behind the desk. Daniel Latham himself was on the floor over by the far wall. He lay faceup, curled in a strange and unnatural position. Mak'Tor knelt next to Latham

k-
amining   e,
as the K   ld
see was   ss
body of

Then Mak'Tor looked over his shoulder at them and snarled. . . .

STAR TREK

The Case

of the

Colonist's

Corpse

A
SAM COGLEY
MYSTERY

BOB INGERSOLL AND TONY ISABELLA

POCKET BOOKS
New York   London   Toronto   Sydney   Singapore

An *Original* Publication of POCKET BOOKS

POCKET BOOKS, a division of Simon & Schuster, Inc.
1230 Avenue of the Americas, New York, NY 10020

This book is published by Pocket Books, a division of
Simon & Schuster, Inc., under exclusive license from
Paramount Pictures.

ISBN: 0-7434-6497-4

First Pocket Books paperback edition January 2004

10 9 8 7 6 5 4 3 2 1

POCKET and colophon are registered trademarks of
Simon & Schuster, Inc.

Manufactured in the United States of America

For information regarding special discounts for bulk purchases,
please contact Simon & Schuster Special Sales at 1-800-456-6798
or business@simonandschuster.com.

To our parents—Jack and Kay Ingersoll and Louis and Florence Isabella—for giving us our imaginations and sense of justice and encouraging us to use them.

ACKNOWLEDGMENTS

No book, not even one written in collaboration, is written in isolation. The authors wish to acknowledge the following people for their invaluable contributions to *Star Trek: The Case of the Colonist's Corpse:*

Gene Roddenberry, who gave us all a universe to play in.

Earl Stanley Gardner, creator of Perry Mason, who gave us a template.

Don M. Mankiewicz and Steven W. Carabatsos, the writers of "Court Martial," who gave us the Samuel T. Cogley character to play with.

John Ordover, our editor, the man who first suggested we take that character and write a Perry Mason novel with him and whose support for the project was unflagging.

Keith R.A. DeCandido, who aided and abetted and made the story even better.

Michael and Denise Okuda, whose *Star Trek Encyclopedia* and *Star Trek Chronology* were more than just invaluable.

Bjo Trimble, whose *Star Trek Concordance* was no less valuable.

Marc Okrand for *The Klingon Dictionary.*

Roger Price, Bill Thom, and Tom Condosta, who helped keep us on course.

Becky Ingersoll, Laura Ingersoll, Robby Ingersoll, Barb Isabella, Eddie Isabella, and Kelly Isabella, who helped keep us sane.

Last, but certainly not least, Thom Zahler, something of a *Star Trek* encyclopedia in his own right, who also kept us on course and who could be called on and counted on any time of the day to supply useful suggestions, insights, and information such as, the Klingon disruptor settings are not disrupt, kill, and purée.

Thanks to all.

The Case

of the

Colonist's

Corpse

1. "Your Honor, I must object!"

Alexander Warren was on his feet as swiftly as if he'd been fired from a photon torpedo tube, practically leaping from behind the prosecutor's table to give emphasis to the objection he had just made.

Samuel T. Cogley looked over his shoulder at the imposingly brawny Warren and noted the prosecutor's face was as crimson as a Big Sky sunset. The older, decidedly not brawny defense attorney chuckled to himself. Even in the far reaches of space, images of Earth were never far from his thoughts. You can take the boy out of Montana . . .

Cogley could see the defense table from the corner of his eye. His executive assistant, Jacqueline LaSalle, had moved Cogley's pen off his pad of paper and put it on the desk, something Cogley would never do. He was obsessive about there being a place for everything and everything being in its place. Pens were not meant to lie on polished tabletops, when there was a perfectly serviceable pad of paper available.

He smiled and looked for a moment at Jackie. Her bright green eyes and wide smile practically jumped out at him from under her red-brown hair. Jackie was telling him their preparations were complete. Cogley tugged once at the bottom of his plain brown suit coat. It was time for the main event.

Cogley walked over to his opponent's table until he almost stood next to Warren. Side by side, prosecutor and defense attorney appeared to be a mismatch. Warren towered over Cogley's thin, five-foot, five-inch frame. Cogley didn't let the mismatch deter him. He fixed his pale blue eyes on Warren and spread his arms wide—his hands open and his palms up to show they were empty. Then he turned back to Judge Faure and gave her a smile that seemed to ask, "Who, me?"

" 'Must'? I'm sorry, Your Honor, I didn't realize that I was pointing my death ray at Mr. Warren."

"I beg your pardon?" Warren asked.

"You said you 'must object,' implying you were being forced into objecting. As I can assure the court, I have no mind-control powers. I can only assume I must have been pointing a death ray or some equally fearsome weapon at you."

The resulting outburst of laughter was even louder than Cogley had dared hope. Even as the judge struck her gavel repeatedly on the bench and demanded that order be restored to her court at once, Cogley knew his comment had had its desired effect: everyone in the courtroom was off his or her guard, unsure of what might come next.

Especially the witness.

As the laughter dwindled, Cogley looked back over his shoulder at the defense table and at his client, Aaron Cole, regretting what he saw. Cole squirmed in his seat, then leaned over to Jackie, his discomfort obvious in the way he moved.

"Ms. LaSalle, is it wise for Mr. Cogley to upset the court this way?" Cole asked her.

Jackie smiled, a look designed to give reassurance to the client. A look she'd had manifold opportunities to perfect.

"Don't worry, Aaron. When Sam gets this way, he has them right where he wants them. Just watch."

Once the laughter had ended, which was obviously taking longer than Judge Faure wanted, Cogley turned to her and spoke before she could.

"I'm sorry, Your Honor. It's just that Mr. Warren was being somewhat imprecise in his speech. Words are still, after all, our tools, our most important means of communication . . . when they are used properly. I guess I just forgot myself."

"If Mr. Cogley wants precision, I'll be more than happy to accommodate him," Warren said, his voice as edged as a Klingon *bat'leth*. Then he continued, putting a slight pause between each of his words, to demonstrate how precise he could be.

"He is asking leading questions of his own witness."

"A most hostile witness, Your Honor, if I may be permitted to demonstrate . . ."

Before the judge could respond, Cogley turned back to the witness stand and looked directly at the Kradian seated there. Sahirn P'Thall stared back at Cogley with a withering glare that the defense attorney would have called cold-blooded, if Kradians had circulatory systems. P'Thall was wearing his family clan's most formal attire, complete with the ceremonial tunic that proudly displayed the family stone in its sash. Cogley also noticed that P'Thall's twin eyestalks did not point at him, but away from him, a gesture by which the Kradian signified that he regarded Cogley as unworthy at best, contemptuous at worst.

"Mr. P'Thall," Cogley started to ask and noticed that both eyestalks turned toward him, even as the Kradian's glare widened so much that his eyes seemed to explode from his eyestalks. "Mister" was not a Kradian form of address; it was, in fact, an honorific that some Kradians found to be not an honor but an insult. If Cogley had harbored any doubts about his assessment of P'Thall's feelings toward humans, they were dispelled.

"Exactly what *are* your feelings toward Aaron Cole?"

P'Thall leaned back in the witness stand and sat up straight, stretching his more than six foot height to its utmost so that he could look down at Cogley. He did not even look at Aaron Cole, but waved his left hand in Cole's general direction in a gesture almost of dismissal.

"That *human* murdered my daughter Daleel P'Thall. How do you think I feel about the *grelth*?"

Cogley didn't miss the pointed emphasis P'Thall had put on the word "human."

"And are your feelings toward me, the *human*"—Cogley put the same inflection on the word that P'Thall had used—"representing Mr. Cole, equally enlightened?"

"You defend the *grelth*. Were it within my power, I would arrange for you to suffer the same richly deserved punishment that your client will endure."

Cogley turned to Judge Faure and smiled.

"As I said, Your Honor, hostile."

"You may proceed, Mr. Cogley," Judge Faure said, and Cogley noticed she seemed to be leaning forward ever so slightly. During his long career as a defense attorney, Samuel Cogley had earned a reputation for three things. The first was for being an eccentric, a reputation enhanced by his borderline obsessive compulsiveness, manifested most noticeably in his love of books and equally strong dislike of computers.

The second was his reputation for indulging in courtroom theatrics. This reputation was widespread, and Cogley was sure it had reached even here, to the vacation moon of Versailles in an out-of-the-way sector of United Federation of Planets space. Especially when his most recent courtroom theatrical, produced while he was representing Captain James T. Kirk in a court-martial, almost resulted in the destruction of Kirk's starship, the *U.S.S. Enterprise*. You don't nearly destroy a *Constitution*-class starship and expect the story won't spread.

However, it was the third thing Cogley was famous for—doggedly getting to the truth of the matters he litigated—that usually prompted judges to allow him to engage in those theatrics designed to ferret out the truth. Those judges who were concerned about justice, anyway.

Cogley had studied Judge Faure during the trial and was fairly sure he knew which type of magistrate she was. The next few minutes would either confirm or deny his assessment.

"Oh dear," Cogley said, "I appear to have lost my train of thought. No matter, I'll start at the beginning.

"Why here, Mr. P'Thall?"

"I beg your pardon?" P'Thall said.

"Versailles. A vacation moon for humans that simulates eighteenth-century France on Earth. It's primitive, doesn't allow spaceships or transporters or anything more advanced than horse-drawn carriages and oil lamps. Perfect for me, perhaps, but on Krador your family clan sells its engineering skills and technological expertise. Why would your family clan come to Versailles of all places?"

"We have started doing business with humans and felt we should learn more about them."

"Then why not go to Earth? Why here?"

"We have found we can learn much more about a species from the recreations it chooses than its usual routines. People tend to be more at ease, more natural when they're on vacation."

"How much could you learn about humans, when you rented an isolated castle on an island in the middle of a lake miles from any of the cities?"

"My family clan is quite large. Not only my wives and fellow husband, but the wives and husbands of our children accompanied us. The castle we rented had to be large enough to accommodate all of us together."

"Did your daughter recommend coming here?"

"She may have. She had been here before."

"In fact, Aaron Cole works here on Versailles and she met him here, correct?"

"Yes."

"Mr. P'Thall, isn't that the real reason you came to Versailles, to meet the human Daleel had fallen in love with?"

"It . . . was a consideration, yes."

"How did you feel about that?"

"I'm afraid I don't understand the question."

"Did you approve of Daleel's romance with Aaron?"

"It wasn't my place to approve. Who my daughter loved was her own choice."

Cogley walked back to the defense table and picked up a thick book. He thumbed through its pages for a moment, as if consulting it for some elusive fact. This was part habit and part theater on the attorney's part.

"Correct me if I'm wrong: the Kradians as a race prize both honor and family?"

"That is correct."

"And you didn't care that Daleel loved a human?"

"No. As I said, who she loved was her concern."

"A commendable attitude, Mr. P'Thall, considering her love for Aaron Cole cost your family both honor and stature among the other clans, as well as a good deal of business."

"It did neither."

"Oh? I thought you had arranged for your daughter to marry into the D'Quas, the family clan of your biggest customer, and when she refused, the D'Quas stopped doing business with you."

P'Thall didn't answer at first, staring pensively at Cogley, who had turned his back on the Kradian and put the book back on the defense table. Jackie then handed him several sheets of paper. Cogley took the papers, then turned back to P'Thall, who looked at him with fury seething behind his eyes. Then, very slowly and very deliberately, P'Thall said, "You were misinformed."

"You do that very well, Mr. P'Thall."

"Do what?"

"Lie."

Warren jumped to his feet and screamed, "Objection!" reaching a volume that startled the courtroom into silence. Cogley turned to the prosecutor and calmly said, "I apologize and withdraw the comment. For now."

He handed P'Thall the top sheet of paper.

"Mr. P'Thall, what is this?"

P'Thall took the paper and read it. At first all expression leeched from his pale blue face. Then the fury that had burned in his eyes consumed his entire face.

"Where did you get this? This was a private correspondence. I will have you arrested for stealing it from my office."

"Correspondence, Mr. P'Thall, has a recipient *and* a sender. In this case, you were the recipient. But after I explained to the D'Quas—the senders of this correspondence—what I needed and why, they were only too happy to supply me with a copy. They seemed delighted at the prospect of spreading word of the end of their dealings with you far and wide. To whoever would listen.

"The letter you're holding is from the head of the D'Quas family, your customer—excuse me, former customer—stating that after your daughter disgraced them by spurning the D'Quas marriage, they were canceling all their contracts with you, isn't it?"

"Yes."

"Come now, Mr. P'Thall, do you really think the jury could hear you when you're talking so softly? No matter, the record can reflect that you said, 'yes.'

"Now these other letters, which other senders were also only too happy to supply, all basically say that because of the manner in which your family disgraced the D'Quas, they were also canceling their contracts with you. Is that correct? Remember, answer loudly."

"Yes." P'Thall spat out the answer.

"So, when you testified earlier that Daleel's romance with Aaron Cole didn't cost your family clan either honor or stature or business with the other clans, that wasn't true, was it?"

P'Thall said nothing.

"Never mind, I think your silence speaks for itself. So you didn't come here just to learn more about humans, did you? You came here because Daleel was already here with Aaron. You came here to break them up, yes?"

"I—we came here to remind Daleel of her duty to her

family, yes. And we were successful. Daleel did break off her relationship with him. That's why he killed her."

"Yes, I've wondered just exactly how you got your daughter to break off her romance with Aaron. But no matter, you said she did and so she must have. After all, you're an honorable man. But what I really wonder is, how do you know Aaron killed your daughter? You didn't see Aaron kill Daleel, did you?"

"You know perfectly well that when my daughter died, my family and I were attending an opera here in New Paris."

"Yes, so you were. And how long did it take you to get to New Paris from your island?"

"As you yourself have pointed out, transportation on this moon is antiquated, intentionally so. I believe the word you humans use is 'quaint.' The trip took the better part of a day."

"So . . . you were nowhere near the island when your daughter was killed?"

"That is correct."

"Then, if you didn't see what happened, how can you be so sure Aaron killed your daughter?"

"No one else could have. Daleel was alone on the island. She didn't wish to accompany us to the opera and stayed behind. Flight isn't possible on Versailles, so the only means of getting to the island is by boat. The records of the harbormaster show that the only boat that went to our island was the one your client hired and that he was alone when he made the trip. As he was the only person who could have been on the island, he must have murdered Daleel, then fled afterwards.

"If you have any doubts about his guilt, ask him why he

went into hiding even before we returned to the castle the next day and found Daleel's body."

"Aaron admits he went to the island. He says Daleel called him on his comm, asking him to come to the island so they could talk it out. But when he got there, he saw she had been strangled and was already dead. He panicked. He figured he'd be blamed and went into hiding.

"That wasn't the smartest thing he could have done. Made him look guilty. But you know what? I believe him."

Before the prosecutor could rise from his chair to object, the disdainful P'Thall made a sound half snort and half laugh, and began to respond to what had not been an actual question. Cogley had read his witness well.

"Your gullibility gets the better of you, human. How can you believe your client, when he was the only other person who could have been on the island and, by simple logic, the only person who could have killed Daleel?"

"Normally, I get to ask the questions, Mr. P'Thall, but since you're grieving over the loss of your daughter, I'll answer yours. Obviously, someone else was on the island."

"How? There was no possible way for someone else to get to the island."

"Someone could have used a transporter," Cogley said.

P'Thall's reaction was immediate. This time, his laugh was full and not combined with a snort.

"Human, your handling of this case notwithstanding, you may be a competent lawyer, but you are clearly not an engineer. Before you suggest the impossible, I would suggest you familiarize yourself with transporter operation."

"The impossible? Why impossible?"

"There is only one transporter station on all of Versailles, the one here in New Paris. As no spaceship is allowed to land on the moon and ruin its sentimental ambience, a transporter is used to ferry visitors from orbiting ships down to this little vacation paradise.

"Our island is on the other side of the moon. An entire moon separates it from New Paris. Transporter beams travel in straight lines and, doing so, cannot bend around the curvature of a moon's surface. While transporters can beam people and materials through a few miles of solid rock, they couldn't beam someone through the entire moon. There's simply no way the transporter in this city could send anyone to our island."

Cogley ran his right hand through his hair, then massaged the back of his neck.

"You've got me there," he said, smiling and nodding demurely. "Well, then, no transporter. Let's talk about the opera you saw. Did you like it?"

"Not especially."

"I didn't think so. You left your seat about twenty minutes before intermission."

"I . . . had a certain biological necessity to which I needed to attend."

Cogley nodded again. "Well, when you've got to go, you've got to go. So . . . you couldn't hold it for the twenty minutes until the next intermission?"

"I saw no need to. As I said, I wasn't enjoying myself."

"But you thought enough of it to wear your most formal tunic with your family stone, just like you're wearing now."

"Objection, Your Honor. Relevance."

"I'm trying to establish the witness's attitude toward humans, Your Honor. It goes to bias, which I'm allowed to explore."

"Briefly, Mr. Cogley. Don't go too far afield."

"That is the farthest thing from my mind."

Cogley went back to his table and took some photographs from Jackie. Her eyes flashed the only amusement courtroom decorum would permit.

"I'm showing you Defense Exhibit E, Mr. P'Thall. Can you tell me what this is?"

"It's nothing more than an image, a photograph, of me at the reception before the opera."

"And you're wearing your formal tunic with the family stone in it, just as you are now, correct?"

"Yes."

"Only it's not quite the same. I noticed that your tunic has a very delicate filigree pattern woven into it. It's really quite beautiful."

"My tailor will be delighted you approve."

"But here's the thing, the tunic you're wearing now has a blue filigree pattern. But, showing you Exhibit F, a blowup of Defense Exhibit E, the filigree weave is more violet."

"I have several such tunics, Mr. Cogley."

"I figured you had. A well-dressed Kradian such as yourself, with as much family honor as you have, would naturally bring more than one tunic on a trip. But let me show you Defense Exhibit G. Do you recognize it?"

"Of course I do. It's an image of me and my wives and fellow husband taken after the opera, as we were being introduced to the lead singers."

"And can you see my problem?"

"You have a great many problems, human. I scarcely know where to begin."

"Then let me clarify things for you. This is Defense Exhibit H. Do you recognize it?"

"Yes, it's a blowup of the previous pic—"

"You stopped in midword, sir. I guess you *do* see the problem after all. The filigree in the tunic in Defense Exhibit H is the precise same blue as in the tunic you wear now. In fact, it's the same tunic as the one you're wearing now, isn't it?

"So here's my problem. How did you come to change tunics from the one in Defense Exhibit E to the one in Defense Exhibit H *during* the opera?"

P'Thall was silent. And Cogley waited. Waited several seconds before he said, "No quick answers? No glib remarks? And you seemed so chatty just a few moments ago."

This time the prosecutor didn't hesitate.

"I object, Your Honor. Mr. Cogley is badgering the witness. Sahirn P'Thall is not on trial here."

Cogley answered without turning away from his witness, keeping P'Thall squarely in his sights.

"That was your mistake, Mr. Warren. You charged the wrong man for the murder of a beautiful and innocent young woman."

P'Thall remained silent.

"No answer? Then maybe you can answer this question: Where *is* the tunic you were wearing in Defense Exhibit E?"

P'Thall stared at Cogley. There was no haughty contempt, no defiance, in his gaze. If Kradians could sweat, the man would have drenched his fine tunic.

"Again, no answer? Well, it doesn't really matter. I think I can answer this question myself.

"Your Honor, Versailles may duplicate old-world France, but even vacationers don't want to be out of contact with the universe. You have quite a modern communications system. The court even has a viewscreen for taking the testimony of witnesses who can't travel to New Paris. With your permission?"

The judge nodded her consent, and the bailiff pushed a button at his desk. Immediately a portion of the wall directly opposite the jury box slid back to reveal a large screen. Cogley gestured to Jacqueline, who spoke into a personal comm box.

"Now, Peter."

The viewscreen came to life, showing a man in his mid-fifties, balding, with gray hair that was interrupted only occasionally by a spot of its former black. The middle-age lines on his face were just starting to change over to the deeper cracks caused by a greater maturity. The man was standing confidently in an opulent bedroom whose furniture and style would have fit perfectly in the palace from which the vacation moon Versailles took its name.

"Mr. P'Thall . . . you recognize my investigative assistant, Peter Lawrence. Can you tell us where he is?"

P'Thall looked at the screen. He stood up suddenly and, with a savage thrust of his arm, pointed at the image.

"How dare you!" he shouted. "You trespass in my bedchamber? Is *nothing* beneath you?"

"I might ask you the same question. But first let me correct your natural mistake. It isn't *your* bedchamber. At least not alone. It's a vacation home. You rent it. We got the permission of the landlord to be there.

"Peter," Cogley said, addressing the viewscreen, "did you find our surprise exhibit?"

"That I most certainly did."

The grinning investigator held up a formal family clan

tunic, similar to the one P'Thall was wearing. Identical to the one shown in Defense Exhibit E.

"Where was it?"

"Hidden in the closet. On a hanger underneath another suit of clothes."

"Can you hold it closer to the camera?"

Peter held the tunic up against his own muscular frame so that its violet filigree weave was clearly visible for all to see. Not even Alexander Warren bothered to object.

"Peter, is that a rip I see on the tunic front?"

Lawrence moved his hand to the rip and pulled back the flap it created so the court could see how big it was.

"*That's* the tunic you were wearing when you went to the opera, isn't it, Mr. P'Thall?" Cogley asked.

P'Thall denied it, but his weak "No" was a stammer that caught in his throat as it came out.

"Your daughter cost you business, reputation, status, honor. The only way you could restore that honor was to remove Daleel from your family."

"No."

"But it wasn't enough to kill her. You also wanted revenge on Aaron Cole for his part in your disgrace."

"No."

"So you came to Versailles and forced your daughter to break it off with Aaron."

"No."

"Then you used a voice chip to fake a communication from your daughter to lure Aaron to the island on a night you knew Daleel would be alone."

"No."

"That night you left your seat at the opera twenty minutes before the intermission so you could be sure you were alone when you transported yourself back to the island and your rented castle. You killed Daleel. You planned her murder so Aaron Cole would be the only suspect, and you killed your own daughter!"

"No."

"Daleel struggled, fighting for her life even as you stole it from her, and in that struggle, she ripped your tunic. You had to replace it and hope no one would notice."

"No."

"Unfortunately for you, I *do* notice things."

"No. It's not true. None of it. That *grelth* murdered Daleel. Not me. I couldn't have done it. I was miles away."

"Miles away, Mr. P'Thall? How many miles? A transporter has a range of over fifteen thousand miles."

In the witness stand, P'Thall stretched to his full height and glared down at Cogley. The sneer was back on the Kradian's face, the contempt back in his tone.

"Your memory fails you, human. That is still quite impossible. Any transporter technician will confirm that I couldn't have beamed from New Paris to the island. Not around the planet and not through it. It can't be done.

"So, then, how did I get from New Paris to the island and then back to New Paris in a matter of minutes? How, Mr. Cogley, did I manage that?"

"How, Mr. P'Thall? I imagine like this."

Samuel Cogley snapped his fingers.

In the next instant, Peter Lawrence, still holding P'Thall's tunic, appeared in the middle of the courtroom.

2. "My God, this must have cost a small fortune."

The awe in Aaron Cole's voice—a tone of reverence usually reserved for the cathedrals and museums of Rome—was as obvious in his words as it was in the wide-eyed expression that dominated his face as he looked at the office. Although, truth to tell, the feeling had started much earlier. It had started when Aaron Cole found the building that housed the office of Samuel T. Cogley, attorney-at-law. Around that building were the gleaming transparent aluminum and metal buildings reaching majestically for the sky that one expected to find in a major city such as Los Angeles. Any of these proud towers would have been ideal to house the offices of a lawyer of Cogley's stature. Cogley chose none of them.

Cogley chose the Bradbury Building.

Surrounded by a forest of skyscrapers of the newest design and materials, the Bradbury Building stood out because it was none of those things. Its exterior was neither metal nor transparent aluminum, but a nondescript combination of sandstone and brick. Its five-story height was dwarfed by the surrounding towers, which reached to the sky as if trying to overcompensate for being next to the Bradbury. They were, after all, just buildings; the Bradbury was history.

It had stood for three hundred seventy-four years, surviving the earthquakes, riots, and fires that felled many of its onetime neighbors. Four floors of corridors went around the rectangle of the building's perimeter and were all open on one side to look down on the open court that made up the first floor. The roof was a massive skylight covering a five-story atrium that let the light dance over the building's yellow brick walls and Belgian marble staircases, staircases made all the more majestic by the foliate iron grillwork that highlighted their railings. The same grillwork also made up the railings along the open walls of the corridors. Two Victorian-style birdcage elevators serviced the building and, although their mechanics had been updated, the ornate grillwork on their cages and shaft exteriors remained the same as they were when they were built.

When he entered the building, Cole walked to the closest of those elevators, intending to ride it up to the fifth floor, where Cogley had his office. But as he moved toward the elevator, he changed his mind. Only by walking up the grand staircase would he have enough time to take in the grandeur of this building. When he reached Cogley's office—an old-fashioned wooden door with an actual doorknob and a pebble-glass window with the legend "Samuel T. Cogley, Attorney-at-Law" painted on it—he still didn't feel that he had spent enough time.

Jacqueline LaSalle ushered Cole from the waiting room into Cogley's inner office. Cogley followed his visitor's eyes as they moved from the massive mahogany desk, adorned with bas-relief carvings along its edges, that dominated the center of the office, to the matching Chippendale chairs in front of the desk, to the oak bookshelves that covered every available inch of wall space and were filled to overflowing with books. None of it—the desk, the chairs, the bookshelves, even the books—were re-creations, but genuine antiques which had been painstakingly restored to their original glory. It was after Cole had taken in the whole office that he let fly his exclamation.

"Yes, it did," Cogley said, smiling and motioning to a leather Chippendale chair in front of the desk. "Thankfully, I have a large fortune. Jackie says you were a little out of breath when you came in. You must have taken the stairs. A lot of people do. The Bradbury just gets to them. It's got a lot of history.

"It's been standing since 1893. A mining tycoon named Lewis Bradbury commissioned it from a draftsman named George Wyman, who had no previous architectural experience. According to the legends, Wyman used a Ouija board—that's a device for talking to the dead," Cogley explained when he saw Cole's blank, questioning expression, "to ask his dead brother whether to accept the commission. His brother told him to accept, it would make him famous.

"It's been renovated a few times, modernized a little, brought up to code, but it's never really changed. Several developers have wanted to tear it down. Some even bribed city officials to ignore the fact that it's on the Registry of Historic Landmarks, so they could replace it with something more in keeping with the times. But they never could. Every time word got out that someone wanted to tear down the Bradbury, the resulting complaints forced those people to abandon their plans.

"It's even been used in lots of movies. You watch movies?"

"I've seen vidcards, yes," Cole answered.

"I don't mean vidcards that you watch at home on your viewscreen. I mean *movies* that you go to theaters to see. Only way to watch them, in the dark, maybe with a drink and popcorn, and surrounded by the ambiance.

"The most famous movie that used the Bradbury was a late-twentieth-century movie called *Blade Runner*. Funny thing about that was, *Blade Runner* took place in a dreary version of Los Angeles that was one man's view of what the future might hold. It was a world where technology had made buildings so large and ugly that they blocked out the sun. In the movie, the only part of the city that looked like it could receive light was the Bradbury.

"I've heard it called everything from foreboding to exquisite. But whatever it is, it's about the only building here in Los Angeles where I feel truly comfortable."

Then Cogley stopped, shook his head, and laughed. "Sorry. When you get to be sixty-five like me, about the only thing you can be sure is still working is your mouth. So you do tend to go on a bit. I'm sure you didn't come here to listen to an old man talk about an older building."

"Actually, I came to do this," Cole took out his minicomp, manipulated the touch screen with practiced ease, then turned the display toward Cogley to show the result of his efforts. The screen flashed the date—December 12, 2267—then verified that an electronic funds transfer had successfully moved from Cole's account to Cogley's.

"Think of it as an early Christmas present. Thanks for everything you did, Mr. Cogley, including letting me pay in installments."

Cogley indicated that the two of them should sit in the Chippendale chairs. As they sat, Cole saw that despite his sixty-five years, Cogley moved with a spry gait. Cogley's hair may have been thinning and his face cragged with the wrinkles of age, but these were the *only* signs of how old he was. Everything else about Cogley spoke of a much younger man, particularly his eyes, which were a pale but bright blue, with a penetrating quality that made you believe he could see through a warp baffle plate.

Then Cole realized not *everything* about Cogley spoke of youth. Cogley was wearing another of his plain suits. It wasn't that the suits were out of style—Cogley's clothes were of a classic cut that was never out of style. But they weren't anything one would think of as current fashion, either. Functional and classic, but not high fashion. Which was probably exactly what Cogley wanted in clothes, something that was functional and comfortable, without caring how they looked or what anyone else thought of them.

Once the two men were seated, Cogley fixed his smile on Cole and said, "I'm the one who should be thanking *you*, Aaron. I like interesting and challenging cases, and your case was both. But tell me, why come here just to do an EFT? You could have done that from Versailles."

"I don't live there anymore. There wasn't much to hold me there, and there were just too many memories. So I've come back to Earth. For a while, anyway. I imagine that I'll get hit by the 'far star' bug again and go see what else is out there. But for now . . ."

Cole's voice trailed off. He really had no more idea what the near future held for him on Earth than he did of what the stars would offer the next time he wandered among them. He had always been the take-things-as-they-come type.

"Anyway, I came here because I thought you might want to know what happened to P'Thall."

"I know he was indicted for killing Daleel. The pompous ass actually tried to hire me to defend him. I turned him down."

"You have trouble representing people you know are guilty?"

"Not at all. If a man in my profession only took on clients he was sure were innocent, he wouldn't have enough of them to earn a living. No, I didn't like P'Thall because he tried to frame an innocent man for his crime. Besides, I told you I like cases that are interesting and challenging. P'Thall's case won't be either."

"No, probably not," Cole said in agreement. "The police checked those things you suggested and found exactly what you said they would. Earlier that day, P'Thall had gone to the New Paris transporter station and arranged to be alone for a moment. He programmed the computer to activate later that night. He also ordered it both to increase transporter power and to strengthen the containment field. Then he had it beam him out of the opera house and bounce the beam off one of Versailles's communications satellites, so that he could beam to his villa on the other side of the moon, even though it was out of direct line of sight. Just like you did to beam Mr. Lawrence from the villa to the courtroom.

"He killed Daleel and noticed that she had ripped his family tunic in the struggle, changed it, then had the transporter station reverse the process and beam him back to the opera house without anyone being any the wiser.

"The police checked the transporter station logs, as you suggested, and found a gap in the logs. Exactly the sort of gap that would happen if someone programmed the computer logs to purge some activity from its memory banks. Ordinarily, it might have been considered just a glitch in the memory banks, but as it happened precisely within the time period you indicated, they don't think that was the cause.

"And, just as you suggested, the Versailles communications grid systems showed two power spikes exactly at the time that P'Thall would have been bouncing his transporter beam off the satellite. The same type of spike that showed up when Mr. Lawrence beamed into the courtroom. You told them exactly what to look for. They looked and found it. Which pretty much seals P'Thall's fate."

Cogley shook his head and smiled. "Actually, it was Peter Lawrence who told them to look for the communications grid spike. He said back when he was with Starfleet, they experimented with bouncing transporter beams off satellites that way and found similar spikes in the comm systems. He said that and the power usage ratios were why Starfleet abandoned the idea."

"I've heard that P'Thall has refused extradition to Krador and will consent to be tried on Versailles. Seems his family is so outraged by what he did, he'll be better off facing trial and punishment under the Federation than on Krador. But what I don't understand, Mr. Cogley, is what made you suspect P'Thall in the first place?"

"The fact that he came to Versailles at all," Cogley explained. "Considering his marked xenophobia, particularly toward humans, the fact that he came to a vacation moon that catered primarily to humans made me wonder whether he had another reason. Killing Daleel and framing you was the most obvious choice. And he made a point of going to an opera that night, even though it was so far away. It made him a perfect alibi. Show me a man with a perfect alibi, and I'll show you a suspect. From there, it was just a matter of figuring out how he could have done it, then looking for the trail he would have left."

"How did you know I didn't do it?"

"I didn't know it, at first. I had a pretty good feeling after I met you, but what convinced me that you didn't do it was meeting P'Thall. I suppose what I should say is that once I met P'Thall, I was convinced that I knew who *did* murder Daleel."

Aaron Cole laughed and realized it was the first time he had laughed in many weeks. He liked being in the office. He felt as if he and Cogley were old friends who were seeing each other for the first time in years.

Cogley was experiencing downtime. He was well enough off that he didn't take many of the cases that presented themselves to him. He would pick those he thought would be interesting, and he had no such cases on his docket at the moment. So he was more than happy to spend some time with Cole.

Later, as Aaron Cole was leaving the office, he stopped to talk to Jacqueline LaSalle. She was a good twenty years younger than Cogley, and wore clothes of the latest vogue that were exactly understated enough to be striking without being flashy.

Cole found Jackie attractive. Not beautiful, but as far as he was concerned that was a good thing. Beautiful women always struck Cole as being somehow unattainable and, for that reason, not interesting.

Jackie had soft features. Cole knew many people, most Vulcans, for example, who had sharp, chiseled, and angular features—as if they had been carved from stone. Jackie was the exact opposite. Her features—nose, chin, cheeks—were all delicate, smooth, and rounded, the perfect setting for her hazel eyes. Her reddish-brown hair, the color of cherry wood, completed the impression of softness. Jackie allowed her hair to hang to shoulder length without artificial curling or straightening. The wave in her hair was natural and not the result of hours of processing.

But, while her look was natural and soft, he knew she was anything but soft. She could, and did, stand up for herself or Cogley or Peter Lawrence when the need arose. Cole found, however, that perhaps the most appropriate thing about her was her height. At five foot five and one-half inches, she was almost the exact same height as Cogley, which meant when they both stood, they saw each other eye to eye. With her clothes, her looks, and her experience, Jackie could have been comfortable in any boardroom in any multisystem corporation in the Federation, yet she chose to work with an aging lawyer on Earth.

Cole asked Jackie whether Peter Lawrence was around. When she told him no, Cole said, "Too bad. I wanted to thank him personally for his help." Then Cole hesitated in front of her desk for a moment before saying, "That's a pretty sophisticated computer system you have there. I thought Mr. Cogley didn't like computers."

"He doesn't, but I couldn't run the office without one. I just don't let Sam touch it."

Cole looked at her. "Do you mind if I ask you a personal question?" he asked.

"Not if you mind that I might not answer it."

"Fair enough. Ms. LaSalle, I don't think I've ever seen two people more loyal to a man than you and Mr. Lawrence are to Mr. Cogley. What prompts such loyalty?"

Jackie leaned back in her chair and smiled up at Cole. "Well, I can't speak for Peter, but for me, the work is interesting. When I was married, my husband and I worked with Dr. Daystrom."

Cole whistled under his breath. For the third time that day, he was both surprised and impressed by what he was learning about Samuel Cogley's office. "Dr. *Richard* Daystrom of the duotronic computer circuit?"

"The same. Anyway, Daystrom wasn't the easiest person to work with. He and William—my late husband—had something of a falling out. When William left, Daystrom fired me and accused us of stealing the basics of the project we had been working on—the M-Project—and offering them to his competitors. It was totally out of character for Daystrom, and we wondered if he was working too hard or having a breakdown or something. We would have ignored his ranting, but no one would dare hire William or me after what Daystrom said. Ultimately, we had no choice but to sue him so we could prove that he was lying.

"Sam represented us against Daystrom and the battery of attorneys Daystrom hired. Ultimately, Daystrom settled out of court. We got enough of a cash settlement to leave us both comfortable, but Sam also forced Daystrom to make a public apology and admit that he had been wrong about us. To this day, it's the only time Dr. Daystrom has ever admitted to anyone that he was wrong about anything.

"A few years later, when William died, the first sympathy comm I received was from Sam.

"And, in addition to the money and the apology, Sam negotiated a promise that his office would always have the newest, most up-to-date computers that Daystrom could supply us with.

"I saw how important Sam's work had been to William and me, so when William died, I came to work for Sam, to help him do the same work for others for whom it was just as important—people who couldn't take on the Daystroms of this universe without Sam's help."

Cole nodded. That sounded like Sam Cogley. He shook Jackie's hand and left the office, sure that he would walk down the stairs to take in the Bradbury again.

As Cole left, Jackie thought, *Why does Peter stay so loyal to Sam?* She knew she hadn't told Cole the full reason for her own decision to work with Cogley. Didn't tell him that along with the cash settlement and the public apology, Cogley also got Daystrom to agree to release William and her from their nondisclosure agreements. Again something Daystrom had never done before. When she had asked Cogley why he had insisted on that part of the deal, he answered that it was insurance. As long as the LaSalles weren't bound by the nondisclosure clause, Daystrom would never dare lie about them again. He wouldn't dare for fear that they would reveal his secrets in return.

What impressed Jackie the most about the whole affair was when Cogley told her the other reason he insisted on that part of the deal. Cogley told them he knew he could insist on it because he knew that neither William nor Jackie would ever abuse the deal. That kind of confidence in her integrity inspired loyalty to Cogley in return.

She believed there was a similar incident in the past involving Samuel Cogley and Peter Lawrence, but she didn't know what it was. Peter never talked about it. All she knew was that it existed and it made Peter a strong ally in Cogley's work.

Work. It was what Sam lived for. Oh, he could relax some, reading one of his precious books or watching one of the antiquated movies he collected. But not for long. She had seen it all too often: if Sam went much more than a week without a new and, more important, interesting case, he would start to get twitchy. And, worse yet, intrusive. One of the last times he had gone on an extended leave because no new cases had come in, he had actually decided that he should try to get Jackie to teach him how to use the office computer.

Sam discovered very quickly how big a mistake *that* had been. Fortunate, because if he hadn't discovered that, Jackie herself might have had to hire him and be his newest client in a murder prosecution. And it would have been very difficult for Cogley to represent her at the murder trial, considering that *he* would have been the victim.

No, she didn't want *that* happening again. She turned to her computer monitor and started to review the incoming mail and communications from potential clients. But she found nothing that Sam would have considered the least bit interesting or challenging.

Jackie sighed as she shut down the mail reader. Nothing yet. But she smiled when she looked into Sam's office and saw that he had moved to one of his Chippendale chairs and was happily reading one of his books. Rereading, actually. *Bleak House* again, although how any attorney could find so much pleasure in reading and rereading the story of the prolonged and unending lawsuit of *Jarndyce v. Jarndyce* that was the centerpiece of that particularly pointed and cynical Dickens novel, she wasn't sure.

Still, Sam was happy for now. And Jackie was sure the docket would change soon. When you were as famous and as successful as Sam, it always did. Maybe not today, maybe not tomorrow, but she knew that Samuel T. Cogley, Esq., would have another interesting and challenging case before too long.

3. Personal Journal of Daniel Latham: December 12, 2267

It's Christmastime back on Earth, and I'm amazed at how little meaning I find those words have for me now.

On Aneher II, as on all the colonies I've spear-headed over the decades, a day is not a day, nor a year, a year. Planetary rotations vary: 24 hours, 16 hours, 38 hours, 29.072 hours. Years, measured by solar orbit cycles, are equally in flux, changing from planet to planet or moon to moon. Finally, the concept of day and year and even hour lose all meaning.

Here, tomorrow is Landing Day—the first anniversary of when our colony reached our new home. But the Aneher day is only 18 Earth standard hours, an Aneher year is only 268 of our shorter days. By our calendar, we've been on our new home a full year. On Earth it's late 2267, still the same year we left.

I understand why Starfleet has stardates. A galaxywide system for keeping time and dates in time and space is essential for its business. But outside of Starfleet personnel, who knows what stardates are? I find its system of compensating for relativistic time dilation and warp-speed displacement confusing, at best. Perhaps a computer can determine a stardate, a feat which requires juggling the warp speed of a starship and its position in the galaxy relative to the galactic core, but I might as well attempt to count the sands on the beaches of Deneb V.

For my purposes, at least the purpose of keeping this journal, Earth standard time—as kept by the calendar clock Helen gave me on our first anniversary, while we were founding our first colony together—suffices. We used it to mark the holidays back on Earth and celebrate them as best we could.

Especially Christmas. Always Christmas.

In just under two weeks, it will be Christmas on Earth. And I find myself caring less about that than I do about the weather patterns on Europa.

It's difficult to keep Christmas when you have no one to celebrate it with.

Daniel Latham's hand paused over the page of the journal book. He looked down at what he had written, almost in surprise. Although he had had the thoughts for months, it was the first time he had ever put them to paper. His gaze moved up from the journal to the lone picture centered on the back of his desk. Himself, his wife, and their daughter, Katherine, in a happier time—a long-ago time.

A time he sometimes had to fight to remember.

He inhaled and exhaled slowly, then brought his pen back down to the book that lay in front of him. That last paragraph was a lousy place to end his journal entry. A maudlin exit line was never good. He was steeling himself to write more when he heard Helen's footsteps coming down the hall toward his office. The expensive high-heeled shoes she usually wore produced a distinctive sound here in the colony of Serenity, where the customary footwear was a work boot. He dropped the pen into his journal and shut it. Then he quickly returned the journal to the upper drawer on his desk.

Latham finished shutting the drawer just as the knob on his office door started to turn. He was glad that colonies such as his rarely bothered with luxuries like motion-sensitive sliding doors, preferring to have fewer things that could break down or go wrong. Having hinged doors not only kept things simpler, today it gave him enough time to put his feet up on his desk and pretend he had been comfortable for quite some time, and start to read the daily report submitted by his second-in-command, Grigoriy Nemov.

It wasn't that he was afraid that Helen would see that he had been writing in his journal again. She knew him well enough to know what he had been doing, no matter what image he presented to her when she came into the office. But things always seemed to go easier when she didn't catch him keeping the journal. When she caught him writing at times that she wanted him to be somewhere else, she could never refrain from skipping the conversation and going directly to screaming at him. If she didn't catch him, he could usually deflect her from screaming. At least at first. What might happen between them after they started talking was as uncertain as the gaming tables on Risa.

"You're not fooling anyone, Daniel!"

Today it didn't help.

As was her custom, Helen Latham didn't just enter a room, she took possession of it. Under most circumstances, she simply allowed her physical presence—her stature, her attitude, her self-assuredness—to overwhelm those around her. And if that didn't work, as it seldom did with Latham, she had a shriek that reminded Latham of a Phylosian swooper.

Well into her fifties, she was a commanding woman. Tall and stately, she had lost none of her beauty to age, although Latham knew she now worked on that more than she once did. Exercise and strict diet kept her figure trim. And while her eyes were a natural green, her hair—now the soft blond of Denevan wheat—had been brunette until a few years after they were married. Still, blond was the color she had kept it all these years, because it hid a myriad of flaws so much better than darker shades.

No matter where she went, she dressed in clothes that were not just stylish, but the most *haute* of *couture*. It didn't matter to her that her clothes, such as the fire jewel red dress she was wearing, were impractical for the colony planets Latham and she lived on; if the possibility existed that she would be seen by others, she dressed to be seen.

Latham didn't move his head as he looked up at Helen over the top of the report. "I beg your pardon, my dear."

He knew it wouldn't work; he wasn't even sure why he had tried, other than that he *always* tried to divert her. *Tried* to avoid the argument. But she was as single-minded regarding this as she was in her choice of clothes.

"It's bad enough that Grigoriy's Landing Eve party starts in twenty minutes and you haven't even begun to get ready, but you make it worse by pretending that you were working on colony matters instead of being in your own world again." As she spoke, Helen moved to the center of the office that Latham kept in the house they shared and made a sweep of the arm to indicate the whole room. She was pointing at the shelving units that covered the walls and the hundreds of books that filled those shelves. Her contempt for them was evident in her expression, a glare as sour as Andorian ale gone bad.

Latham tried to sidestep the issue by rising from his chair and sidestepping his wife, moving past her and toward the door of his office. "You're right, Helen. I'll go get ready now."

"Don't get condescending with me. You haven't cared about me for years. If you did, you certainly wouldn't have brought me here, to a planet we have to share with *Klingons*!" "Klingons" was only one word, but Helen Latham had said it as if it combined every curse word ever spoken since time began.

Latham knew what Helen—what the entire colony—thought about having to colonize Aneher II side by side with Mak'Tor and his people. And while he did not begrudge the Klingon Empire's right, under the Organian Peace Treaty, to colonize this world alongside the Federation, he did admit to himself that things would be easier if Mak'Tor's colony was not here.

Unfortunately for those whose primary concern was simplicity, Aneher II lay within the Neutral Zone that separated Federation space from that belonging to the Klingon Empire. Under the terms of the peace treaty that both sides in the Federation–Klingon conflict had found forced upon them by the Organians earlier in the year, neither the Federation nor the Klingons could send starships into the Neutral Zone. The problem was that planets like Aneher II—planets rich in natural resources such as dilithium, zenite, pergiuim, and topaline—also lay within the Neutral Zone. Both sides required these resources, and even the ethereal Organians, who had evolved beyond such requirements millennia ago, understood those very corporeal needs. So they provided in their treaty that disputed planets would be awarded to the side that demonstrated it could develop them most efficiently. So planets such as Aneher II, Maggie's World, and Sherman's Planet were colonized by representatives of both the Federation and the Klingon Empire simultaneously.

It was for this reason that the Federation specifically requested that Daniel Latham head up the Serenity colony on Aneher II. For decades he had spearheaded Federation colonies, going to new worlds with the initial colonists to help them get started. Then, when the colony was under way and self-sufficient, he would move on to the next world. It had been a very lucrative proposition for him, though he had stopped caring about the profits years ago. Despite Helen's repeated urging that he retire and that they live in a manner befitting their earnings rather than claw at the dirt of each new wasteland world the Federation foisted on them, he took on each new assignment more than willingly.

He simply liked the challenge that each new world presented. Liked it far more than living the type of life more in keeping with the style of clothing that Helen favored.

Now the Federation had given him his most difficult, but also his most interesting, challenge. Moreover, he had to colonize Aneher II in such a way as to anticipate what type of development would satisfy a race of noncorporeal sentients—beings who were pure thought, who had abandoned physical bodies long before his own race even existed—and convince them that he was doing a better job at developing the planet than Mak'Tor's colonists.

Latham did not stop walking toward the door while he thought about his wife and the colony and how both came to be on Aneher II. Before he could reach it Helen screeched, "Typical. Ignore. Evade. That's your solution to everything, isn't it, Daniel? No concern at all about what *I* might think."

Latham stopped by the open door and, without looking back at his wife, said, "I suppose I might care about what you think, but for the fact that you haven't had a thought that didn't begin and end with 'Helen Latham' for years."

"How dare you say that to me!"

"Because you make it so easy, Helen! Now, if you really want us to make an appearance at that party, I suggest you let me change. And, as appearances *are* what you care about, for the sake of those appearances, I suggest you start practicing your smile now."

Latham went through the door and walked away from the office. He did not turn back, nor did he need to. He could tell by the loud sound coming from behind him that he was not the only person in the house that night to be glad the colony used hinged doors. Sliding doors were so hard to slam.

He knew he hadn't avoided yet another argument with his wife, merely postponed it. Of late, postponing an argument was as much of a victory as he could hope for.

"O'Dell, aren't you afraid of health code violations?"

The bar sat in the Aneher Neutral Zone, a buffer that separated the Federation colony from the Klingon encampments, where inhabitants from both sides traveled freely. Unlike the Neutral Zone in space, the Aneher Neutral Zone was a matter not of Organian fiat but of common sense. Nether colony could possibly thrive if both sides were constantly at war. Latham and Mak'Tor set up the Neutral Zone as an area where the colonists of each faction could learn to coexist rather than to live in isolation and mistrust.

That, anyway, was the hope, although neither leader deluded himself into thinking the hoped-for coexistence would always be peaceful.

Ronald Sayger didn't go in much for alien drinks such as Saurian brandy or Altair water. A shot and a beer were his drinks of choice. Usually together. And this night, he had made lots of choices. He had no idea how many glasses of *warnog* the Klingon sitting at the table next to his had put down. Sayger had lost count of the Klingon's intake shortly after he had lost track of his own. But the Klingon had matched him glass for glass, he was sure of that much.

Just as he was sure that he didn't like the bastard's swarthy skin, which made it look like he was constantly sweating, or that damned devil's beard he and the other Klingons wore. And just as he was sure that he could not only match the Klingon drink for drink, but blow for blow.

"What do you mean 'health code violations,' Ron?" O'Dell, the bartender, asked.

Sayger looked directly at the Klingon at the next table and said, "I thought you were supposed to take out the trash *before* you opened for business."

K'Vak, the Klingon at the next table, turned his head slowly in Sayger's direction. He fixed a scornful snarl on his face, even as he instinctively reached to his side for the *d'k tahg*, which was not there because Mak'Tor's regulations required he check it before entering the bar. He realized he was glad the dagger was not at his side—he needed no weapon to deal with this mewling animal. K'Vak took a long swig of the *warnog,* wiped his mouth with the back of his arm and said, without looking away from his glass, "If you cannot hold your liquor honorably, Earther, then it is *you* who should leave this establishment!"

Sayger stood, which put him directly in front of the Klingon. "What would you know about honor? You and the entire Klingon race are a bunch of gutless, sneak-attacking bushwhackers with about as much honor as a Joranian ostrich!"

K'Vak started to get to his feet but had only half risen when Sayger threw what was left of his beer into the Klingon's face. From his half crouch, K'Vak leapt at Sayger, screaming, *"qaHoH!"*

Sayger, who had been ready for the attack, brought the heavy, unbreakable beer glass down hard on K'Vak's head before the Klingon could reach Sayger's throat. It took only seconds for K'Vak to regain his senses and resume the attack, but by the time he did, the entire bar had erupted into several fights, which quickly spread into one large brawl.

When the security forces from both the Federation and Klingon colonies finally arrived at O'Dell's, neither force could do more than contain the fight to the one bar. Security didn't bother trying to keep the fighters from damaging O'Dell's. The rules imposed by both Latham and Mak'Tor required that any bar that permitted a fight to break out in it be shut down temporarily. Shut down as punishment or shut down for repairs, it hardly mattered. So security let the fight play itself out inside the bar.

Tomorrow there would be a jurisdictional hearing to sort it all out. A perfect way to begin Landing Day.

4. Personal Journal of Daniel Latham: December 13, 2267

Landing Day. What's supposed to be a day of celebration in our colony, and I have to start it with a jurisdictional hearing.

Lord, I hate these things. Sitting in judgment of another person is hard enough, but it's still ahead of sitting in judgment to determine exactly who gets to sit in judgment.

Morning was his favorite time of the day, on Aneher at least. The sunsets on Helzar IV were among the most spectacular he had ever seen, what with the way the sunlight broke up in the dusty atmosphere and spread prism light everywhere it touched. And when the orbits of Alpha Centauri A and B brought them close enough that both could be seen in the noon sky, the display was nothing short of breathtaking.

But on Aneher, it was definitely the mornings—not so much for what could be seen, but for what couldn't be seen. Aneher II was closer to its sun than Earth was to Sol, and its atmosphere was thinner. By day the waters of Lake Cochrane, which supplied the colony of Serenity that had been put on its shores with so many essentials, heated under the sun. Because Aneher didn't have a thick atmospheric layer to contain the heat, at night the air cooled. *More* than cooled. At night Aneher was frigid. As a result, in the morning, when the winds blew off Lake Cochrane into the still chilled air of the colony, the resulting fog did not come in on Carl Sandburg's "little cat feet." It was more like on the massive paws of a Vulcan *sehlat*.

It came almost every morning, as thick as *plomeek*, and seemed to cling to everything it touched. Latham could stand in his office in the colony's city hall and stare out the window that looked over the main street of the colony without being able to see the buildings that were next door to him. So Latham, almost every morning, stood by that window and watched the swirling gray eclipse his colony like some death shroud. It looked as if his office were all the world, that existence simply ended three feet outside his window, swallowed up in the slate-colored miasma.

As Latham watched, the rays of Aneher's sun started to break through the murky fog and began to turn its quicksilver veil into a translucent haze and then, finally, a mist. He saw the light pass through the melting fog and stream from the sky down to the ground. Soon the colony would be bathed in the full Aneher dawn, and the pall of fog would be gone. A daily ritual of nature that Latham enjoyed watching as much for its beauty as for the images of renewal and reaffirmation he often found he desperately needed.

It was also the most enjoyable time of the day on Aneher II, before the colony's proximity to its sun and its thin atmosphere conspired to drive the temperature up to thirty-eight degrees Celsius by midmorning.

And before most of the colonists were awake.

This morning, Latham was not at his window. He sat at his desk surrounded by the plainness of his office. Four walls, a hard floor, a desk, some chairs, a credenza upon which his attaché case lay open and empty, and a computer that was, fortunately, not damaged by the dust that had accumulated on it after being unused for days—that was all that filled this space. Unlike his study at home, the office did not have any personal effects other than the pictures on his desk. No shelves. No books. Furniture that was standard issue for Federation colonies. Nothing that proclaimed the room was his.

It was how he had kept his office on every colony he had founded. It was a way of reminding himself that what he did in his house was his concern, but what he did in his office was business. Not only his business, but the business of the colony—whichever colony it had been—and the many colonists who had come with him. He found the colonies ran better when he kept them stark, efficient, and businesslike, so he arranged his offices to be the same. It was a system that had worked well in the past, but now, for the first time in his decades of pioneering, he found his office wasn't businesslike, only sterile.

He sat at his desk writing. First he wrote in the journal he kept with him at all times. Then he began to write in a different book, one he had brought with him from his study. Although "writing" seemed to be something of an exaggeration. He was doing more crossing out than actual writing. No sooner would he compose a paragraph than he would reread it, scowl, and drag his pen over several lines to scratch them out. For every sentence he wrote, he seemed to discard three.

That was his way: pen, ink, and paper. It always had been. He may not have had his reading books or his personal furniture in his office, but there were always plenty of pens for him to write with and pads of paper for him to write on. He couldn't dictate his thoughts into a computer's voice-recognition program and let some duotronic coding format his spoken words into writing. Not and get them to come out right, anyway. When he tried, he froze. Even typing on a keypad didn't work.

For him, the only way he could write was to put pen to paper and create the words with his own hands. Later, when he finished his draft, he read it aloud into the computer. His father and his friends had used to chide him for the inefficiency of his system, but it got the job done, and that was what mattered.

He was drafting a report to the Federation about some suspicions the senior staff, himself included, had that the Klingons were substituting personnel in their colony and doing so surreptitiously.

Aneher II's closeness to its sun and its extreme heat made working the planet difficult at best, particularly outdoor activities such as mining and farming. The conditions left his own people spent by early afternoon. But that did not seem to be the case in the Klingon colony. Although the Klingons prided themselves on their toughness and durability, the fact that they didn't seem to wither at all in the Aneher sun seemed strange.

More than strange, suspicious. And the colonists' suspicions were only fueled by the frequent supply sleds that came to the Klingon colony.

Unlike Serenity, which produced most of the food it ate via hydroponics, the Klingon colony received regular supply sleds, which brought foodstuffs from the High Council. Foodstuffs and, the senior staff at Serenity had come to suspect, more.

The sleds were supposed to be drone ships on preprogrammed routes that were to be used only for transport.

But Serenity suspected the sleds were also smuggling in new colonists to replace those miners who had expended themselves working in Aneher's extremes, so that the Klingon colony would always have fresh workers and look far more efficient than it actually was.

There was nothing wrong with sending new colonists. Nothing in the Organian treaty forbade such substitutions. But the practice was not efficient, and not likely to convince the Organians that the Klingons were better suited to colonize Aneher II. So the Klingons were hiding their personnel substitutions by smuggling them in and making it look as if the original settlers were handling their colony without any help.

For weeks, Serenity had collected evidence to back their suspicions. Now they thought they had sufficient proof that they could take the matter up with the Federation, hence Latham's report.

Latham, in particular, wanted to stop the practice. If the Klingon High Council wanted to risk the lives of its people in its conquests and wars, Latham couldn't do anything about it. But if he could bring to light this particular risk the Council was inflicting on its people—reveal how the Council was shipping people wearing environmental suits like so much cargo in the holds of transports that lacked both independent controls and life-support systems—he might be able to stop it from claiming any more lives. Still, for some reason, try as he might, Latham could not write the report accusing Mak'Tor of this practice.

He was blocked.

In the past, when he felt unable to write, he came to recognize that the blockage came about because something was wrong in what he was writing. Usually, he didn't even know *what* was wrong, at first. All he knew was that it would keep him from going forward until he figured out what it was.

He turned back one more time to the book lying on the desk in front of him. The remnants of his many false starts seemed to mock him. He brought his fist down on the desk in frustration. The book jumped up and his pen flew through the air in lazy somersaults that he found even more annoying than the unfilled pages before him.

He sat staring at the book, now slightly askew from its fall back onto the desk. Today this book, where he drafted his most secret thoughts, made him feel more impotent than Helen at her worst did.

He continued to stare, unaware of time passing until the clock in his computer sounded its gentle alarm. He looked up and noted the time with a soft curse. Any moment now, Grigoriy Nemov would be arriving for their meeting. Grig would have Security Chief Louis Alexander's report of last night's fight. The one that Latham and Mak'Tor would be discussing at the jurisdictional hearing later in the morning. He didn't have time for his writing now. He closed the book and hastily put it in the attaché case behind him. As he did, he ordered his computer to come out of hibernation mode and bring up his mail. The monitor flashed on and displayed the latest mine yield reports that Homero Galdamiz, Serenity's chief mining engineer, had sent him the day before. Latham had just enough time to look at it and feign an expression of interest before Nemov entered the room.

"Daniel, here is Louis's report of the incident for last night," Nemov said. As usual his voice boomed from him like that of an enraged power-cat. He retained a slight

Russian accent. He crossed the room, moving more quickly than his large frame would have seemed to allow. As he walked, his fingers moved over the report he was bringing to Latham. He was familiar with Latham's office, knew it for the barren furniture wasteland that it was, and so was not paying attention to his progress. He was therefore surprised when his foot bumped something on the floor.

"Your pen," Nemov said, bending down to pick up the pen, which Latham had not even realized had bounced off his desk and fallen to the floor.

"Thank you, Grig. I must have knocked it on the floor while I was reading Homero's report. Didn't even notice."

"Well, here is the report of the incident *and* your pen."

Latham reached over his desk and took the report that Nemov offered him. As he did, Nemov let the pen drop from his hand and fall to the desk. It made a slight noise as it hit the bare wood. Latham looked up at Nemov and caught the briefest hint of a smile before the Russian made his face go blank. *Yes, it* was *on purpose*, Latham thought.

He set the report down and noted that it looked like an orphan lying in the middle of his empty desk. Good. Maybe the symbolism wouldn't be lost on Nemov. He lifted his pen with his right hand and, showing complete indifference to the report Nemov had offered, pushed the cap over the tip hard, so that it produced a noticeable click. Then he opened his attaché case and returned the pen to its holder. When he was finished with his ministerial duties, he finally picked up the report, moved his arm to where he could see it properly, and started to read.

Nemov looked down, towering over him.

"Did you want something, Grig?"

"Dickens, I see."

Latham glanced up from the report, followed the direction of Nemov's eyes, and realized the man was looking at the book in his attaché. "I'm impressed. You actually recognize a book."

"I see the matched set in your study often enough."

"I'm sure my reading habits *aren't* what was on your mind."

"No. I—"

"Don't bother yourself, Grig," Latham said, and looked up directly at Nemov's face. "I *know* what's on your mind. And I have no intention of discussing it again." Latham moved his glance down and started to read the report. Without looking back up at Nemov, he added, "That will be all."

"Daniel, you're not really plan—"

"I said that will be *all*. I don't want to discuss it now."

Nemov turned on his heel like a cadet doing an about-face and walked out of the room, muttering something under his breath. Latham noted that the disadvantage of having a voice that carried as well as Nemov's was that, even though Nemov was whispering, Latham could hear every word he said.

None of them pleasant.

"QaSuj'a'neS?"

Mak'Tor looked up from his desk at his second-in-command without letting his irritation show. It had been a simple enough question, but Mak'Tor knew it was more. For one thing, Khogo didn't really care whether he was disturbing his commander, never had cared. And Mak'Tor noticed the slight pause Khogo put between the question

and the honorific suffix *neS*. Slight but deliberately calcu-
lated to remind Mak'Tor that, while Khogo's phrasing
might be deferential, he didn't really mean it.

No, it was a question designed to provoke Mak'Tor,
and he had to be careful not to allow the provocation. If for
no other reason than to deny his second the satisfaction of
knowing he had succeeded.

Mak'Tor shifted his glance briefly, moving it from
Khogo across his office. It was stark, bare of all furnish-
ings except those that were necessary for his duties as
colony head. It even lacked a window. The Earthers
would call it Spartan. A Klingon would simply call it
standard.

His eyes fell on the one embellishment he allowed in
the office, a *bat'leth* that was no longer battle worthy because one of its curved blades was broken. He had broken
it honorably, when he was commanding the battle cruiser
Kavek on a mission to provide reinforcements to a cargo
ship that had come under heavy attack from Orion ma-
rauders. He had broken the *bat'leth* with a *chaQ* to the ribs
of an Orion captain, even as the captain sank a knife deep
into the Klingon's leg, causing a wound that forced him to
walk with a pronounced limp to this day.

The High Council had given him a special commenda-
tion for his victory that day, but it had removed him from
active duty. In the past, he would have been reassigned to
be the military governor of one of the Empire's conquered
planets. But since that *toDSaH* Kor had lost the military
base on Organia, the entire Empire was forced to suffer the
indignity of the Organian Peace Treaty.

Now, instead of being a proper military governor,
Mak'Tor was the head of a colony. A head who had to live

near and placate the Federation. It was *not* the Klingon way, at least not the old Klingon way. But as long as it was the order of the High Council that he oversee the colony, honor required this course. Even as Kor, who caused this insult to the entire Klingon Empire, was given command of one of the new *K't'inga*-class battle cruisers.

Mak'Tor wanted to spit as he thought of Kor. It was his fondest wish that when the Klingon Empire finally recognized Kor's cowardice, Kor would never find himself in *Sto-Vo-Kor*.

All that flashed through Mak'Tor's consciousness in nanoseconds, and he turned his head back to Khogo.

"What do you want, Khogo?"

Khogo handed his superior a report of the previous night's altercation. "The information you need for today's hearing."

"You don't approve of the hearings, do you, Khogo?"

"I may speak?"

"So formal? You've never been reluctant to express your true opinion in the past." Then Mak'Tor sighed and waved his hand in a tired gesture. "Speak freely."

"No, I do not. I do not understand why we must accommodate the Earthers. Why we simply do not take this world from them."

"And thereby lose it and its mineral wealth, under the terms of the treaty, Khogo? I doubt the High Council would allow either of us to see our next birthdays."

"Then why a procedure to determine under whose law the criminal shall be prosecuted? If a Klingon has wronged an Earther, he should be punished under Klingon law. And if an Earther were to dare wrong a Klingon, he should also suffer Klingon punishment."

"Latham and I decided that a mechanism for determining which colony would get jurisdiction over infractions that occurred in our Neutral Zone was desirable in order to keep what passes for peace between our people. We established the jurisdictional hearings to make that determination, even if they are an inelegant solution that no one truly likes.

"When we had our first hearing, I informed Latham that you called it a *veQDuj*. To his credit, Latham had studied enough Klingon to know the word meant 'garbage scow,' but he didn't understand your use of the term. I explained that in some parts of the Empire, the word had come to have a second meaning: 'a ship that, although necessary, is without honor.' You would be interested to know that he told me humans have a similar phrase. They call such things a 'necessary evil.'"

"I may not think much of the Earthers, Mak'Tor, but I do appreciate that to be an elegant turn of phrase. You and Latham would do well to remember that however necessary you believe it to be, a 'necessary evil' is, nonetheless, still evil.

"Now I believe you should go to the hearing, *la"a'*."

Mak'Tor again noted that slight hesitation between the sentence and the honorific that ended it. And the deliberate use of the word *la"a'*, "commandant"—the commanding officer of a place—instead of his true military rank *la'*, "commander." Khogo may have claimed to hate most things human, but he seemed to have picked up a decided inclination toward the human practice of sarcasm.

When it was over, the jurisdictional hearing went as Mak'Tor had predicted it would from the reports. Both

Sayger and K'Vak were found to be responsible for the fight, K'Vak for making the first attack and Sayger for baiting K'Vak into attacking. K'Vak was remanded to human custody for trial and punishment, while Sayger was delivered to the Klingons. But the morning still left a bad taste in his mouth, like *gagh* that had been allowed to die before eating and he intended to do something about it.

As Latham walked past on his way out of the hearing room, Mak'Tor grabbed his arm and spun him so that the two were face-to-face. "A moment!" Mak'Tor phrased it as a command, not a request. Neither Louis Alexander, the head of Federation security on the planet, nor any of the members of the Federation ruling council made any effort to leave. He dropped his hand so that it brushed against the disruptor at his side, looked Alexander directly in the eyes, and snarled, "Alone!"

Alexander started to move toward Mak'Tor, but Latham held up his hand and nodded toward the door to tell them he would be fine and they should meet with him later. Outside.

After the others had left the hearing room and they were alone, Mak'Tor looked at Latham and said, "I do not like these jurisdictional hearings. They waste time. Their outcomes are a foregone conclusion. No Klingon would ever dishonor himself by lying to escape punishment, especially your weak, *human* punishment. And no human would ever admit his guilt and subject himself willingly to Klingon punishment. We take testimony. The Klingon tells the truth, the human lies, and we pass judgment accordingly."

"I'll ignore the racial slurs and the fact that K'Vak's going into a primarily human bar was at least as provocative as anything Sayger might have said and do you a favor, Mak'Tor: agree with you. I think we do need to find an alternative to the jurisdictional hearings. But not now. It's something we can discuss later."

Mak'Tor grabbed Latham's right wrist and squeezed it tightly. "Why not now?" he demanded.

Latham stared directly into Mak'Tor's face with an intensity that belied the paleness of his blue eyes. Then he lifted his right arm so that his wrist, Mak'Tor's hand still around it, hung in front of Mak'Tor's face. Neither man said anything at first, silence filling the room until Mak'-Tor released the wrist.

Latham's hand went to his wrist. "Because now I have something *more* important to do. When I'm finished, we'll have a lot to discuss."

Latham turned, walked toward the door, and without looking back or stopping, said, "I'll let you know when I'm ready." Then he went out the door and into the hallway.

"So, did you give in, like you *always* do?" a voice demanded before Latham moved halfway down the hall. He turned his head and saw the colony's computer expert, Chiaki Iino.

Chiaki may not have been as tall or as brawny as the miners or farmers who made up most of Aneher's population; he was, in fact, almost as wide as he was tall. But Chiaki didn't let his relative lack of stature keep him from standing up for what he thought was right. He never gave up, and he never backed down. It was one of the things that Latham admired in his computer expert.

Usually.

Latham looked down the hall, didn't see Mak'Tor, and

was glad that Mak'Tor must have gone out the other door in the hearing room and left with his staff. Latham was sure that Mak'Tor suspected the unrest in Serenity, but he really didn't want the Klingons to overhear this conversation and have those suspicions confirmed. After Latham confirmed that Mak'Tor was not within hearing distance, he turned back to Chiaki and for the second time that morning found himself saying, "Not now."

"When? After you've sold out *everything* we have to the Klingons?"

"I know you're upset, Chiaki. I know Ron was your partner. But go home. Sleep it off. Before you say something—"

"I'll regret? What I regret, Daniel, is that you care more about the Klingons than you do about your own kind! I regret that you turn your own people over to those bastards for their 'justice'! That I still have the scars and the limp I got when you threw me into their forced labor camp! That despite what's happened to me and so many others, you still indulge in this barbarity with Mak'Tor! Even to the point of giving them Ron!

"Yes, I regret all that. But what I *really* regret, Daniel, is that no one has taken a phaser to you yet!"

Iino turned on his heel and walked away angrily. And each time Iino's limp forced him to favor his left leg, Daniel Latham winced.

5. "He's not the only one, you know."

Latham had been watching Chiaki walk away from him, so he didn't notice that someone else had approached from the other direction and was speaking to him. He recognized the voice and its slight accent and shook his head. He really wasn't in the mood to talk to Nemov at the moment. He wasn't in the mood to talk to anyone, and especially not to Nemov. Still, how did the saying go? If wishes were starships . . .

Latham turned and looked over his shoulder at his second-in-command. "You have a point, Grig?"

"*Da.* Chiaki is not the only person who would like to take a phaser to you. There is much unrest in Serenity."

Latham turned his head so that he looked forward, then rubbed the base of his neck. When this was over, he'd have to go to his office for a painkiller. "I meant a point you hadn't made *before.*"

"It is not a laughing matter, Daniel."

"I'm sorry," Latham said, still not looking at Nemov. "I didn't realize I was laughing."

Nemov repositioned himself so that he stood directly in front of Latham, so that he would not be ignored. At that distance it would have been hard for Latham to miss him. Nemov stood six feet one inch and had worked his way up the ranks of mining colonization. Although middle-aged, he still possessed the broad shoulders, powerful thick arms, and barrel chest that had marked the days when he actually worked in the mines rather than oversaw their operation. His curly black hair was not thinning, and it, plus the full beard he wore, made him look like the bear that used to symbolize his Russian homeland; Latham found the streaks of gray that were invading both in increasing force did little damage to the ursine image.

"And still you continue," Nemov said, the tone of confrontation as hard to miss as his burly frame. "Your people do not appreciate having to share this planet with those barbarians."

Latham noted the emphasis Nemov had put on the words "your people." As if he were Moses leading the tribes of Israel to the promised land. Still, he imagined that Moses got more respect from his followers than Latham generally enjoyed, and that included the time when the Israelites were building the golden calf. "You make it sound as if it were my choice, Grig. Yes, I'd prefer it if Mak'Tor and his colony weren't here, if for no other reason than that it would make my job so much easier. I don't have that luxury. *None* of us do. So we make do as best we can. And 'my people,' as you put it, knew the setup before they came."

"They did not know you would send them to slavery in Klingon prison camps. And today of all days. Our first Landing Day. Our holiday. By sending Ronald to the Klingons, you have spoiled celebration for all."

"Ronald spoiled it for himself. He knew the rules when he started the fight."

"As I try to explain, Daniel, *no one* likes your rules. They cause more difficulties than they are worth."

"Well, when they get colonies of their own, they can set their own rules. But until that time, I don't see any need to have another round of a conversation we've had repeatedly in the past."

Latham turned and started to walk away. The door that would let him outside was nearby, and to show Nemov that if the Russian had anything more to say, he didn't want to hear it, Latham started to whistle the opening bars of *Eine Kleine Nachtmusik* as he approached it.

"Daniel," Nemov said in a voice that was loud enough to show he didn't care what Latham did and did not want to hear.

Latham stopped. He exhaled in a sigh that he was sure was just loud enough for Nemov to hear, rolled his eyes up, and said, "Yes, Grig?"

"There is another matter we should go over." And then his tone dropped to a whisper. "Something *important*."

Latham turned back to face Nemov and was surprised to find him looking hastily up and down the corridor. But not as surprised as he was by Nemov's expression. They had their differences, but Nemov always tried to hide his feelings behind a smile. No matter what he said to Latham, he tried to say it with a smile. The contrast between Nemov's words, which of late had been increasingly critical, and the broad smile he usually tried to effect as he said them was jarring. Not as jarring as the definite scowl that hung on Nemov's face.

Nemov held up a report. "These are the crop yield projections. See?"

Latham came over to Nemov and pretended to look at the report. It wasn't what Nemov wanted to discuss and he knew it. "If they continue as is, we'll have to adjust the allocations."

"Yes, I see."

"Not here. Too crowded," Nemov said in an even softer whisper, a whisper that Latham knew carried only as far as his ears and no farther. As Nemov spoke, his eyes looked not at Latham but down at the report in his hands. Latham glanced down at it and saw that it did not have crop-yield projections on it, but rather the words YOUR OFFICE. LATER. WE SHOULD GO SEPARATELY.

"Grig, I've got other work waiting for me back in my office," Latham said, and walked toward the door. He reached for the knob, and to let Nemov know that he understood and would meet him in his office, said, "Send it to my computer there and I'll read it as soon as I can. Shouldn't take me too long to walk back, as long as nothing interrupts me."

Something did.

Rather, some*one*.

"Latham!"

Another voice from behind him, its tone indicating someone as upset as the others that had accosted him that day. Latham laughed softly under his breath and wondered what the world's record for most angry voices in one day was. After a moment of reflection, he figured that he might not have the world's record, but he sure as hell had Serenity's. And it was a record he hoped he would lose. Soon.

As with Nemov earlier that day, Latham didn't need to turn and see who was talking. *Not yet midmorning,* he thought as he wiped the sweat that only a few moments' walk had already sent streaming down his forehead, *and already it's thirty-six degrees out. Probably more.* Only one man would actually approach him outside and expect to have a discussion under the blazing sun, so there was little doubt in his mind that it was Homero Galdamiz behind him. There was even less doubt in Latham's mind as to what Serenity's chief mining engineer wanted.

"Latham, we got a response back from Starfleet about our request to modify our minin' techniques," Galdamiz had spoken as soon as Latham had stopped walking, not allowing Latham time to turn around to face him or even offer him a greeting. Galdamiz obviously wanted nothing to distract him. Nothing that could deflect him from his purpose. "Starfleet turned us down. Know why?"

Latham didn't turn to face Galdamiz. If the engineer wanted to talk to Latham's back, Latham was glad to oblige him. Instead, Latham looked up at the large glowing ball of Aneher. It almost seemed to fill the sky. Then he turned his glance to the ground and removed the polarized glasses everyone had to wear when they went outside during Aneher's day so that the star's powerful rays didn't damage their eyes. He could see the heat rising off the ground in undulating waves that seemed to make the colony around him shimmer, as if it wanted to flicker out of existence.

"Of course I know why, Homero. Because that's what I recommended Starfleet do. We've gone over this before, and nothing has changed. Not since yesterday. Or the day before." Latham turned and looked Galdamiz directly in the eye as if to emphasize what he had to say. "Or any of the *other* times we've had this conversation."

Galdamiz stared at Latham with a seething anger that threatened to escape his control at any moment. The engineer was compact but firm and tight, as if someone had taken a six-foot-tall Olympic athlete and compressed him until he stood only five foot six. His short, muscular, build was perfect for working in the mines. His face had sharp, angled features except for his brow, which was rounded and pronounced, almost simian in appearance. When he looked at you from under his brow, he almost seemed to be looking out from one of the shafts he thrived in. Although he had the dark hair and swarthy complexion common to his Latin American ancestors, Galdamiz's visage—what could be seen of it beneath the smudges that the mines had left on him— seemed to have paled from the years he had spent working in those mines and out of the sunlight. As a result, the contrast between the thick black hair on top of his head and the equally thick mustache and his paling skin was striking. Even disconcerting.

But it was the other effect that working in the mines seemed to have had on Galdamiz that never failed to amaze Latham. Somehow years of laboring in mines where environmental conditions could go to extremes of either hot or cold, depending on the planet being mined, had given Galdamiz some sort of internal thermostat. He could live comfortably in almost any conditions. Even now, the Aneher sun was making sweat flow from Latham like Columbia Falls of Deneva, but Galdamiz's face didn't have a single drop on it.

His temper, on the other hand, reacted to the heat in ways his body could not.

"You stabbed us in the back, Latham! You've seen my reports. Conventional minin' doesn't work. We gotta surface mine. My men can barely function in this heat."

It was true, the heat did impair the mining yields, and Latham knew it. The heat outside the mines was oppressive. And inside, where phaser drills heated up the rocks, it was even worse, probably rivaled only by Dante's Seventh Circle. Neither being inside the mines nor being outside them offered any respite for the miners.

Sodium supplements helped some, but not enough. Even with them, the miners could not do full-day shifts before their bodies threatened to collapse. Not even with the shortened days on Aneher II.

Latham knew it was true, but he also knew there was little that could be done.

"You know my decision, Homero."

"You're killin' us. Maybe not literally. Not yet, anyway. Why won't you even talk about other minin' techniques?"

"Because the only one you've suggested, what you euphemistically call 'surface mining,' is tantamount to strip mining. And the runoff from strip mining would pollute Lake Cochrane, which we need to survive. Every one of your so-called alternatives would destroy this planet's ecosystem."

"Starfleet approves surface minin'."

"Yes, for asteroids and moons. Planets incapable of supporting life, where the ecology doesn't need to be preserved. We don't have that option here."

"Bunk. Starfleet *does* allow surface mining on Class-M planets."

"In special cases, none of which apply here. Mak'Tor and his people haven't had to resort to your 'other techniques.'"

"That's 'cause the Klingons work till they drop without any regard for their safety. Then they keep comin' back for more. Me? I'm not gonna force my guys to do that."

"I can hardly prove to the Organians that *we* can colonize this planet more efficiently than Mak'Tor if we destroy it in the process."

"So, instead, you're just gonna give the planet to the Klingons?"

Galdamiz stopped. He realized his diatribe was having no effect. He took a quick breath and smiled at Latham. Maybe a different, nonconfrontational tactic would penetrate the duranium of Latham's skull. "You know, Daniel, you hand this planet to the High Council, and Starfleet's not exactly gonna Kronos with glory."

Latham noted the shift in Galdamiz's tone. It was softer and had one of his trademark puns. Galdamiz continued, even as Latham evaluated what was probably still just under the surface in the speech. "But the hell with Starfleet," Galdamiz said, "Daniel, I'm askin' you as a friend. Me and a lot of my guys came here from Janus VI. With the Horta diggin' the tunnels for Vanderberg's people, they're all makin' fortunes down there. My guys came here because Starfleet promised *us* a fortune in bonuses. But we can only collect them if we make our minin' quotas. Your stubbornness is takin' food out of our mouths."

And that was it. Galdamiz had left a fortune behind on Janus IV and wanted to rape this planet to ensure that he could make it up here. That was something Latham couldn't allow. "I'm sorry, Homero, the answer is still—"

Latham didn't finish his sentence. He was too busy ducking the right hook that Galdamiz aimed at his head. While Latham was regaining his composure, Galdamiz rushed at him and launched another attack.

It didn't last long. Latham had been on far too many backwater, rough-and-tumble colonies not to have learned how to defend himself. Even if not all of his methods were approved of by the Marquess of Queensberry.

When Galdamiz picked himself up off the ground, he stared at Latham for a moment, then staggered a few steps away, stopped and glowered. The hatred in his eyes was visible even under the ledge of his jutting brow. "Maybe I spoke too soon when I said you weren't killin' us yet. You force my guys to work in these conditions much longer and they probably *are* gonna start droppin' off. And I'm warnin' you, Latham, we're not gonna take that lyin' down."

Latham watched Galdamiz limp away, nursing his grudge. He made sure that Galdamiz was well clear of the area before he started walking down Main Street toward his office. He didn't know what was wrong with the people of Serenity. Yes, it was hot, a condition that always made people short-tempered. But even with the heat, it almost seemed that there was something in the water that made people even more prone to violence.

Latham shook his head. *Something in the water,* he thought, laughing at himself. That was the sort of paranoid thinking he had come to expect of Starfleet, not of himself. He had been on far too many colonies, had been far too grounded in the day-to-day concerns of simple survival to succumb to such high-flying theories. To be sure, the heat and the daily contact with a race of people most of his colonists regarded as mortal—even murdering—enemies was enough to put anyone on edge. And the majority of his people were hardly expert in dealing with either of these extreme conditions.

He continued down Main Street toward his office in City Hall. Generally Latham walked through the colony quickly. The less time he spent out in Aneher's rays, the better. But today he moved more slowly. He may have won the brief fight with Galdamiz, but not without paying a price. He wasn't a young man anymore. The combination of the heat and the fight had winded him, and he wasn't recovering with the speed he might have liked. All of which did not put him in the best of moods as he walked. His ill humor was only heightened when he began to feel that he was being watched and knew exactly *who* was doing the watching. He turned around.

"Do you always just stand around and watch when your boss is being attacked?" Latham asked of Louis Alexander, the former Starfleet officer who headed up Serenity's security.

Alexander, who had, in fact, been leaning against the wall by the front door to his office watching the confrontation between Latham and Galdamiz, smiled as he straightened up and started to walk toward Latham. "Don't know why you're complaining, Dan. I was doing you a favor."

"Me?" Latham asked in a tone that conveyed both incredulity and demand.

Alexander centered the wide-brimmed hat on his head. He didn't actually need the hat. Everyone in Serenity used a sunscreen that could, at least, block the burning of Aneher's rays, even if it could do nothing about the star's pervasive heat. Alexander had once explained to Latham that he wore the hat because it cast most of his face in shadow, which he found very useful when he had to go head-to-head with either another colonist or a Klingon. When his face was hidden so his expression couldn't be read, the person he was facing off against tended to give him the benefit of the doubt and do what he asked.

When he had finished adjusting his hat so that it sat precisely where it gave maximum coverage to his head and face, Alexander looked out from under its brim at Latham.

"Yes, you. Sure I could have stepped in, but I figured it would be better for you to let Homero know he couldn't take you. Unless, that is, you want him to take a swing at you every time you piss him off."

"And what if I couldn't take him?"

"If I thought you were in any trouble, I would have stopped it, like any good referee."

"Most reassuring. Exactly how far were you prepared to let it go before you stopped it?"

"Considering how well you did, I guess you'll never know. Listen, you want me to haul Homero's butt in?" Alexander asked, gesturing toward the building he and Latham had come from, where both the colony's jail and hearing room were located.

"No. As you said, he's learned he can't take me. That should keep him from repeating his mistake. Besides which, he's already upset enough that the mines are behind schedule. I can't imagine that slowing things down even more by putting him behind bars will do anything to calm him."

"Your call, Dan," Alexander said. "Probably the right one. But if you *really* want to keep people from taking a swing at you, you should do what most of the rest of us are doing." Alexander patted the type-2 phaser that hung from the belt around his waist.

Latham shook his head. Yet another conversation he'd had several times before was being revisited. "This isn't Dodge City, Lou."

"Where?"

"Never mind. The thing is, walking around armed when the heat's making us all quick-tempered is a mistake. One I'm seriously considering fixing."

"All phasers are set on stun except in an emergency, Dan. You know that."

"And switching them to kill takes how long? It can be done as you draw the thing."

"Most of your people think living next to the Klingons is a mistake. Side phasers are the only things that make them feel safe. You try to take them away and you'll have a colonywide revolt on your hands. And I can't say I'd be on your side in it."

"I appreciate the warning. Now I have one for you. I haven't made any decision yet, although I'm *strongly* leaning toward banning all phasers, but if I should make that policy, I expect you to back and enforce it fully."

Latham and Alexander stood facing each other. They were about the same height, so they stood eye-to-eye, staring. Alexander was much younger than Latham and they both knew it. He had joined Starfleet directly out of the Academy, put in his twenty, and retired on full pension. When he had grown bored living the retiree's life, he decided to enrich his life and supplement his income by accepting the job as Serenity's chief constable.

Alexander was also in far better shape than Latham. He had spent every day of his life maintaining his body as it had been on the day he graduated from the Academy. They both knew that, too.

Most important of all, Alexander could have taken Latham. Easily. And they both were well aware of this fact, as well. Still, Latham did not back down. Just as he had done earlier with Galdamiz, he more than held his own, returning Alexander's stare without blinking or looking away.

Alexander smiled and pushed his hat back on his head so that his face was no longer hidden in its shadow and Latham could see his smile. "Yeah, I guess you would, at that. You know what your problem is, Dan? You're a hard man to like sometimes, but you're an even harder man to hate."

"Thanks. I only wish more of Serenity agreed with you."

"Dan, about that. I know you won't carry a phaser, but you *do* still have the ones I gave you, don't you?"

"Yes, Lou. Both the one in my office and the one in my study back home. I'm not completely unreasonable."

The two men laughed and went their separate ways. Alexander hadn't said what he was going to do, but Latham knew that it wouldn't be long before the security officer found and confronted Galdamiz. Just because the head of mining had learned he couldn't take Latham in a fair fight didn't mean that Alexander wouldn't do his job and remind Galdamiz that trying again wouldn't be a particularly smart idea.

Latham headed in the opposite direction, toward his office. As he walked, he looked around at the colony. At the end of Main Street, perched on a hill that fronted Lake Cochrane, was his house, a stately, almost palatial, Georgian colonial. Federation officials had said time was of the essence when they set up the colony. They made no secret that they wanted the colony up and running immediately so that they could beat the Klingons and secure Aneher II, with its mineral wealth, as a Federation world. To that end, they had sent a team from the Starfleet Corps of Engineers along with the replicated materials the transports brought. In only a month's time, the engineers used the materials and the most efficient building techniques their decades of colonization experience had devised to construct the stores, municipal offices, and other buildings that were essential to the colony's survival. By the time the colonists arrived, the town of Serenity was waiting for them.

The engineers also built temporary housing units. These were simple corrugated metal huts that the colonists could live in while they designed and then built houses to suit their own tastes and needs. But for the most part, the engineers didn't build the colonists's houses for them.

Still, there was one exception. One house was included in the initial set of buildings the engineers erected. Helen Latham had insisted on that as a condition for her—on their—going to Aneher II. Other houses had waited, but the self-styled queen of Serenity got her symbol.

The rest of the colony was more of a work in progress. The corrugated metal huts that had been built as temporary housing were becoming more and more permanent. The same heat that hindered the miners all but destroyed the colonists' desire to build more formal houses. They came home from the mines or the farms exhausted and overheated. The last thing they wanted to do was work some more out in the sun, building a house. Not when the huts were comfortable and air-conditioned. A few dozen houses had been finished, but for a colony of ten thousand that was a very small number. For the most part, the lots behind the huts contained the skeletons of houses that had been started but would probably never be finished. They'd just stay partially built, their frames baking under the Aneher sun.

* * *

"Well, you certainly took your sweet time coming here," Nemov said as Latham entered his office. Latham could hear the annoyance and pique that shaped the words.

"I had a run-in with Homero out on Main Street. Literally."

"Shall I have him brought in?"

"No. It was just a frustrated man letting off a little steam. And I think Lou is having a little talk with him. It'll be all right." Latham crossed the room to his desk and sat down. As he did, he looked at Nemov, who was standing in front of the desk. No, not standing, pacing. Latham took the time to study Nemov as he walked: his expression, his posture, his body language. All indicated that whatever Nemov had on his mind was of vital importance. "So what was it that you had to talk to me about in here, that we couldn't discuss back in the hearing room?"

Nemov said nothing at first. Instead he walked over to the office door, looked out to make sure no one was in the outer office, then shut the door. He walked back to the desk and sat down. Then he leaned forward as far as he could, so that his face was as close to Latham's as possible. He spoke in a measured tone, just loud enough that Latham could hear him but too soft to be heard by anyone else. "Daniel, I think we have a spy in the colony."

6. Latham did not move.

Other than to blink several times, he just sat looking. Not at Nemov. Not really at anything. And not staring. His eyes weren't fixed on anything. He just looked straight ahead as if at something that wasn't quite there. A completely blank expression was fixed on his unmoving face. He was not aware of time passing, and did not consciously attempt to form any thoughts about what he had been told.

Still time did pass and several thoughts came, then ran, unbidden, through his mind.

At first, he could not believe what Nemov had told him. These were his colleagues. His hand-picked team. Most were his *friends*. How could *any* of them betray the colony? Betray him? How *dare* he or she—whoever it was—sell out the colony? And for what? A few extra credits? Thirty pieces of silver? It was intolerable. Still, so many of them had come here seeking quick riches. And with the unexpected hardships and competition on Serenity, such riches were promises not even Latham and his experience could guarantee. That he could fail saddened him, but it also made him realize that what Nemov had said was, quite possibly, true. Someone in Serenity could well be supplying information to the Klingon colony.

And then, in the first sign of life that Latham exhibited after Nemov had dropped his thermite bomb, Latham laughed.

He had once read that there were five stages to grieving: denial, anger, bargaining, depression, and acceptance. He realized, even as he tried to stop the laughter that seemed to grip him uncontrollably, that with the exception of bargaining, the same reactions had just run through him. And maybe the laughter was his form of bargaining: let him get this one moment of amusement out of the situation before he addressed it in earnest.

"It's hardly a laughing matter, Daniel," Nemov said in a parent-to-child kind of tone that Latham had heard from him before. But Nemov had never been hesitant about criticizing Latham; at any time and about any thing. "It is probably the most serious matter we've ever had to discuss."

Latham looked up at Nemov's face, which had a decidedly serious expression that complemented the somber tone Nemov had affected. It *was* a serious matter. He inhaled slowly and deeply, using the same technique that helped stop hiccups, in an attempt to control the laughter. At the same time, he studied Nemov's expression again, as if trying to draw Nemov's somber frame of mind into himself so that he could match it and expel his own inappropriate reaction.

"Sorry, Grig. Nervous laughter."

"Nervousness, at least, is a fitting response. If what I fear is true, our entire effort here could be undermined."

"Grig, you almost sound like Homero," Latham said almost as if he wanted one last attempt to put off the subject. Then he sighed and asked, "What have you got?"

Nemov handed Latham a report and said, "Read the entries, you'll see."

Latham didn't like reading off screens. Even with his

Retinax treatments he had trouble positioning the damned things so that his eyes would focus on their small print. It was another reason he preferred reading and writing the old-fashioned way. He held the report out at arm's length, then slowly brought it toward him until his eyes were able to distinguish individual letters on the screen instead of orangish blurs. As he did, he sneaked a quick glance at Nemov to confirm his suspicions that his second-in-command secretly enjoyed watching his discomfort. Then, he started to digest the information.

He thumbed the screen scroll to the entry Nemov was talking about and read it. Immediately, memories of an embarrassing week came flooding back to him.

It had been three months ago. A data stream glitch had transposed two numbers in the colony's monthly yield report to the Federation Council. The yield reported, while not untoward, was better than anything they had been able to manage so far.

An innocent enough mistake except that, as Finagle's Laws seemed to dictate, things got worse. The Federation sent its own monthly report to the Organians, using the incorrect information. When the mistake was finally caught, the Federation was rather put off that they had to send a correction. After all, the Federation had originally noted with pride its superior crop yield as evidence that they were more than equal to the Klingon Empire when it came to colonizing harsh and inhospitable planets.

Latham looked at Nemov. "Okay," he said to the Russian, "so we left the Federation with egg on its collective face. I *still* don't see how this proves anything."

"By itself, it doesn't," Nemov answered. "But I take it,

while you were preparing for the hearing this morning, you did not have time to read your subspace mail."

"No," Latham said in agreement and immediately turned to the computer console on his desk. "Computer, display subspace mail."

"Working."

Latham had always found the voice programmed into the Federation computers irritating. It emulated a human female voice, but it had a tinny quality and its inflections always struck him as being slightly off. Not a lot, but just enough to remind him that it was a mechanical approximation of a human female voice he was hearing, not an actual human voice. He found the voice disquieting rather than soothing and reassuring, as the long-ago and nameless technician who had originally picked this voice had no doubted intended it to be.

Latham's subspace mail for the past several hours appeared on the monitor. He skimmed the mail until he came to a progress report the Klingons had filed and which the Federation had forwarded to them.

Like Serenity's reports, it listed the Klingon's accomplishments on Aneher II and compared them to Serenity's progress. Like the Federation's own reports, this document from the High Council served the dual purposes of information and propaganda. It didn't surprise Latham that Serenity did not come off well by comparison to the Klingon colony. That was, after all, the intent of the report.

But he couldn't find what item convinced Nemov that there was a spy in—

And then he saw it.

The date.

The report used the Klingon calendar, naturally. But Latham could convert the Klingon dates into Earth standard dates. The original transmission from Qo'noS occurred between the time that the Federation sent its own report for that period and the time the Federation had been required to send the corrected report with its updated wheat crop yield.

But the High Council's report used the *correct* wheat yield figures. Not the figures in the Federation report, which is what would have been available to the High Council at the time. Rather, it used figures the Federation did not even have in its possession at the time.

Figures the Federation didn't know yet. Figures the High Council could not have known unless someone who had access to the correct wheat yield computations had supplied that information to someone in Mak'Tor's colony. Someone in Serenity who discussed these figures and was familiar with them.

Someone whose business required that they know them.

Someone on the senior staff.

For the second time that day, Daniel Latham sat in his chair not moving. His eyes were directed at his monitor screen, but was not looking at it. In his mind, he was looking past the monitor, down Main Street to the palace that sat at its end. And for the first time in more years than he could remember, he was grateful that Helen always insisted that their house—the same, identical house on each new planet they colonized—be built first. He wanted to be there now, to be away from here, his office, this situation. He even imagined himself in the warmth of his study, surrounded by its fabricated cherry wood shelves, losing himself in the friendly books they held.

He wanted desperately to be there, reading them. And in his mind, he started to do exactly that; one by one, starting with his favorite book, the one whose opening line seemed so appropriate to his own life right now. "Whether I shall turn out to be the hero of my own life, or whether that station will be held by anybody else, these pages must show." That was where he wanted to be: in his study, and from there to Blunderstone in Suffolk and on to London. And the books held the people he wanted to be with: David Copperfield and Miss Trotwood, Agnes and Mr. Micawber. Hell, even Mr. Murdstone and Uriah Heap.

Anywhere but here. With anyone but . . .

"Daniel?"

Latham was, again, not aware that time had passed. He gathered it had, because of the stress that Nemov had put on his name, an irritated emphasis that indicated that he had said it several times and was growing tired of repeating himself.

"I'm sorry, what did you say, Grig?"

"I said, 'Will we let that son of a bitch Mak'Tor get away with this?' "

Latham shook his head. Then he said, even as he tried to contain a chuckle, "Mak'Tor? What makes you think Mak'Tor's behind the spy? No, it's not his style."

"*Not his style?* He's Klingon, Daniel. All they know is treachery."

"No. Oh, I agree that's the popular conception of Klingons, but I've been working very closely with

Mak'Tor for several months now and I've come to know the man."

Latham held up a hand to stop the protest from Nemov that he was sure was coming. "Klingons may be warriors, but most of them have a highly developed sense of honor and tradition that they value above all else. I've found Mak'Tor and most of his colony to be more honorable than many humans I've encountered."

Nemov looked at Latham with disgust. "How typical of you, Daniel, taking the Klingon's side."

"Oh, I believe you, Grig, that someone on the senior staff is supplying information to someone in the Klingon colony. I just don't think Mak'Tor is a part of it. Mak'Tor's a warrior. Yes, he'll meet you *mano a mano* on the field of battle, but he'd want it to be a fair fight. He'd find no honor in fighting a weaker opponent. And he wouldn't go in for sneaking around in shadows, spying on you to learn your weaknesses before that battle. He wouldn't want to know. He'd consider that an unfair advantage. And the same is true of our . . . competition on this planet. Make no mistake about it, Mak'Tor wants to win. Wants to prove that the Klingon Empire is better suited to colonize Aneher II than the Federation is. But he wants to do it honorably, in a fair competition. He doesn't want to subvert one of our people and pay for snippets of information that he could use in the competition. He wouldn't consider that fair or honorable. Spying just isn't his way."

"If not Mak'Tor, then who?" Nemov asked.

Latham leaned back in his chair. He steepled his fingertips and closed his eyes, thought for a bit, and then said one word, "Khogo."

"You're sure?"

"I've dealt with several of the higher-ups working under Mak'Tor. Khogo is the only one I can honestly say I don't like. Khogo doesn't have any honor. His main concern is his own ambitions. He doesn't approve of the Klingons having to share this planet with us any more than you approve of our having to share it with them. He thinks Klingon–human relations should go in a decidedly different way. It . . . irks him that Mak'Tor goes along with the limitations the Organians have imposed on them. He'd like nothing better than to supplant Mak'Tor so he could be more proactive in shaping Klingon–human relations."

For a moment, Latham didn't say anything. Then he nodded and added, "Yes, Khogo. I'd say he's responsible for a lot of the things we don't like that are going on in the Klingon colony."

Nemov leaned forward, bringing his large head within inches of Latham's own, and fixed his own stare into Latham's eyes. "What are we going to do about it?" he said with a delivery that reminded Latham more of a demand than a question.

" *'We'* are going to do nothing. *I* am going to think about it between now and tonight. And tonight I'm going to talk to Mak'Tor about it."

"Tonight?" Nemov said and the expression on his face changed from one of determination to one of horrified surprise. "But tonight is Landing Day celebration. As head of the colony—"

"I'm sure Serenity can drink its fill without me. It will give everyone more to drink. But we need to do something about this immediately. And Mak'Tor has a right to know, too."

"Still, tonight . . ."

"What about tonight, Daniel?" Both Latham and Nemov turned to look toward the door to the office in response to the question. They saw Helen Latham standing in it with a scowl on her face and her arms crossed. Latham recognized the body language. Helen knew she was about to hear bad news and was preparing herself not to take it well.

"Daniel is meeting with Mak'Tor tonight."

Helen rushed into the room like a charging Geskana player and was screaming long before she reached Latham's desk. "What do you mean you're meeting with Mak'Tor tonight? You have responsibilities and obligations tonight that—"

"That will have to get along without me," Latham said. He tried to sound as pleasant as he could, even as he interrupted his wife's diatribe. "I'm sorry, I'd like to be with you, my dear, really I would. But duty calls. You'll have to be the social butterfly without me tonight. I'm sure you can manage. It *is* what you live for."

"Don't you take that tone with me!"

"I will take whatever tone is necessary to end this conversation, Helen. If you want me to participate in any part of tonight's festivities, I'll have to make my meeting with Mak'Tor as early as possible. And for that I'll have to start preparing for it now. Good-bye."

"But—"

"Do not waste your time, Helen," Nemov said, and put his hand on her arm. "Daniel may be a fool, but he's a *stubborn* fool. You cannot convince him he is wrong."

Helen started to speak, then she looked into Nemov's face.

Latham saw the gentle touch that Nemov gave Helen as

well as the special, private look they shared. *Do they have to make it so obvious?* he thought as Nemov let her out of the room. He knew the two of them would be starting their celebration even earlier than the rest of the colony. He realized there was quite a bit he had to think about before his meeting tonight with Mak'Tor.

Latham wasn't aware how long it had taken him to finish his writing. He remembered how that morning, he had seemed to scratch out as many sentences as he wrote, as he tried to accuse the Klingon High Council and Mak'Tor of risking their people by using supply sleds to transport replacement miners. He remembered each and every false start he had made.

Now the writing flowed from his hand as effortlessly as the ink flowed from his pen. It was all a matter of perspective. His meeting with Nemov made him realize he was looking at the problems from the wrong way. He'd been trying to fix the blame on the wrong party. Once he knew how he should be looking at things, he was able say what he had to say easily.

He even realized there was more that needed to be in his report than the simple smuggling.

When he finished, he capped his pen with a satisfied smile and looked down at the book lying before him. The report was basically done. One last proofreading pass, then he'd read it into his computer so that he could send it to everyone who had to read it, both on Serenity and in Starfleet. But not now. He always liked to put some time and distance between draft and the final proofreading. When what he had written was too fresh in his mind, he tended to miss things. And he couldn't afford to miss anything on this.

Latham put the book into his attaché case. He'd take it home, have a quick dinner, and proofread it when he'd finished. That should give him enough time.

His thoughts of dinner reminded him that it was getting late. Both here and in Mak'Tor's colony. If he wanted to meet with Mak'Tor tonight, he had better set the meeting up now.

"Computer."

"Working."

"A communiqué to Mak'Tor," he said, and realized that now not even the computer's nonhuman voice was grating on him. "Make the subject 'Our Mutual Friend.'"

Homero Galdamiz was multi-faceted, very much like the firegems he had once mined on Epcir Prime. Few in Serenity knew that, as a child, he had been very interested in computers before the promise of quick riches, coupled with the fact that he enjoyed a workout, had drawn him to mining. In one of his earliest mine postings, circumstances had forced him to double as the colony's computer officer. And even though he had a talent for computers, he didn't enjoy working them. So, before he left Epcir Prime, he used his computer skills to alter his record and remove all mention of his having worked the machines. With no mention of these skills on his record, he'd never have to double again. He had even taken to exaggerating the natural apocope of his speech, because it made him seem less like someone who would work in computers.

But he had maintained the skills, studying in secret and practicing them in each colony he worked. Because one simply didn't know when those skills might come in handy.

As they had in Serenity.

One of the computer skills he had developed enabled him to write a virtually undetectable backdoor program that gave him access to every computer in the colony.

When Khogo had approached him about spying for him in Serenity, Galdamiz accepted. Eagerly. At least that way he could earn some of the fortune that Latham's unenlightened attitudes was costing him.

His skills had, until today, served him well by keeping his activities secret. Or so he thought. Then he read the computer mail that Latham sent to Mak'Tor. Mail that outlined Latham's belief that someone on his senior staff was spying on the colony and turning information over to Khogo. The mail ended with Latham's asking that Mak'-Tor meet with him that night because there was "much they had to discuss."

Galdamiz erased the computer mail off his machine, then sent a spike virus back to Latham's computer to wipe it off that machine as well. Latham might notice the spike, but probably not. After all, Latham didn't use his computer much. And the risk that Latham might notice the spike was far less than the risk of leaving the mail on Latham's computer, where anyone might find and read it.

When Galdamiz received confirmation that his spike had wiped the offending message off Latham's computer, he modified the parameters on the backdoor program in Latham's computer. Now, instead of looking for certain key words and forwarding files that contained them to his computer, the backdoor carried out Galdamiz's new order: to route copies of *all* new files that showed up on Latham's computer to his own. Then he did the same with the backdoor into Nemov's computer.

It increased the risk that someone—most likely Chiaki Iino—might find the backdoor and trace it back to him. But the risk that Chiaki might find him was more than off-set by his need to keep constant scrutiny over Latham and Nemov, so that if they discovered him he'd have enough warning to flee.

When he had finished his security precautions, he pulled his personal communicator. He turned it over, opened the back plate, and adjusted the tuning of his comm, switching it to a low-band frequency that operated through standard space instead of the usual subspace channels—a frequency that neither the Federation nor the Klingon Empire had much occasion to use.

But he did, when he had to talk with Khogo.

The Klingon answered Galdamiz's call and did not attempt to mask the irritation in his voice. *"What is it?"*

"They're on to us."

"On to us?"

"Latham knows that someone's spyin' for you. He hasn't figured out it's me yet. But that's probably only a matter of time."

"I can see how that would be of concern to you, human. Why do you risk communication with me over this matter?"

" 'Cause Latham's also told Mak'Tor about his suspicions. In fact, he and Mak'Tor are meetin' tonight. An' you know what they're goin' to talk about? *Us!"*

Khogo didn't respond immediately, and Galdamiz was sure he was doing what Galdamiz had seen him do so many times when they had met in person to exchange information for credits; Khogo was stroking his beard.

Then, after what seemed an eternity to Galdamiz, Khogo

spoke again, and Galdamiz could swear he heard laughter in the Klingon's usually harsh voice.

"Let them meet," Khogo said. *"I'm sure they know nothing about us."*

"An' if they do?"

"If they do, they do. It won't matter. I'll deal with them—both of them—as I deal with all my enemies."

7.

Outside, in the skies above Serenity, a fireworks display filled the dark with its pyrotechnic wonders. All over Serenity, its citizens—those who weren't in the bars and well on their way to celebrating Landing Day in an entirely different manner—looked up with the wide-eyed gaping and vocalized "oohs" and "aahs" that such displays usually earned.

They came by the thousands.

Some stood on the beach that lined Lake Cochrane so that they could get the best view of the fireworks as they were launched from the small boat that floated in the lake. They watched as the rockets arced upward and exploded into multicolored blossoms, then they looked down quickly to see those same colors reflected in the water.

Some sat on the hills to the west of the city and looked to the skies. Others took the more relaxed way and lay back on the hills, so that they, also, could look up at the fireworks, but without any effort. There were even some who chose to look at the one they were with and didn't really care about what was in the sky.

Most, however, stood in the streets of Serenity staring and pointing up. They milled through the colony's arteries looking more like ants swarming around their hill than a group of people. Most chose to stand where they were and hope their spot afforded a good view of the fireworks. Those that did move, if they could at all, did so slowly. Too many people on too few roads insured that moving was more a matter of starting and stopping, dodging and weaving, maneuvering to avoid bumping into someone

Every street was packed, Main Street most of all. It wasn't as bad as Bourbon Street during Mardi Gras in full swing, but that was only because Serenity had far fewer people than New Orleans. Tonight, other than the few who had to work, the entire population of Serenity, ten thousand strong, was out in the colony somewhere. Before the night was over, children would revel in the fireworks and celebration and then enjoy staying up well past their bedtimes, and with their parents' blessing. Those same parents would celebrate not only Landing Day but the fact that for a night, they got to be children again. The security forces would break up countless fights and make several arrests. Tomorrow nothing would be accomplished in the colony as it recovered from the night before. No one cared. And no one would have wanted it any different.

They had worked hard the past year, under conditions that were trying, arduous, even unbearable, and they had borne them all. Maybe they hadn't exactly prospered in Serenity, but they had persevered and been productive. In the first year of a colony on a planet that was little better than hell itself, being productive was more than just an accomplishment. It was a cause for celebration.

So a celebration it was. Maybe not as loud as Mardi Gras or as crowded as New Year's Eve in Times Square or even as colorful as Coronation Day on Troyius, but it was the best that Serenity had. And that was more than good enough for its people.

Daniel Latham did not see the fireworks.

His study hung over Lake Cochrane with a two-story picture window that ran from ceiling to floor and gave a spectacular view of the water that provided life to the colony. Tonight, the window gave an equally spectacular view of the many-hued fireworks, both the colorful bursts in the sky and their equally colorful reflections in the lake below.

Daniel Latham did not see them.

He sat at his desk, ignoring the display. He was finishing the final proofreading of the words he had written earlier that afternoon. When he finished that, he would read the report out loud, so that his computer could transcribe it into its memory. Then he'd be able to send it out.

Just as he preferred writing by hand, he also preferred dictating his finished product. Scanning the page directly into the computer would have been faster, but not as satisfying. Nor as accurate. Optical character recognition programs may have been close to three hundred years old, but in many ways the technology was no better now than when it had first been invented. The process of scanning text and converting it into binary information the computer could understand and display on a monitor also created errors that ranged from minor mistakes to things that could only be called abnormalities. Anytime the computer did not recognize something for any reason—and he had to admit that often it was his handwriting—it tried to approximate what had been written. Latham found that when he scanned, he had to spend as much time correcting these "best guesses" by an artificial intelligence as he would spend simply dictating what he wrote directly into the computer. So tonight, even though time was of the essence and he had to press ahead so that he could complete his task before his meeting with Mak'Tor, he intended to dictate the report.

He had ordered his computer to play Beethoven's Seventh Symphony, one of the longest and possibly the most beautiful of the old master's works. He ordered it loud, to cover up the noise of the fireworks. He wanted no distractions as he sat at his desk, read to his computer, and made any final edits he thought of. Nothing that would take him away from what he wanted to do.

Unfortunately for him, the music had worked too well as a bar to distractions. He was not aware that Helen was coming into the study until she opened the door.

Latham moved quickly, with the practiced fluidity of a maneuver he had performed many times. He closed the book he had been writing in, picked it up, spun on his chair's swivel to face the bookshelf directly behind him, and slipped the book into its waiting space on the shelf. It slid neatly into an empty hole between two other books in the middle of a seventeen-volume set, all matched and identically bound.

Usually, he would have heard Helen's distinctive footsteps coming down the hallway and from far enough away that he would have finished the maneuver and turned back to face the door before she entered his room. But he had expected her to be out partying with the rest of the colony. As a result, when he turned his chair back to face the front of the room, he found Helen already well into his study, confronting him.

She loomed before him, looking almost twice as large as she was because of the thick, quilted overcoat she wore. As was usual with Helen, the coat was more than she needed. Aneher II got cold at night, but the coat she had on was one designed for an ice planet. But that was Helen, she never wanted to be uncomfortable.

"It's always about *you*, isn't it, Daniel? Here Serenity is having its biggest celebration and instead of being out with your people, as their leader should be, you've sequestered yourself in your little hidey-hole writing. Selfish as ever!"

Helen reached down and plucked the pen from Latham's desk and pointed its uncapped nib at him as if it were a spear she wanted to thrust through his heart. "The next time you want to hide what you're doing, you should remember your pen!" she said to him in a voice that easily drowned out both music and fireworks. "I've lived with you too many years not to know your damned habits. You *never* leave your pens lying around uncapped, unless you've been writing! Wouldn't want all that valuable ink to dry out, now would you? I swear, Daniel, I think you care more about your pens than you do about me!"

"That wouldn't be hard," Latham said before he could stop himself. Helen's face turned scarlet, and she threw the pen at Latham like the missile she probably wished it had been.

Although the pen bounced harmlessly off Latham's chest, it didn't do so without effect. He looked at her and could feel his own face reddening as brightly as hers had. He reached up and pointed across the room. "There's the door, Helen. *Do* let it hit you on the backside on your way out." Then he added, not as an afterthought, "Preferably hard."

Rather than go toward the door, Helen moved with a swiftness that surprised Latham, especially considering that she was wearing a pair of her stupid, impractical high heels. Even before Latham realized what she was doing, Helen was standing in front of him and glaring down at him as she said, "Don't you *dare* dismiss me, like I was some . . . some . . ."

"Commoner? But that's exactly what you are." Latham stood up so that she had to look up at him and continued. "I don't think there's anyone more common than you. A cheap, philandering slattern whose only attributes seem to be an overinflated sense of self-importance and an ability to make your voice more shrill than a Merakian squeal-worm."

"How . . . dare . . . you—"

"As if on cue."

Helen's response was sudden and explosive. Her right hand shot out and slapped Latham across the face, producing a sharp sound that, like her voice before, was loud enough to be heard over both the music and the fireworks.

Although his cheek smarted, Latham did not reach up to touch it. He stood staring at Helen, an anger as intense as the pain he felt on his face burning in his eyes.

Helen had hit him only once before, shortly after the tragedy that had claimed their Katherine. He had sworn to her then he would never allow her to do that again. Now, although he didn't know that he could hate anyone as much as he hated Helen at that moment and didn't know what he was going to do to live up to that vow, he moved toward her.

Only to find, again, that Helen had, again, moved more quickly than he could have imagined.

"Don't come near me, Daniel!" Helen said, punctuating her command by pointing the phaser she had taken from his desk drawer directly at his head.

Latham blinked once, in bewilderment. Their marriage was a sham, but he couldn't believe it had gotten so bad that Helen would actually pull a phaser on him. Then he saw the look of pure hatred that filled her face and made her, for the first time since he had met her, actually ugly. Then he looked at the phaser in her hand, in particular at the controls on the back of the grip.

And he laughed.

"Stay back, Daniel! I . . . I mean it!"

Latham noted that the hatred in Helen's face was quickly being replaced by fear. He realized that the strangeness of his reaction—his laughter in the face of a phaser—was making her uncertain. Of what he would do next. Of his sanity. He saw the determination in her face waver and the hand that was holding the weapon shake.

Then, in a movement every bit as quick as any Helen had managed, he reached out and took the phaser from his wife.

"You stupid bitch," he said while pointing the phaser just to the left of her head and pressing the trigger. Nothing happened. "That thing isn't even charged. I only keep it because I promised Lou Alexander I would.

"Of course, it's not like *you* knew that, is it?" he said, and dropped the phaser. He found that the hatred he had felt for his wife only seconds earlier was gone. To be sure, he was still as angry with her as he had ever been with anyone in his life, but he didn't hate her. She wasn't worth the effort.

"I expect you to be gone when I return tonight, Helen. I don't care where you go, frankly. Off planet would be preferable, but I doubt you can arrange it on such short notice. Have someone tell me where to send your things, as I doubt I'll ever have the desire to talk to you again.

"You are, of course, not welcome here any longer. I'll make sure Lou Alexander is apprised of your antics tonight, and I'm sure he'll be more than happy to enforce the order. Perhaps it's unfair of me to kick you out of your own house, but what can I say? Rank hath its privileges.

"One more thing, you can expect me to make the divorce as difficult as possible. I intend to see to it that you get nothing. And even in these enlightened times, between your indiscretions, your infidelities, and your attempt to kill me, I don't think I'll have any trouble convincing a judge that you simply aren't entitled to much."

"Daniel, I . . ."

"Save it, Helen. I really don't care what you have to say anymore. And please, spare us both the scene. One way or the other, you *are* leaving here tonight. Either under your own power or in Lou's restraints, charged with attempted murder.

"Your choice."

For the second time that night, and one of only a handful of times in the past several years of their marriage, Latham's words to his wife—or his *ex*-wife, as he suddenly realized he should start calling her—achieved his desired effect. Her face blanked, as if all life and expression had spilled out of it, and she left.

No words. No crying. No scene. She simply left. His

study and his house. She went out to wander the streets of Serenity alone.

Latham didn't think she would be alone long. Only until she found Nemov. Then, not only would she no longer be alone, she would also stop being quiet. When she found Nemov she would have all the time and audience she wanted for her words and her crying and her scenes.

It was over. Their marriage. Their life. It wasn't sudden or unexpected. This day, this result, had been a long time in coming. And yet, even though Latham couldn't say the end had been unexpected, in some ways he still hadn't expected it.

He looked down at the phaser pistol lying on the bare surface of his desk, its control knob turned to the kill setting. No, he hadn't expected it.

Maybe no one does.

8. It wasn't his house anymore.

Not tonight, anyway. And maybe it never really had been.

It had been Helen's design in the first place, a blueprint she conceived and helped draft on one of their earliest colonies. A house that was simple enough to be reproduced easily on each colony world, yet elegant enough to befit her perception of herself. She had insisted on its being built first and reproduced exactly on each new world they colonized. Other than Latham's study, centered as it was around his preferred, antiquated styles and, of course, his bookshelves, nothing in the house had ever really been Daniel Latham's.

Her design. Her showplace. Her palace.

Never his. He only lived there.

Even tonight, even after he had ordered Helen out of the house and told her never to return to it, it still felt like *her* house, not his. In fact, tonight it was worse. Latham felt out of place in his own house.

Nothing felt right to him. Not even his study—his only refuge—offered any comfort. He didn't know what he was going to do. He didn't know where he was going to go, but he knew he couldn't spend the night in the house.

But he didn't want to pack anything, either. The streets were so full of celebrants that simply walking through them was going to be a challenge, and he didn't want to add to that challenge by carrying a suitcase. Even his attaché case, which was smaller and lighter, was more than he wanted to carry through the crowd.

He pulled the book he had been writing in from the bookshelf and lay it on his desk. Then he took a small portable workstation from a bottom desk drawer and found himself surprised at how much dust had collected on it. He turned it on and pressed the icons on the faceplate keypad to activate the text scanning program. His facility with the unit might have surprised the other members of the senior staff, who always joked about Latham's hatred of machines. It was never that he hated them or was unable to use them. He was, in fact, quite adept with them. They were, after all, what everyone who worked with him used, so he knew he had to be able to use them, too. He simply preferred not to use them whenever possible.

Tonight was one of those times when it wasn't possible. He wanted to take his report from his study back to his office without carrying his attaché case, or even the book it was written in. He had to scan it.

When he finished, he had the unit link with his office computer so that the document would be there and waiting for him when he reached his office. He shuddered as he thought, almost fearful, of what he'd find later, when he called the document up on his computer and saw what approximations the scanning program's character recognition mode had made of his handwriting this time. *Oh well,* he thought, *I've rewritten this report so many times, I almost know it by heart.* Which meant he'd also be able to use his memory to correct and supplement whatever anomalies had scanned into the computer.

He turned off the unit and slipped it into his pocket. Then he slid the book back into its space on the bookshelf. He walked across the room to the door and was about to turn off the lights in his study, when he saw the phaser pistol still lying on his desk, hardly the appropriate place for *that* little item.

He crossed the room back to his desk and picked up the phaser, using only the index finger and thumb of his right hand on the grip, as if he feared he would be contaminated if any more of his body touched it. Then he dropped it into one of the other throwbacks to olden times in his study: the wastebasket.

He went back to the door, and this time he did turn off the lights, throwing the whole house into darkness. Much like the life it had once symbolized.

Helen Latham left her house alone. She didn't stay that way for long. She walked only far enough away from her house to be sure that Daniel couldn't see her—and to work up what seemed the appropriate amount of tears—before she summoned Nemov on his personal comm. They arranged to meet, discreetly, in Nemov's house. By the time she arrived, Helen had control of both the needed tears and herself.

"This is bad," Nemov said, as he and Helen embraced in his living room. They kept the lights off so that no one would be able to peer into the house, and closed the curtains so that they wouldn't be suddenly and unexpectedly caught in the light of the fireworks for all of Serenity to see. "You actually pulled a phaser on him?"

"I . . . I just lost control," Helen answered between the pants that had come as she stopped crying. "Don't you see, Grig, I couldn't bear it anymore. Living with *him* and not being able to show my feelings for you. I knew as long as Daniel was alive, we could never be together. I . . . I just didn't know what I was doing. Thank God the phaser wasn't charged. Otherwise I don't know *what* might have happened!"

"No, Daniel doesn't keep his personal phaser charged, just the one in his office. But you are right, things are coming to a head. It is perhaps time we had it out with Daniel."

"What, go to him *tonight?* No, Grig, I don't think I could."

"No. Not us. Me. Promise me *you* won't see Daniel tonight."

"I promise."

"Good. This is for him and me. To be settled between men. You don't . . . mind, do you?"

"No. No, not at all. Thank you."

Helen looked at Nemov and saw that he was looking toward the window. Staring, in fact. If the curtains had been open and he could have seen the town, Nemov would have been staring in the direction of City Hall and Latham's office. Helen reached up and put her hand gently on Nemov's chin, then even more gently guided his eyes back toward her. When he did look in her eyes again, the love in them was obvious.

Nemov brought his head down and the two embraced, then kissed. Nemov tried to tighten the embrace but found that Helen, instead, maneuvered his hands to the straps of her gown.

Helen had already left as Nemov dressed slowly, thinking about things. So, Daniel had put Helen out. He realized he wasn't completely disappointed by that news. It would speed matters up, make Helen come to him all the faster.

As Nemov put on his pants, he looked out the window to the crowded streets. Helen was out there in those crowds somewhere. Nemov didn't like having to send her out to look for a room in one of Serenity's boardinghouses. But they had both decided she couldn't stay at his house. Not tonight. It wouldn't look right.

He wouldn't have been able to be here for her anyway. He had things to do that night. Not the things that might be expected of the second-in-command on Serenity's night of celebration. These were private matters between him and Latham. Where he stood. Where Helen stood. Things that had to be settled—how had Latham put it?—*mano a mano*.

Out on the streets, Helen Latham had grown tired of many things. Thinking about which of the limited number of inns and boardinghouses in Serenity would be the least uncomfortable if she had to stay in one tonight; and she *didn't want* to have to stay in one tonight. Considering what excuse she'd give for why she wouldn't be sleeping at home. Having to say hello to everyone in the crowds who passed her. Worse, having to smile and greet them as if nothing were wrong—"Hello, Ms. Stilger" "Yes, it *is* a wonderful celebration" "No, I don't believe I've ever seen more beautiful fireworks"—was certainly high on the list of things she had tired of. Having to accommodate these yokels, to pretend they were her equal, had grown as irksome as when she once walked on the beaches on Alcaria and had to spend the better part of an hour picking the sand ticks off her legs.

Higher still on her list of things that had grown wearisome was the memory of Daniel. Smug, superior Daniel. Condescending, arrogant Daniel. She bristled at the thought that he'd had the last word before she left.

That was the thing she really couldn't tolerate, that Daniel had had the last word. She'd have to do something about that.

True, she had promised Grig that she wouldn't go back to Daniel that night, but she hardly considered that binding. There were, after all, any number of ways she could get to Daniel's office without being seen.

Yes, the more she thought about it, the more she knew, Daniel simply *couldn't* have the last word. She *would* have to do something about that.

Louis Alexander read the message that Latham had beamed to his terminal over and over. *Dammit, Daniel, you're overreacting!*

Well, maybe overreacting was a bit strong. According

to the report, Helen *had* pulled a phaser on Daniel, after all. But even so, ordering Alexander to collect *all* the phasers in Serenity because he didn't want any more private ownership of phasers in the colony was excessive.

No, Alexander decided, he had been right. That *was* overreacting.

He had to talk to Daniel. He didn't know when his duties this night would permit it. The celebration and the celebrants were both going strong, were, in fact, only a short hair from getting out of hand. He was needed out here on the streets. But as soon as he could, he *had* to go to Daniel's office and talk to him.

He just hoped Daniel would listen. Alexander was angry enough that, if necessary, he was prepared to do quite a bit more than just talk.

Khogo didn't understand the colors in the sky. Oh, Galdamiz had explained the Landing Day celebration as well as what fireworks were to the Klingon second-in-command, but Khogo still did not understand them.

Celebrating a simple arrival and not a great victory seemed a waste of time to him.

And these fireworks. Not as practical as the *kor'tova* candle he had lit as a youth to commemorate his intention to follow the noble warrior's path, the fireworks' only purpose seemed to be to fill the sky with bright colors and loud sounds. Didn't the humans realize that an enemy could easily launch an attack under the cover of the noise and confusion that their fireworks created? No, apparently not. No more than they realized that the gunpowder wasted in the fireworks would have served them far better in weapons, no matter how antiquated those weapons might be.

Still, the humans were preoccupied with so many trivial things—their parties, these fireworks, and the way Galdamiz was obsessed with the meeting tonight between Mak'Tor and Latham. Galdamiz was so worried about whether he had been discovered as a spy for the Klingons that he completely missed the *real* intent of the plan.

The cursed humans were *supposed* to find out that they had a spy in their midst. That had been Khogo's desire all along. The meager information Galdamiz's petty spying supplied Khogo was of little use. The true purpose had always been about maneuvering the two people on Aneher he wanted to be rid of into their proper places, so that the next step of his overall plan could be executed.

Finally, the maneuvering was complete. Tonight, Mak'-Tor and Latham were supposed to meet to discuss the spy. Such a meeting could only be difficult. One could expect it to produce shouting and recriminations and bitter feelings—ill will and explosions every bit as spectacular as the humans' fireworks.

Khogo walked out of his office and down the corridor toward the transporter room. With a contented smile on his face, Khogo manipulated the transporter controls and set the coordinates for Latham's office. Later Mak'Tor would use this transporter. By the time Mak'Tor arrived, however, Khogo's plan would be well on its way toward ridding him of both Mak'Tor *and* Latham.

It could all just go away if it weren't for Latham.

Homero Galdamiz was not out in the Landing Day celebration, as he didn't feel much like celebrating. His world was coming out of its orbit, and one thought kept coming back to him over and over: *It could all just go away if it weren't for Latham.*

Outside, the town of Serenity was dark but for the occasional fireworks that lit up the sky. Inside his office, it was darker, as there was no light save the occasional explosion that shined through his window. In his own mind, it was darker still.

Galdamiz sat in his office chair with his right elbow resting on the chair arm and his head cradled in his right hand. His eyes were closed, and he rubbed his forehead repeatedly, almost obsessively while he thought, *it could all go away if it weren't for Latham.*

He kept his eyes closed so that he wouldn't look at the fireworks. Why did he want to see them? They were bright, colorful, optimistic. Everything that, at the moment, his life was not.

At first, he had been flattered when Latham asked him personally to head up Serenity's mining operations. Not only was it a great compliment—or so he thought at the time—it would also look good on his résumé. Latham and he seemed to see eye-to-eye on things, right down to keeping their offices sparse. Latham said it was for greater efficiency; Galdamiz kept his existence Spartan because he just didn't see the reason for moving everything from his home to a colony only to have to move it all back again when the colony posting was finished.

But he had come to realize he'd been wrong about Latham. Latham and he couldn't see eye-to-eye if they were both Nimporian Cyclopes in a staring match. He wasn't sure if he ever disagreed with a man as much as he disagreed with Latham. Hell, the two of them probably couldn't even get together enough to agree to disagree.

A particularly loud explosion shook Galdamiz's office and startled him so much that he opened his eyes. Without conscious thought his eyes took in his office. In his mind's eye, he contrasted his office with the lavish furniture his wife had probably filled their home back on Earth with by now.

When he and the other miners on Janus VI first started working with the Hortas, they all knew they were going to be richer than they could possibly imagine. He subspaced his wife back on Earth and they discussed how they were going to invest their newfound riches. They decided on real estate. They bought a bigger, grander house for his wife and their children to live in—and him when he finally retired. They bought equally grand furniture for the house. And they bought, as well, several investment plots on colony worlds around the quadrant. When Starfleet promised him incomprehensible bonuses for bringing in the mines on Aneher II, they bought more of everything. It seemed that not only had their starship come in, it could hit warp ten.

But he hadn't figured on that bastard, Latham. Hadn't figured that Latham would actively block the only way mining Aneher II could be profitable.

Latham, what is it? Profits are without honor in your kingdom? Galdamiz shook his head. Not even one of his puns could make this situation tolerable. He had walked away from the fortunes being earned on Janus VI to join Aneher and now he was being prevented from earning a bigger fortune on Aneher.

And all the while, the subspace communications, the ether mails, the calls on their personal comms, even the old-fashioned dunning letters—all of them once requesting, but now demanding, money—were coming in. And kept coming in. He and his wife were going to lose it all, and it was all that bastard Latham's fault.

Galdamiz opened the bottom drawer of his desk to take out the bottle of Tellarian fireale he kept there. He also pulled a not particularly clean glass out of the drawer. Cleanliness didn't count for much. Whatever germs might be on the glass wouldn't last long when bathed in fireale.

Closing the drawer, he said, "Computer, bring up any new files on Daniel Latham's computer." Even as the computer said, *"Working,"* Galdamiz also spoke and drowned out the computer voice, "Let's just see what you're up to tonight, Latham." He didn't say it to anyone, just said it aloud for the satisfaction of hearing his own voice and knowing there were still *some* things in his life he actually controlled.

The computer went about its business, and Galdamiz poured himself a large drink. He leaned back in his chair and started to swallow the burning liquid. As he did, his eyes fell on the fully charged phaser pistol that was hanging on a coat hook near his door. He almost never went outside without the type-2 phaser strapped to his hip. But when he was in his office, he kept it on the hook rather than wear it while he sat.

Galdamiz drained his glass, poured another drink, and read the few new files that his backdoor program had pulled from Latham's computer. When he finished reading them, Galdamiz drank his second fireale even quicker than he had the first. He poured a third drink, bigger than either of the first two, then sat for a time drinking a bit more slowly and staring at the phaser. The phaser disappeared and reappeared, as his office went from dark to fully illuminated by the fireworks explosions that flared through his window.

It could all just go away if it weren't for Latham.

Chiaki Iino was more than a little drunk. Tonight was supposed to be a celebration, not just of the colony's landing on Aneher, but of him and Ron.

Neither he nor Sayger were sure exactly when they met. They had seen each other many times on the ship during their transport to the colony, but neither had ever really fixed in their minds the day when they first spoke. Any more than either could remember whether that first conversation was anything more meaningful than a guarded "excuse me" for accidentally bumping into each other in some corridor. No matter when that first meeting had occurred, at the time neither had known there would be a reason to note the date or time.

So, for want of having an exact date to fix upon to commemorate the start of their relationship, they chose instead Landing Day, the day they arrived in Serenity and started their life together. As Iino had joked, "At least this way, neither of us will ever forget our anniversary."

Tonight they had planned an evening together, just the two of them. To hell with trying to weave their way through the crowded streets or craning their necks up so they'd be stiff the next day just so they could watch some fireworks. They had their own celebration in mind, their own kind of fireworks.

"Had" being the operative word now.

All their plans had vaporized as spectacularly as the skyrocket charges overhead.

Iino knew that Ron had started his celebration one

night too early. He also knew that Ron may have been as much at fault for starting the previous night's bar fight as the Klingon who had beaten Ron senseless. But of the two, Ron had, by far, gotten the worse of the fight. Ron had simply not been a match for the Klingon, not even with his mine-sculpted body that Iino so admired.

So, yes, technically Ron may have been partially responsible for the fight, but what the hell was that Klingon bastard doing in O'Dell's anyway? It was a human bar. Any Klingon who went into it knew he was asking for a fight. No, as far as Iino was concerned, Ron had already suffered enough and there was simply no excuse for Latham to have turned him over to the Klingons.

So, shortly after he got off work, Iino went to one of the bars at the edge of Serenity's town center and sat in a dark back corner, where he hoped few other than the bartender would see or interrupt him. The practically empty bottle of blended scotch that sat on the table in front of him showed that he had not been nursing his drinks, either. Time after time, he'd pour two fingers of scotch in his glass, lift it to his lips, and as he downed each drink, have the same thoughts running through his head.

He thought of Ron standing in the prisoner's dock, the railed circle in the middle of the Klingon courtroom. When he had stood in the dock several months earlier, it had reminded him of the bar in the English courtrooms, but that was where any similarity between the fair trials of English system and the Klingon trials ended. He thought of the Klingon spectators surrounding the prisoner's dock, howling their disapproval and banging their staffs on the ground any time the proceedings didn't go exactly as they wanted. Of the robed Klingon judge wearing the traditional clawed gauntlet that he used to hold the electrified ball Klingons wielded instead of a gavel. Of the way the judge would slam that ball onto the bench, to regain what passed for order in the kangaroo courts the Klingons held. And each time he had these thoughts, he'd swallow the jigger in a gulp, then slam the glass down on the table as hard as the judge had struck the ball against his bench.

When his trial had ended—with the same predictable guilty verdict Ron's trial had this morning—Iino was sentenced to several weeks' hard labor in the dilithium mines on the Klingon side of Aneher II.

The Klingon miners were allowed to use sophisticated, phaser digging equipment. The prisoners had to hack the raw dilithium out of the ground with picks, shovels, and frequently their own hands. When a prisoner fell short of his quota, or it simply appeared that he would, the Klingons were quick to apply persuasion at the end of a painstik. It was while falling after being prodded with a painstik that Iino broke his leg. The Klingon medical facilities were unsophisticated, and whatever care they did offer was reserved for their own people. They healed Iino's leg just enough for him to continue to work in the mines, but no more. To this day, he still walked with a limp.

Iino tried to pour another drink for himself, but found the bottle was empty. He motioned for the bartender to bring him a new bottle, but all the bartender brought was a scowl.

"You've had enough, Chiaki. Go home and sleep it off."

"*I'll* tell you when I've had enough," Iino said, a lion's snarl behind his words.

"No, *I'm* letting *you* know: you've had enough. Last thing I need is for a fight to break out in here so I get shut down like O'Dell's." The bartender, a beefy man who could more than take care of himself, mixed just enough concern and determination in his voice that Iino could tell, even through his stupor, that he had overstayed his welcome.

Iino reached into his pocket, pulled out a handful of credit chips, and fumbled with them as he tried to find the correct change to pay for his tab.

"Forget it, Chi," the bartender said. "Tonight yours is on the house."

Iino looked at the bartender, regarding him with the same disdain he had showed when he scraped a Styrisian slime grub off the bottom of his boot. He took the handful of credits and slammed them on the table as hard as he had the bar glass.

"I don't want your charity!" he said in a tone that tried for a snarl but came out more as a slur. Then he stumbled out of the bar into Serenity. The streets were crowded and Iino bumped into several people, never with an apology. The only thing that kept him from falling was that there was simply no room for him to do so.

He wandered with no real thought of where he was going, somewhere in the general direction of his house. And then he saw Daniel Latham going into City Hall.

Oh, that's right, Iino thought, *Latham's damned meeting with Mak'Tor.* The sight of Latham brought such a surge of anger, he suddenly realized he was thinking more clearly than he had in hours. Certainly since he had received the communiqué from Latham about the meeting with Mak'Tor.

He had been sitting in his office watching as the computer system ran its daily systemwide diagnostic scan; the perfect activity for him in the mood he was in. He could watch the diagnostic displays show their constant progress and claim he was doing something, while actually he was brooding over Ron.

Latham wanted Iino to program the colony's transporter to beam Mak'Tor directly into the office, so that the Klingon didn't have to walk through the crowded streets that night.

True to his duty, Iino programmed the transporter to make the transfer that night. Then he checked that the diagnostic was going well, ordered the computer to send the diagnostic's results to his terminal, and left work early to start drinking for the day.

Why doesn't this surprise me, Latham? Iino thought. *Always solicitous to the Klingons before your own. God forbid that Mak'Tor should be inconvenienced by walking through the crowds before your secret meeting tonight. And how much of our dignity will you give him tonight?*

As Iino watched Latham enter City Hall, he realized that he never hated anyone as much as he hated Daniel Latham at that moment.

The first thing Latham had done when he got to his office was pull the phaser out of the desk drawer where he kept it and put in on the corner of his desk. He figured Lou Alexander would be in to see him sometime that night after the message he had commed to Lou's terminal. Latham wanted the phaser to be there and waiting, so that Lou could take it and get the thing out of his office without any further delay or trouble.

Then Latham called up his report onto the computer to see what kind of a garble the scanning had made of the document. He read it quickly and saw that it wasn't too bad. He'd be able to dictate a corrected version easily enough. Probably even be able to make some last-minute improvements on the fly, as he dictated.

He leaned back on his chair, propped his feet up on his desk, and began the task of dictating the report so that he could both correct it and make those final improvements in it. He did it with the single-minded determination he brought to so much of his life. By the time he had almost reached the conclusion of the report, he wasn't even aware of how much time had elapsed since he started.

Or that the door to his office was slowly opening.

9. "Hey, you seen Latham anywhere?"

Galdamiz was standing on the streets not too far from City Hall. Unlike most of the people around him, he wasn't looking at the fireworks overhead. Instead he had been walking around the colony and scanning the crowds looking for someone. When he saw Iino, he cupped his hands around his mouth and shouted out his question. He didn't get any reaction from Iino, only a blank expression, as if Iino hadn't heard him above the noise of the fireworks and the crowd.

Galdamiz started walking toward Iino and tried again, this time cupping his hands around his mouth and shouting the question. "I said, I'm lookin' for Latham, you seen him anywhere?"

Iino still didn't answer. He walked toward Galdamiz, put his hand up to his ear, and shook his head to indicate he couldn't hear whatever it was Galdamiz was saying.

Galdamiz couldn't help but notice the pronounced stagger in Iino's step as the computer expert walked toward Galdamiz. *Yup, pretty much what I heard—he's been drinkin' all day.*

Galdamiz had heard rumors from the other miners that Iino started drinking early and stopped only when the bars wouldn't sell to him anymore. Seeing Iino almost fall down as he tried to walk didn't do anything to disprove those rumors. Iino was definitely taking the whole Sayger thing hard.

Hell, so was Galdamiz. Sayger was one of the best workers down in the mines.

When Iino was close enough to Galdamiz that he wouldn't have to go hoarse shouting above the noise of the celebration all around them, he said, "I couldn't hear you, Homero. What did you say?"

"I'm lookin' for Latham. You seen him anywhere?"

"Probably in his office."

"His office?" Galdamiz looked over his shoulder back at City Hall. "What the hell's he doin' there?"

"His . . . big meeting with Mak'Tor tonight."

"His meetin' with Mak'Tor? Why would Latham be meetin' with the Klingons *tonight* of all nights? Other than that he's shown he couldn't Kahless about what we think?" Galdamiz noticed that even as drunk as Iino was, he still grimaced at the pun.

"Don't know why," Iino said, and Galdamiz noted that Iino's usually precise speech was clipped and slurred. "All I know is, Latham ordered me to set up the transporter to beam Mak'Tor in from the Klingon colony for a meeting tonight."

Galdamiz shook his head and was about to say something else when an accented voice from behind them interrupted.

"It's true."

Both Galdamiz and Iino turned suddenly, surprised by the booming voice that had come from down the street. They saw Nemov walking up to them. Galdamiz started to walk toward Nemov, but Iino slumped a bit and leaned against a wall behind him. So Galdamiz waited with Iino until Nemov reached them.

"What's true?" Galdamiz shouted to Nemov.

"What Chiaki said. Daniel is in his office meeting with Mak'Tor." Galdamiz was amazed that the Russian didn't even have to shout to be heard above the explosions and celebration.

"He's meetin' with the Klingons on *Landin' Day*?"

"*Da.*"

Galdamiz shook his head again, then contorted his face, scrunching it up into an expression of disapproval. "That's not right. No one should be workin' tonight. Not even Latham." As if to signify its agreement, the night sky above them suddenly erupted with a spectacular display of exploding colors and sounds.

"It's what Daniel wanted," Nemov said, shrugging his shoulders and spreading his hands wide in a gesture of apparent helplessness. "This very afternoon, I told him not to. He insisted. What could I do? Drag him out of his office?"

"Hey, why not?"

Nemov looked at Galdamiz for a moment. Then he cocked his head to one side and opened his eyes so wide that their whites could be seen even under his thick, bushy eyebrows. "What are you saying?"

"I'm sayin' why don't we go an' drag him out?"

"You can't mean it," Nemov said, even as a skyrocket produced an ominous-sounding rumble behind them.

"Of course I mean it. Look at 'em," Galdamiz said gesturing to the crowded streets around them. "Maybe all those people out there don't know Latham's not out here with them now, but that's just for now. Tomorrow they'll start thinkin' about the celebration, an' then these people— *Latham's* people—are gonna realize their leader couldn't even be bothered to show up for their party. An' that ain't right, Grig. Latham's sendin' the wrong message."

Nemov shook his head violently and waved his arm at Galdamiz. "It's maybe the *worst* idea I've ever—"

"No, I *like* it," Iino interrupted, suddenly standing very erect and alert. "Let's show him that those Klingon bastards shouldn't always come first. That sometimes the good of *his* people is more important."

"Are you both out of your minds?" Nemov asked, but found he was talking to no one. Galdamiz and Iino were already walking away from him and toward City Hall. Toward Latham's office. Nemov ran after them, but the two men continued to walk away from him, talking to each other and laughing.

Nemov increased his speed and passed the two men, then turned and stopped so that he was standing directly in their path. "Homero, Chiaki, think about it. If you do this, Daniel will be furious."

"It's better than havin' him ignore me all the time. At least if he's mad, I know he's noticed me. Just think of it as my notice *operandi*."

Galdamiz and Iino continued walking toward City Hall. Nemov watched them move away from him.

"Wait!" His loud bellow cut through the din that surrounded them. "Wait for me."

Galdamiz stopped. He saw that Iino was still walking, so he reached out and tapped him on the shoulder. Iino looked at him, and Galdamiz gestured back at Nemov with his head. Then Galdamiz turned around to face Nemov and, out of the corner of his eye, saw Iino do the same.

"So you're joinin' us now?"

"Not 'joining,' no. I want to be there to keep order if Daniel gets too angry."

Nemov, Galdamiz, and Iino walked together the rest of the way to City Hall. As they did, it struck Iino that the three of them—walking three abreast, looking grim and determined, and sporting phaser pistols on their hips— looked rather like characters from one of those old vids that Latham used to force on them. What were they called? Westerns? Yes. They looked like some western posse moving through town.

The three of them moved through the door and into City Hall, then down its mostly dark corridors. The corridor that ran from the colony's transporter room to Latham's office was the only area in the building that was lit. They walked together in silence, and when they reached the door to Latham's office, Galdamiz grabbed the knob and threw the door open.

When they did, Galdamiz gasped and Nemov swore.

The office was a mess. Papers and a few books were scattered about the floor. Latham's desk chair was lying on its back behind the desk. Daniel Latham himself was on the floor over by the far wall. He lay faceup, curled in a strange and unnatural position. Mak'Tor knelt next to Latham, looking down at him.

The three men looked first at Latham, then, almost immediately, they looked at Mak'Tor. He seemed to be examining Latham, but none of the men could be sure, as the Klingon had his back to them. What they could see was that Mak'Tor knelt over the still and crumpled form of Daniel Latham.

Then Mak'Tor looked over his shoulder at them and snarled.

10. "Look out, he has a phaser!"

The words still hung in the air when three turquoise rays lanced from the phaser pistols Nemov, Galdamiz, and Iino held. The rays arced across the office and struck Mak'Tor full in the back, bathing him and the room around him in their blue-green field. Mak'Tor threw his head back. His upper body, which had been bent over Latham, straightened up and stiffened. His two arms suddenly flew out to his sides and shook.

The Klingon started to rise, although shakily, pulling his left leg forward so his foot lay flat on the floor, then pushing up on the leg in an effort to stand. For a moment, it looked to all three men as if Mak'Tor was going to get to his feet.

He didn't turn toward them, concentrating all of his efforts on the once simple task of standing. But he *was* moving up. Neither Nemov, Galdamiz, nor Iino could believe it. Three direct phaser hits, and it still looked as if he were going to get up.

Mak'Tor had gotten to a half-crouch, and his right knee was just starting to rise off the floor. Then his left leg collapsed under him and he crumpled to the floor. He fell face down, almost on top of Latham. He had crumpled into a balled-up mass, a position that looked every bit as unnatural as Latham's.

Nemov, Galdamiz, and Iino approached Mak'Tor slowly. Warily. None of them had any combat experience with Klingons. Even after living on the same planet with a colony of Klingons for almost a year, none knew the full extent of a Klingon's physical capabilities or whether even three phaser stun blasts would be enough to keep Mak'Tor down. So at every step of their cautious advance, the three men trained their phasers on Mak'Tor and did not allow them to waver even slightly from their target.

But the Klingon didn't move.

Nemov stood over Mak'Tor for a moment and looked down at him. He could see the deep rhythmic breathing that indicated the Klingon was probably unconscious. Both Galdamiz and Iino held back.

"Looks like you may be in charge now, Grig. What do you wanna do?" Goldamiz asked.

Nemov extended his right foot and kicked Mak'Tor in the side. Hard. Mak'Tor did not move or react, and the rhythm of his breathing did not change. Having satisfied himself that the Klingon was truly unconscious, Nemov extended his right foot again, almost as forcefully as he had when he kicked Mak'Tor, and pushed the Klingon's crumpled bulk. Mak'Tor rolled onto his back. He lay there, now supine, eyes closed and unmoving. All three men looked down at the stunned Klingon and the type-2 phaser pistol lying on the floor next to Mak'Tor's right hand.

"Good call on that phaser, Grig," Iino said. "You probably saved all our lives. Where do you think he got it?"

"It's probably Daniel's."

"Shootin' a guy with his own gun. Man, that's *cold*. Guess nothin' phasers those damn Klingons."

Both Nemov and Iino turned toward Galdamiz and glared at him. Both gave him withering looks that told him, in no uncertain terms, his humor was not welcome at the moment. To change the subject, Galdamiz asked, "How is . . . Latham?"

Iino noticed there was a hesitant catch in his voice as Galdamiz asked the question. But the catch seemed to Iino almost to be forced. It was as if Galdamiz were affecting the concern in his voice instead of actually feeling it.

Nemov stooped down and knelt over the unmoving Latham, just as Mak'Tor had done earlier. He reached out, took Latham's left shoulder in his hands, and gently moved Latham's body until he was lying on his back. When he was finished, Galdamiz let a soft, long whistle escape his lips.

The front of Latham's shirt had a large hole in it. The smooth edges around the hole showed that it was not a rip, but the result of a phaser's ray that had struck Latham squarely in the chest and burned through his shirt. A phaser capable of burning cloth—one that had *not* been set on stun. But what the men could see behind the hole in the shirt told the full story. An equally large hole was in Latham's chest. The heat of the ray blast had seared his skin and almost instantly cauterized the wound. One that had burned its way through Latham's chest and scorched his heart underneath. One that had been instantly fatal.

Nemov moved his right hand up from Latham's shoulder and pressed it against the carotid artery in his neck. He held it there for several seconds and did not move. Then he shook his head to signify to the others that he felt nothing.

Daniel Latham was dead.

Chiaki Iino was the first of the three to look up from Latham's corpse and scan the office again. His eyes moved around the room, taking in the details. Galdamiz saw what Iino was doing and asked, "What do you suppose happened?"

"It looks as if the meeting went badly and they started fighting. During the fight, Mak'Tor must have taken Daniel's phaser and used it against him."

"What were they fightin' about?"

"We may never know," Nemov said as he stood up and also looked around the office. He cocked his head in a gesture toward Mak'Tor. "I doubt *he* will ever tell us."

"What's next?" Galdamiz asked. Both Galdamiz and Iino looked at Nemov for instructions, silently reminding the Russian that he was in charge of the colony now.

"Word of this must not spread. Not yet," Nemov said. "Obviously people must know. But I don't want to spoil their celebration. There will be time enough for them to learn and for mourning tomorrow. But for now, I want as few people to know of this as possible."

"Gotcha. But who *should* know?"

"Louis Alexander, naturally. And Helen. I should tell her this myself."

"I saw Lou near Thom's Pub just before we came here," Galdamiz said. "He should be somewhere around there. I'll go get him and bring him back."

"Couldn't you just comm him?" Iino asked.

"Naw, Grig's right, we gotta keep this secret," Galdamiz explained. "People might overhear us and this would leak all over. We probably shouldn't use the comms at all for now."

"Agreed," Nemov said with a tone that indicated he not only agreed with the plan, but appreciated Galdamiz's initiative. "When you find him, bring him back here. But as you said . . ."

"I know. I'll be as tight-lipped as an Aldebaran shell-mouth."

Galdamiz exited the office and walked down the corridor. After he had gone several feet, he looked back toward Latham's office. The door was still shut, and there was no sign that either Nemov or Iino was looking through it. *Good*, he thought, *they aren't watchin'*. He continued down the corridor, but passed the front door and made his way toward his own office. He fully intended to go get Alexander, and soon. That was, after all, the excuse he gave to get out of the office. But there were a few things he had to attend to first.

After Galdamiz left, Nemov turned to Iino and said, "I'm glad Homero went. We have to discuss something, but I didn't want to talk in front of him. He wouldn't have kept it . . . confidential, as you will."

Nemov walked over so that he was standing next to Iino and whispered into the man's ear. "I don't want the rest of the colony to know this, but Daniel and Helen had a big fight this evening. She left him. Now she should come back and make it look like nothing had happened. Serenity should remember Daniel and Helen as they were, not breaking up just before his death. She should go back home, before the rest of the colony learns what happened between them.

"Go find Helen. She may still be out enjoying the celebration. Or she may have already gone to one of Serenity's boardinghouses. Try Ellington's first. Helen always regarded it as the cleanest in Serenity. If you find her, get her alone. Tell her you have a message from me, and make sure *no one* else is around. Then tell her she should go home and wait for me there.

"Tell her something has come up which makes it important that she return home. She'll protest. Tell her it is all right for her to go home now. But *do not* say more. *Do not* tell her what. No matter how careful you are, someone may overhear you. I don't want the news leaking out now. Louis and I will be there as soon as possible to let her know what has happened.

"It is important you get her back to her house alone. We must keep people from learning the news for now. Let the celebration go on tonight. Tomorrow will be soon enough.

"When you have found her, come back and let me know she is there."

Like Galdamiz before him, Iino went out into the crowded streets of Serenity on the errand, leaving Nemov alone in the office with the corpse of Daniel Latham and the unconscious Klingon. He wondered how long it would take Galdamiz to find Louis Alexander and return.

As it turned out, both Iino and Galdamiz returned to the office at almost the same time, a little more than twenty minutes later. Iino returned first and a few minutes later, Galdamiz came back, accompanied by Alexander. Nemov could tell Galdamiz had Alexander, because the chief of security announced their arrival even before he entered the office. "Dammit, Grig, I got a drunk city out there that any second could make the Tarsus IV food riots look like an Academy hazing prank. What's so damned import—"

Alexander stopped short when he saw the condition of the office and the two unmoving bodies lying on the floor. He could see the signs of the struggle in the office and the phaser wound in Latham's chest that his years of experience in Starfleet security told him was fatal. He knew immediately, but he still, almost beyond his control, found himself saying, "Ah hell, Daniel. Is he . . ."

When Alexander's voice trailed off, leaving his question unfinished, Nemov answered it anyway. *"Da."*

Alexander went to Latham's body and knelt over it. He picked up Latham's right wrist and checked it for a pulse, more to get himself under control than to verify what he already knew. "Who found the body?" he asked.

"We all did," Galdamiz said. Even as Galdamiz spoke, Alexander unslung the strap of the tricorder that was hanging from his shoulder and used it to analyze both Latham and his wound. "We were comin' to get Latham," Galdamiz continued. "We were tryin' to get him to go out to the celebratin' instead of meetin' here with this Klingon." He found himself speaking louder so that his voice would be heard over the high-pitched, two-tone whine of the tricorder. "When we came in, we found Daniel like that and that Klingon son of a bitch kneelin' over him. Grig warned us the bastard had a phaser, so we shot him."

"A phaser?" Alexander asked.

"Yes," Nemov said. "It looks like Daniel and Mak'Tor fought, and Mak'Tor used Daniel's phaser in the struggle."

"Yeah, he usually kept it in his desk, but Daniel told me

he was going to leave it out on his desk for me. Dammit, Daniel!" Alexander said, and slammed his fist against the floor. "Why didn't you just issue an engraved invitation to anyone who wanted to hurt you?" Then he looked at the various screens and displays on his tricorder and became businesslike again. "Yeah. Energy signatures on Daniel are consistent with a Federation phaser, not a Klingon disruptor," Alexander said. Then, he pointed the tricorder at the phaser that was lying on the ground and the same two-toned whine again filled the office with its ominous reminder of what had happened there. "And not just any phaser—*this* phaser. It's been fired recently and its energy signature's the same as the one on Daniel. This is the murder weapon all right."

"So what's next?" Iino asked.

"Next?" Alexander said, even as he walked around the office scanning everything with his tricorder, so that he'd be able to replay a video of the murder scene anytime he wanted during his investigation. "Next I start my investigation. I need statements from the three of you. Not tonight. Tomorrow's soon enough. Right now, I need to get Mak'Tor here back to a cell in my office, but I'd just as soon not be seen doing it. You were right to keep this under wraps, Grig, and I mean to see it stays that way. Don't want a riot on our hands."

"The transporter? We can carry him to the transporter and beam him over to your jail without anyone observing us."

"My thoughts exactly, Chiaki," Alexander said. He quickly scanned Mak'Tor's unconscious body and said, "I don't think he's gonna be waking up anytime soon, so I'll need help carrying him. And we need to seal off this room as a crime scene."

"I will beam the four of you over to the jail," Nemov said. "Then I will lock the office behind me and join you. There is one more thing. I told Helen to wait for me at her house. I need to go there to tell her what has happened."

"Damn! I forgot all about her. You're right, we do need to tell her. But that's not something you should do alone, Grig. When you're finished here, come to the jail. We'll go tell Helen together."

"It is not necessary—" Nemov started to say in protest, but Alexander cut him off.

"No one should have to do that alone."

Helen Latham was waiting for them in her living room. If there was any room in the house that was hers— uniquely and markedly hers—it was the living room. This was the showpiece, the room where, even in the backwater colonies she'd been forced to live in, she displayed her taste, her style, her breeding. Like her clothes, the furniture was strictly *au courant*. The newest, the most elegant vogues in home decorating were showcased for all to see, proof that Helen Latham knew what was fashionable this year in the trendiest settings back on Earth. It didn't matter that several light-years separated her from the trendsetters, she always knew where they were going and was only one step behind them.

This year the vogue was Kretassan. The living room of Helen Latham's colony home had been made over with the chairs, tables, and divans that could be found in the most stylish of homes on Kretass. The resulting look thrilled Helen. It was beautiful furniture made up of thin, delicate lines and elegant, rounded shapes that set off the lines to perfection. The Kretassans may have had a reputation for being officious, but the beauty of their society and its accoutrements could not be denied.

It was fortunate, however, that the living room was used as a showplace and not for actual living. It was never intended to be practical, and this latest makeover was no exception. Kretassan furniture may have been beautiful, but it was exceedingly uncomfortable. So much so that, even though Helen had been waiting for Nemov for several minutes, she was never once tempted to sit while she waited. So Helen Latham was standing in the middle of her oh-so-stylish living room when Nemov and Alexander entered.

"Grig, Lou," Helen said, as they came into the living room where she waited. "What is it?"

"It is Daniel, Helen. I am sorry. He is dead."

"Dead?" Helen stared first at Nemov and then at Alexander, fixing a blank expression on her face that showed no trace of what was going through her mind. For a moment, she was silent. Then she said, "Ho . . . how?"

"Murdered. Mak'Tor shot him with a phaser."

"A *phaser*. I don't understand. Why a phaser?"

"The Klingons don't carry their disruptors with them into City Hall, Helen. Looks like Mak'Tor shot Daniel with his own phaser."

"His own—"

The next thing any of them knew, Helen Latham was lying on the floor in a crumpled heap. Alexander looked down at her and struck his own forehead with the heel of his right hand. "Ass! I shoulda been gentler with her."

"Daniel has Saurian brandy in his study," Nemov said. "I will get her a glass."

Before Alexander had a chance to respond, Nemov was

gone. He crossed over to the study, disappeared into it, and returned a few seconds later with a snifter. Alexander was sitting next to Helen. He had picked up her head and he was supporting it in his lap. Nemov handed him the glass of brandy, which Alexander pressed to Helen's lips and helped her to drink.

When Helen had recovered, Alexander looked down at her and said, "Helen, I'm damned sorry. I shoulda taken it easier on you."

"Nonsense, Lou. You were . . ." Helen paused for a second, as if allowing her head to clear. ". . . only doing your duty. It's I who should apologize to you, fainting as if I were a silly old woman."

"It's understandable, Helen," Nemov said. "You just learned Daniel was murdered. But I promise you as new head of Serenity, no matter how it may split the planet apart, we *will* try Mak'Tor in Federation court for Daniel's murder."

Outside, the skies over Aneher II exploded as the fireworks display reached its spectacular grand finale. But in Serenity, the fireworks were only just beginning.

It had been several days. Several *long* days. Several unending days in which Samuel T. Cogley had had nothing to do. Nothing except to grow restless and twitchy and intrusive. Jacqueline LaSalle had been able to deflect him with his books for only so long. Now he wanted to get involved in *something*, even if it was her work. She had been desperately trying to think of something else for Sam to do. She had sent Peter Lawrence out to see if he could find a new book that Sam had never read before.

Jacqueline's thoughts were interrupted when the comm on her desk chirped to indicate an incoming call. She answered the call, then put the caller on hold. She smiled broadly—almost beamed—as she went into Cogley's office.

"Sam, it's Elliam Hareel from the Federation legal department. He's got a case he'd like us to take on. Seems a Klingon has been accused of murdering the head of a Federation colony on Aneher II."

11. Captain's Log: Stardate 4521.7

The repairs to the Enterprise *have been finished and her stay in spacedock is all but concluded. The damage that Norman and the androids on Mudd's planet did to the ship when they hijacked her was minor. So I was surprised that Starfleet had us put in at Earth's Spacedock for repairs that could have been handled at any well-equipped starbase. I learned later the* real *reason the* Enterprise *was summoned back to Earth is that we're scheduled to provide transportation for a party that's going from Earth to a Federation colony near the Klingon Neutral Zone. Ordinarily, I wonder about the wisdom of using starships for such milk runs, but Starfleet received a specific request that the* Enterprise *provide the transportation and frankly, I couldn't be more delighted, both because of the identity of the passenger and because I learned it early enough that I was able to arrange for a proper reception. Our passenger is not only an old and dear friend, but a man to whom I owe my career.*

Samuel T. Cogley used to describe himself as a "meat and potatoes kind of guy," although he had stopped doing so when he realized very few understood what the rather dated expression meant. When meat could range from Deltan musk elk to Tarsian seal steaks and potatoes encompassed Catuallan barsaki roots, it was hard to get across that the phrase meant "simple and unadorned." Still, for the most part, those were the types of meals that Cogley preferred. A dinner of Kansas beefsteak, Idaho russets, sweet corn on the cob, and a glass of aged lager satisfied him more than the finest cuisines of planets whose societies revered gastronomy.

But even those with the simplest of tastes can still enjoy the occasional exotic luxury. For Cogley that exotic taste was for Denobulan caviar. He found that it had a much lighter flavor, more delicate texture, and far less salty taste than the famed beluga caviar of the Caspian Sea. It was the one food, extraterrestrial or domestic, for which Cogley once thought he had an addiction.

James T. Kirk, captain of the *U.S.S. Enterprise,* smiled as Cogley spooned another helping of Denobulan caviar onto a cracker and popped it into his mouth. It was at least Cogley's tenth helping, not that Kirk was counting. Nevertheless, Kirk was glad to see his friend enjoying his hospitality.

It was rare that Kirk got to entertain. Although he had some good friends on the *Enterprise*, they were still the officers and crew who served under him. He had heard that the captain of the first warp-capable ship to bear the proud name *Enterprise* used to schedule regular meals with his senior staff as a form of socializing. It may have worked well for Jonathan Archer, but Kirk knew he could never do anything like that. He believed that protocol demanded that there always be a certain distance between the captain and the crew, even the senior staff. Wining and dining them would not have qualified.

Kirk had few friends outside of his command. His family relocated from Iowa to the Tarsus IV colony when he was a young boy, and he left his childhood friends behind. Whatever friends he made on Tarsus IV died when Kodos the Executioner seized power, declared martial law, and killed several thousand of the colonists during the food crisis.

At the Academy, Kirk was no more successful at finding friends. In his first year, he had been called "a stack of books with legs," the perfect description for the serious-minded cadet who had only one goal in his life: the center seat. It was the kind of no-nonsense drive that was not conducive to friendship. It was the reason an upperclassman named Finnegan used to torment Kirk with endless practical jokes. When Kirk left the Academy he really had only two good friends, Gary Mitchell and Ben Finney. Neither friendship ended well.

Kirk and Mitchell served together on several posts, culminating in Kirk's requesting Mitchell serve on the bridge of the *Enterprise*. Kirk had been forced to kill Mitchell after Mitchell was exposed to a powerful energy barrier and mutated into a malevolent and godlike being. An unmarked rock grave on Delta Vega became the only testament to their friendship.

Kirk was only a little luckier with Ben Finney; he didn't kill Finney, although it had looked for a time as if he had. They met at the Academy, where Finney was an instructor while Kirk was a midshipman, and became friends. Finney even named his daughter after Kirk. Later, while Kirk was still an undergraduate, he took a practicum course that included a posting on board the *U.S.S. Republic*, the same ship where Finney was also serving after he left his instructor's job. It had seemed an ideal situation to Kirk, at first. But Kirk hadn't known then that one day he would relieve Finney on watch and find his friend had left a circuit on the atomic matter piles open. Or that he would have to report Finney's lapse. Or that Finney would receive a reprimand on his record and be moved to the bottom of the promotion list. Or that the bitterness Finney felt about the incident would fester for seventeen years while he saw himself passed over for promotion time after time and saw Kirk become captain of the *Enterprise*. Or that Finney would come to hate his former friend so much that, when Finney was serving as the records officer on board the *Enterprise*, he would fake his own death and frame Kirk for his murder. Or that Kirk would become the first starship captain ever to stand in a court-martial.

No, his friendships with Gary Mitchell and with Ben Finney both ended badly. Indeed, the only good that had come out of either—save the memories of some happier times—was that Kirk met Samuel Cogley, when the lawyer successfully defended Kirk at his court-martial.

Just as Kirk had few friends, he also had very little family of his own. Being the youngest starship captain in Starfleet gave him numerous opportunities for liaisons in the ports of call he visited, but little time for long-term commitments. His brother, Sam, and his sister-in-law had been killed by the neural parasites of Deneva, leaving him with only three surviving relatives, Sam's three sons. Kirk's responsibilities to his ship and crew kept him from really interacting with Peter, Julius, or Alexander. Even Kirk's own son, David Marcus, was a stranger to him—as mutually agreed between Kirk and the boy's mother, Carol Marcus.

So Kirk truly enjoyed those occasions when old friends came on board his ship and he could play host to a small, intimate gathering. The grand and gala receptions his duties as starship captain forced him to hold held little interest for him. In a little over a month, the *Enterprise* was scheduled to transport a group of Federation ambassadors to the Babel conference, and Kirk was not looking forward to it. The endless full-dress uniform affairs such missions always required were too formal, too restrictive. No, he preferred entertaining one, maybe two or three good friends, where all felt more free to be themselves.

In a larger, more formal gathering, for example, Sam Cogley wouldn't have felt so free to enjoy his—what was it now, his twelfth?—helping of the caviar Kirk knew was a favorite of his. And, Kirk wondered, would even a man of Cogley's well-known eccentricities have felt comfortable in a larger setting?

"I'm not saying computers are worthless. I'm just saying they're stupid."

Kirk's years of service in Starfleet, particularly as a starship captain, had trained him to conceal his reactions, no matter what. So he remained placid even in response to what Cogley had just said to the small party that Kirk had set up in one of the *Enterprise*'s rec rooms. And, even as he maintained his noncommittal expression, Kirk moved his eyes to each person around him one at a time, surreptitiously checking their reactions to Cogley's pronouncement.

Mr. Spock, his half-Vulcan first officer, as Kirk expected, showed even less of a reaction than Kirk had. Vulcan, where Spock was raised, was home to a race of extremely logical beings. They hid their emotions whenever they could. Spock, being only half Vulcan—and half human—tried all the harder.

Montgomery Scott allowed his eyes to widen and his jaw to drop. His position as ship's engineer meant that he worked with computers almost as much as Mr. Spock, who doubled as the ship's science officer. To be sure, Scotty allowed his irritation to show when the computers didn't purr like an obedient kitten, but he still relied on them. In some ways he loved them almost as much as he loved his engines.

Chief Medical Officer Leonard McCoy had a decidedly amused expression, and Kirk could swear he was trying to stifle an outright laugh. Kirk knew why. Bones was born and raised in Georgia by a family that still honored and respected the "old South" traditions of the region. But with those traditions seemed to come the antebellum hot-bloodedness that used to result in duels. Where Spock tried to hide his emotions, McCoy wore them as openly and proudly as one would display the Silver Palm with Cluster. So, while McCoy respected Mr. Spock as an officer, he found the Vulcan's logical demeanor and lack of emotion irritating. Indeed, McCoy had an ongoing personal, if friendly, feud with Spock, the main purpose of which seemed to be to try to coerce an emotional reaction from the Vulcan. To date, the tally of the feud was decidedly in Spock's favor, but that didn't stop McCoy from taking every possible opportunity to get a rise out of Spock.

"Well, Mr. Spock," McCoy said in challenge, "Mr. Cogley here has just insulted your precious computers. Don't you have anything to say in response?"

"Not really, Doctor, no," Spock said with a voice that was as calm as an impulse drive. "In fact, I agree with him."

"*What?!*" both McCoy and Scott virtually shouted at the same time.

Spock turned to face the two Starfleet officers, with his customary arms behind the back posture. "If you had listened to Mr. Cogley's major premise, it was that a computer is a tool the reliability of which is dependant entirely on its own programming. I happen to agree with that proposition." Spock turned back to Cogley. "Have I correctly summarized your position, sir?"

"You have indeed, Mr. Spock. Why, we have only to look back at our own recent history to prove the point. When I represented Captain Kirk at his court-martial, the most damning piece of evidence against him was your own ship's computer logs, which showed that the captain had jettisoned an ion pod with Ben Finney still in it while the *Enterprise* was at yellow alert and not red alert. On the surface that would seem to be a most reliable piece of evidence. But we all know Captain Kirk didn't eject the pod until after the red alert had sounded. The computer lied, because Finney wanted to get revenge on your captain and so faked his own death by reprogramming the ship's computer to show Kirk ejecting the pod prematurely."

Cogley spooned another bite of the blue-green caviar onto a cracker and ate it before he continued. As he did, he quickly looked around the room to see where his own senior staff was. Peter Lawrence was on the far side of the room talking to a gray-haired man who had been introduced to Cogley as Lieutenant Commander Giotto, the chief of security on the *Enterprise*. Cogley smiled at the onetime and present Starfleet security officers deep in conversation together. *No doubt swapping war stories, some possibly about real wars*, Cogley thought.

Jacqueline LaSalle was in another part of the rec room talking with other crew members. He noted they all wore the blue tunics indicating they were in the ship's science division. He figured they were engaging in shop talk that Cogley himself could never understand until he heard Jackie say, "Peter has called this 'The Case of the Klingon Killer,' but that presupposes our client is guilty. I think of it as 'The Case of the Colonist's Corpse.' " *Poor Jackie,* Cogley thought, *she probably wants to talk computers with them, and all they want to talk about is that nut Cogley and his cases. But at least she and Peter seem to be entertaining themselves, I don't have to cut this short on their account.*

"And the incident with your ship's computer wasn't the only time you've encountered a computer that was only as good—or as bad—as its own faulty programming. There was that whole affair with the computer Landru on Beta III."

"How did you learn about that?" Kirk asked with an openly astonished expression on his face that stayed there until he realized that he was violating his own rule about concealing his reactions.

"Tut tut, Captain," Cogley said while smiling wryly and shaking his head. "Let's just say that I have my ways."

Kirk looked past Cogley at Peter Lawrence. "Yes, I suppose you do," he said.

When Cogley and his party came aboard, Lawrence stood out for two reasons. At six feet two inches tall, he towered over both Cogley and Jacqueline LaSalle. And

Kirk recognized Lawrence from when the two served together briefly on the *Republic*. Kirk had liked Lawrence then and was happy to find that feeling hadn't changed.

Back then, Kirk was a little surprised that Lawrence was in security. Lawrence didn't look the part. Even all those years ago, Lawrence had already started to go salt-and-pepper and his hairline had begun its retreat. Now his hair, what there was of it between the receding widow's peak and the bald spot on the back, was more salt with highlights of pepper. Although Lawrence was trim and athletic, he didn't have the chiseled muscles so many security officers had. He struck Kirk as looking more like a stockbroker who had decided to get into shape after facing a midlife crisis than someone who had always been in condition.

However, as soon as Kirk had looked into Lawrence's eyes, he knew Lawrence was born for security. They were deep, intense, and penetrating, and missed little when they looked at you.

Lawrence had been a good security guard for Starfleet and, Kirk was sure, was proving to be just as good an investigator for Sam Cogley.

"My point is, Captain," Cogley continued his argument, "I'll bet that if you think about it, you'll be able to come up with a few other computers that were less than perfect because of their programming."

Kirk smiled again and realized that, without even thinking hard, he could remember a few. Norman and the androids on Mudd's planet, which they had just left, certainly qualified. As did the Earth deep-space probe *Nomad*, which had reprogrammed itself by combining its programming with an alien space probe. "One or two," he said, nodding in agreement.

"Mr. Cogley, I didn't see much of you this afternoon," Dr. McCoy said. "Were you preparing your defense?"

"No. I won't really have much to prepare until we arrive at Aneher II and I can start interviewing the principles involved. The cold reports I received secondhand from Starfleet don't really help very much. So I've been doing a bit of reading."

Kirk smiled. "You read a lot of books."

"I do indeed."

"I'm afraid that most of the reading in my life has been devoted to my career. Textbooks, the exploits of Garth of Izar, that sort of thing. The writings of Abraham Lincoln are probably the most pleasure reading I've ever done. I was wondering if you could recommend some good works of fiction I might try?"

Cogley put his forefinger under his nose and regarded Kirk for a moment, as if studying him. "Let me see," he said. "Devotion to duty, heroism, self-sacrifice." He smiled and pointed his finger at Kirk. "Have you ever read *A Tale of Two Cities* by Charles Dickens?" he asked.

"No. But if you recommend it?"

"Oh, I do," Cogley said. "And now, Captain—"

"Jim," Kirk interrupted.

"Jim. If I could ask you a question in return?"

"Be my guest."

"My staff and I are already on board the *Enterprise*. We could be under way for Aneher II. Why are we still in Earth orbit?"

"We're waiting for another passenger that the *Enterprise* is to transport to Aneher II. The prosecutor in the case, in fact."

"Not . . ."

12. Captain's Log: Stardate 4522.4

We have taken our final two passengers on board and are en route to Aneher II. The first of the two passengers is Manuel K. Carabatsos, the judge who will preside over the upcoming murder trial on the colony. The second passenger, the prosecutor who Sam's going up against, is someone who makes even stronger that feeling of "old times." For she, like Sam, is an old friend.

Areel Shaw sat across the small table from Kirk in the same rec room which, the night before, had held the party for Sam Cogley. This night's gathering was more intimate—Kirk and Areel were alone in the room.

Ordinarily, this rec room, like the others on the ship, would be filled with any number of the four hundred thirty crew members on board the *Enterprise* during their off-duty hours, all of them searching for some diversion to fill those idle hours. Even Spock could be found in the rec rooms from time to time, usually indulging in a game of three-dimensional chess or playing his Vulcan lute. But for this night, Kirk had exercised captain's prerogative and commandeered the room so that he could entertain Areel alone.

Areel Shaw was as beautiful as ever. The soft blond hair and attractive figure she'd had when they first started dating those many years ago were unchanged. Kirk also noticed that Areel was wearing the same dress she had been wearing the last time they met over a small rec room table. That was back on Starbase 11, when she recommended that Kirk hire Samuel Cogley to represent him at his upcoming court-martial. Kirk suspected that her wearing the same dress now wasn't because her salary as a Starfleet JAG officer didn't permit her to buy a new dress. At that last meeting, Areel had recommended that Kirk have Cogley represent him, then dropped the bomb that she had been assigned by the Starfleet judge advocate general to prosecute him. When Kirk recognized the dress, he also recognized that Areel had worn it as a subtle and silent way of apologizing for what had happened the last time they had met and asking if they couldn't put it behind them and start anew from that point.

Kirk held up a glass and inclined it slightly toward Areel. It was the traditional indication that a toast would follow and Kirk honored that tradition by saying, "Here's to—"

"Old friends?" Areel interrupted, finishing the sentence quickly.

It wasn't the finish Kirk had intended. Areel and he had, at one time, been more than simply friends. They had, in fact, been lovers, and he had intended his toast to be a little more personal than "old friends." But he let it slide. Most of the women with whom he'd had relationships— Areel, Carol Marcus, Janice Lester, Janet Wallace—were very much like him: strong-minded and career oriented, and looking to excel as doctors, lawyers, or scientists. His relationships with women tended to end as examples of the old principle that opposites may attract, but likes repel. Things would be fine, at first. But eventually their mutual careers would start to come between them. Kirk wanted what he wanted, and what he wanted always took him to the stars. The women also wanted what they wanted, and their careers didn't include the possibility of starship travel. Or waiting patiently at home like the wife of some sailing ship captain of old. When their careers inevitably took them down different paths, they went their separate ways. And despite what Shakespeare said, parting was not always sweet sorrow.

The parting with Areel had been amicable enough. There had been some arguments, but nothing that had kept them from remaining friends. Still, the fact that she did have to prosecute him that one time might have made Areel feel a little awkward about being reminded of exactly how close they had once been.

"Sorry the atmosphere is a little 'regulation,' " Kirk said while looking around him at the very plain and by-the-book accommodations of the *Enterprise*'s rec room.

"Are you kidding me?" Areel said in a sweet voice that mixed in a melodious laughter. "I'm Starfleet, too. Not just Starfleet, but a JAG officer. 'Regulation' is what I live for."

"Be that as it may, I hear Starfleet's still trying to adapt those Xyrillian duplication chambers so they can be used in starships. It's too bad they haven't succeeded yet. It would have been nice to be able to offer you dinner in surroundings a little more hospitable than this."

"You sell your ship—and yourself—short, Jim. This is fine."

"Maybe. But 'fine' doesn't tell you that there are no hard feelings about . . .

"Sorry," he finished, when he noticed that Areel had rather pointedly turned her attention down to the meat she was cutting and away from him.

"No, it's *I* who should apologize to you, Jim. Not only for accepting the case against you, when I should have withdrawn because of our personal history, but for letting it affect me today." She stopped cutting her meat, stopped eating altogether and looked directly into Kirk's eyes. "It's just that—well, I guess I'm a little sensitive about your case. Don't get me wrong, you were innocent of the charges and I'm delighted that Sam got you off. It's just that for the past several months, I've had to live with all the kidding from the other lawyers in my office about losing a case to 'that nut Cogley.' It doesn't matter that Sam may be the best criminal defense attorney in the Federation, losing to someone with his reputation for eccentricity carries with it a certain derisive stigma that, frankly, I've grown tired of.

"That's why I was so delighted when Starfleet agreed to my request to prosecute this new case he's defending."

"You *asked* for the case?"

"Yes."

"Why?"

"It's what we call in the office a 'dead bang' case. This Klingon, Mak'Tor, was found kneeling over the body holding the murder weapon. I can't tell you how much I'm looking forward to beating Cogley on this case, so that I can shut up everyone in the office."

Kirk smiled, nodded, and said, "I see." Then he, like Areel had done before, turned his attention to cutting his food, although not quite for the same reason. She had done it to interrupt him. He did it because he needed to look away, otherwise Areel would have caught him studying her. There had been a certain intensity in her tone, something that told Kirk her reasons for wanting to beat Cogley in this case were stronger than simply wanting to put a stop to some office jests. No, there was something more. He didn't know what. He didn't know why. He just knew it was there and that the next several days were not going to be easy ones for his two friends.

Per the orders she'd received from Starfleet and the strongest possible recommendation from the United Federation of Planets, Areel Shaw had turned over the contents of her file to Samuel Cogley. She didn't simply go over the file with Cogley, she gave him a physical copy of what was in it. Everything he was entitled to under the rules of discovery: the results of Louis Alexander's investigation and anything that might be deemed exculpatory.

Alexander's investigation consisted of video recordings he had taken with his tricorder. There was a video of Daniel Latham's office that night with the strewn papers and upended furniture, as well as the dead body of Daniel Latham and the unconscious form of Mak'Tor next to Latham, the murder weapon by Mak'Tor's right hand. There were copies of the scans Alexander had run proving the phaser next to Mak'Tor was the murder weapon. Another video showed what Alexander found in Latham's study at home, after he and Galdamiz had spoken with Helen Latham and gotten her permission to look at the study for possible clues.

The centerpiece of the investigatory file was the video depositions and interviews. Although both Khogo and Mak'Tor refused to speak with Alexander because "it is not what Klingons do," he did interview Grigoriy Nemov, Homero Galdamiz, and Chiaki Iino. In three separate interviews, each man described, in turn, how and why they went to Daniel Latham's office on Landing Day and what they found there. At the end of the interviews, at Alexander's request, all four went to Latham's office. There Alexander asked Iino—because he was the "best actor" in the group—to re-create what they saw when they entered. Iino showed them where they stood and what they could see. Then, with Alexander standing where the three members of Serenity's senior staff had stood, Iino duplicated Mak'Tor's movements, when they found him kneeling over Latham's body. Iino showed Alexander how the Klingon was kneeling beside Latham's body and turned his head to look at the three men when they entered. Iino re-created Mak'Tor's efforts to stand and attack them, even after he had been shot with three phasers.

The interviews ended with Nemov's curt *Da,* and Galdamiz's enthusiastic "Pretty much dead on," when Alexander asked them if Iino's re-creation matched their memories of what they saw that night.

During the night when Areel Shaw dined with Captain Kirk in the rec room, Samuel Cogley, Jacqueline LaSalle, and Peter Lawrence reviewed the file she had given them. The next morning, they met in one of the *Enterprise*'s briefing rooms. The only mission *Enterprise* had was transporting the participants in the upcoming murder case to Aneher II, and Kirk hardly needed to meet with his senior staff for any reason during this milk run. So when Cogley and Areel asked to use the *Enterprise*'s briefing room to hold a pretrial conference, he agreed quickly and with ease.

Designed for meetings of a captain and his senior staff, it was little more than a room with a large table and chairs that took up almost the whole room. There was a three-sided viewscreen in the middle of the table, so that everyone in the room, no matter where they sat or stood, could see it.

Areel had suggested they use the briefing room, instead of meeting in one of their cabins, so that Cogley could have his entire staff with him at the meeting. That way, she explained, he wouldn't have to repeat everything they talked about to his staff later. A seemingly magnanimous gesture, the significance of which wasn't lost on Cogley. It was symbolic, meant to convey exactly how strong Areel felt her case was. She had no problem being outnumbered in the room—Cogley, Jacqueline LaSalle, and Peter Lawrence on one side and little Areel Shaw all alone on the other. Three against one didn't scare her.

"So, Ms. Shaw," Cogley asked, almost before everyone had a chance to sit down in the briefing room, "what do you have?"

"What do I have?" Areel asked, the note of incredulity in her voice was obvious. She knew Cogley has famous for his theatrics and flamboyant tactics—she had even experienced them firsthand during Captain Kirk's court-martial—but the brazenness of Cogley's question had still taken her aback. She pressed some buttons on the table's console, so that the viewscreens in the center of the table displayed the faces of Grigoriy Nemov, Homero Galdamiz, and Chiaki Iino, images taken from their interviews with Alexander. "What I have is the fact that your client was found kneeling over Daniel Latham with the murder weapon in his hand."

"My 'client' is a person, Ms. Shaw, he has a name: Mak'Tor. I realize it's much easier to judge and condemn nameless defendants than actual people, so using names isn't convenient for prosecutors such as yourself. But, then, I'm not here for *your* convenience, am I?"

Cogley looked at Areel and gave her a little, wry smile that seemed to say, *No hard feelings, I'm sure.* Then he saw from Areel's expression that his gentle barb had struck home. He had found, after many years of experience as a defense attorney, that in these dealings it was never a bad idea to make sure the respective parties remembered their respective functions and interests.

"And I know full well what Nemov, Galdamiz, and Iino said they saw that night. What I'm more concerned about is what they *didn't* see."

"Didn't see?"

"None of them claimed they saw Mak'Tor shooting Daniel Latham, did they?"

"No."

"Do you have any physical evidence proving Mak'Tor shot Latham? DNA scans on the phaser that match his, for example."

"Nothing conclusive."

"How about fingerprints? Were Mak'Tor's fingerprints on the phaser?"

Areel looked at Peter Lawrence. As a former Starfleet security officer, he would have known the answer to the question. She studied his face quickly and satisfied herself that, yes, he *had* told Cogley the answer to this question.

"Klingons don't have fingerprints, as I'm sure Mr. Lawrence has told you."

"Yeah, he did," Cogley agreed.

"Then why are you asking me questions you already know the answers to?"

"To show you exactly where your case is, Ms. Shaw. You have no eyewitnesses to the murder. You have no physical evidence to prove Mak'Tor fired that phaser. You have circumstantial evidence. Hell, you don't even have a motive for the murder, do you?"

"Latham's office showed they argued and got into a fight. Mak'Tor shot Latham during that fight. The motive is in that fight. As for the case being 'circumstantial,' as you put it, what murder case isn't? Unless we can get Daniel Latham to stand up and identify who shot him, of course the case will be circumstantial. But we've both seen defendants convicted on much weaker cases."

Areel looked down at the viewscreen for a moment, and a thoughtful expression came over her face. It struck Cogley that she was trying to determine whether this was the appropriate time to say something. Then she returned her attention to Cogley with an expression that Cogley could see indicated she had made up her mind.

"Mr. Cogley, if *your client,*" the emphasis that Areel put on the words didn't escape Cogley's notice, "did get into a fight with Latham and if Latham pulled his phaser on him, there are extenuating circumstances. We could probably agree to a plea bargain to voluntary manslaughter."

"A plea bargain? Before I've even met Mak'Tor? Isn't that a little premature, Ms. Shaw? Or are you that uncertain about your case?"

"I'm simply trying to do you a favor, Mr. Cogley."

"Or Starfleet's bidding. I'm sure Starfleet and the Federation would like nothing more than a quick end to this case. Especially one that ends in Mak'Tor's conviction. Probably make their ongoing negotiations with the Organians all that much easier."

Cogley leaned back in his chair and templed his fingers in front of his face, barely hiding the smile that lay behind them.

"Just as I imagine if we proved someone else killed Daniel Latham, say a Federation citizen, those negotiations would not be helped. Anyway, there will be no plea bargain until after I've had a chance to talk to Mak'Tor. And I doubt even then."

"Samuel Cogley, you are the most infuriating man I've ever met!" Areel said as she stood up to leave the briefing room.

"Wait until you get me back into a courtroom."

"That went well," Jackie said after she, Cogley, and Lawrence had returned to Cogley's cabin.

Cogley noted the obvious tone of sarcasm in Jackie's voice. "It wasn't supposed to," Cogley said to reassure her. "I was checking on something I'd heard. Wanted to find out if it might be true." Then he turned to Lawrence. "How about it, Peter, did you get enough for an opinion?"

"You know I did, Sam. The same one you got."

"An opinion?" Jackie asked. "An opinion about what?"

Cogley turned to Lawrence and said, "They were your rumors, Peter, so that gives you the floor."

"Some of my old contacts in Starfleet have been hinting that Areel was set up in the Kirk court-martial."

"Set up? In what way?"

"Think about it, Jackie. Areel—Kirk's old girlfriend— is tapped to prosecute Captain Kirk at his court-martial. Under ordinary circumstances, she should never have prosecuted the case, considering the conflict. Then Sam, one of the best defense attorneys in the Federation, goes with Areel to Starbase 11 ready to represent Kirk even though Kirk's never even heard of Sam. Obviously Kirk didn't ask for Sam, so who did? Finally, Areel suggests Sam to Kirk to ensure that he accept Sam's representation. These things didn't just happen. The rumors are that Starfleet sent Sam to represent Kirk and told Areel to recommend him."

"But why would Starfleet do that? It's almost as if . . ." Then the puzzled expression on Jackie's face left and was replaced by one of comprehension. "Oh."

"Exactly. Starfleet *wanted* her to lose the case. Not overtly, of course. But how embarrassing would it be if a starship captain—and not just any starship captain, but the highly touted, youngest starship captain in Starfleet—were convicted for cowardice on duty?

"Oh, if she had won, Starfleet was prepared to take its lumps and punish Kirk to the full extent of the law. And beyond. But imagine how much easier it would be for all concerned, if she didn't win the case."

"Do you think Areel knows?"

"That she was set up? I doubt anyone's told her. But she isn't stupid. What I've heard is that she suspects what happened."

"And that explains what happened today," Cogley said. "There was a certain intensity in our Ms. Shaw. And then there was that premature plea offer. She *didn't want* me to take it. That's why she made it today, when she knew I couldn't accept it. She wants to prove herself, both to herself and to Starfleet. She wants to beat me—*needs* to beat me.

"And the problem is, it won't be hard for her to do it. All that talk about circumstantial evidence was so much puffery, because we don't have a lot going for us. It's not enough that we're going to be facing what's likely to be the most hostile jury ever called into a courtroom. Areel Shaw is an excellent prosecutor. And she has an even better case."

13. Captain's Log: Stardate 4523.1

We have left our passengers on Aneher II, along with a small contingent of security officers handpicked by Lieutenant Commander Giotto and me who, through their training and temperament, would help maintain the peace among a potentially volatile civilian population. I can only hope it is enough. For though I have some apprehensions for the well-being of my old friends, the Enterprise *cannot stay in orbit around Aneher II to provide additional security. In light of the unrest that the situation on Aneher II has created, Starfleet has ordered us to patrol the area near the Federation–Klingon Neutral Zone.*

Our path is taking us into a sector of the galaxy that has been under dispute between the Klingons and the Federation since initial contact. The Battle of Donatu V was fought here twenty-three years ago. The results were inconclusive. We are presently approaching Deep Space Station K-7, which is now within sensor range.

Kirk, Spock, and Ensign Pavel Chekov sat around the table in the same briefing room that Samuel T. Cogley and Areel Shaw had occupied the day before. Kirk was using the time to check on the level of training and knowledge of the young ensign, who had recently been transferred to bridge duty. Truth be told, Kirk was also making sure that he, himself, was current on the status of this hotly disputed sector. The three were discussing the situation on Sherman's Planet, when the face of Lieutenant Uhura, the ship's communications officer, appeared on the three-sided viewscreen in the middle of the table.

"Captain, I'm picking up a subspace distress call . . . priority channel. It's from Space Station K-7."

Kirk's reaction was immediate, as was that of Spock and Chekov. Even as he ordered, "Lieutenant Uhura, call a red alert. Go to warp factor six. Kirk out!" all three were already rushing toward the door to the briefing room. Behind them they could hear Uhura's voice calling a ship-wide red alert and ordering all hands to their battle stations.

A priority-one distress call! The call indicated more than an emergency, it foretold a total disaster. The last time a starship had responded to a priority-one from a deep space station, it was to search for the bodies after a cataclysmic hull breach. As Kirk dashed down the corridor toward the nearest turbolift, he began to imagine worst-case scenarios that could have prompted such a distress call, starting with the Klingons attacking the station. His mind was able to conjure several more possibilities, some even worse. Kirk didn't know why the priority-one had been issued. He only knew that his hope of being able to stay near Aneher II to provide any assistance that Sam Cogley or Areel Shaw might need was gone.

"Hot as Vulcan," that was the phrase Peter Lawrence was fond of saying whenever he complained about the dry, hot Santa Ana winds that blew through the San Gabriel

Mountains and slammed into Los Angeles every summer. As Samuel Cogley and his party arrived in Serenity, however, he suspected that whoever coined the phrase had never set foot on Aneher II.

They had arrived at midday, when the Aneher sun was directly overhead and beat down on the planet with unrelenting fury. And even though they beamed directly into the courtroom, which was air-conditioned, Cogley found the heat was so pervasive that he swore he began to feel hot before he had finished materializing. He knew the reputation of Aneher's weather before he arrived on the planet and had, he thought, dressed accordingly. A lightweight, light-colored suit made out of a nice breathable cotton. He knew there were materials designed to absorb and then disperse heat rather than allow it to pass through to its wearer, but they were expensive materials, the efficacy of which Cogley doubted. He could afford them, to be sure, but he knew people who had used them, Peter Lawrence for one, and Peter still complained bitterly about the heat and wasting a week's pay on a fancy suit.

No, for Cogley a nice old-fashioned cotton would do.

"Mr. Cogley, welcome to Serenity," Grigoriy Nemov said to him as he finished materializing. Nemov had extended his hand to Cogley. Despite the fact that Nemov was a massive-looking, powerfully built man, his handshake struck Cogley as limp and unenthusiastic. "You must be Areel Shaw and Judge Carabatsos," Nemov said to them, and pumped their hands in a firm, two-handed clasp. "And you would be Ms. LaSalle and Mr. Lawrence." Nemov turned sideways and gestured toward the other people who were standing in the room. "May I present my senior staff, Homero Galdamiz, Chiaki Iino, and Louis Alexander.

"But I see Mr. Lawrence and Mr. Alexander already know each other," Nemov said as Lawrence and Alexander greeted each other warmly. "Did you serve together, perhaps?"

"Yes, Peter and I did a tour on the *U.S.S. Price* a few years back. How many years ago was it, Pete?"

"I don't think *either* of us want to admit that," Lawrence said

"But where's the rest of our party?" Cogley asked, when he noticed that no more people were beaming into the open room they all stood in.

"You mean the extra security detail that *Enterprise* is sending down to baby-sit us?" Nemov asked, and Cogley noted the slight edge of scorn in his words. The colony, it seemed, did not appreciate the implication that it could not provide for its own needs. "We gave *Enterprise* coordinates for our security office. They have been sent directly there. One of Mr. Alexander's men is greeting them. We had *Enterprise* beam you into our courtroom. It's one of the rooms big enough to handle multiple person beam-ins, and I thought you would want to see it."

Not really, Cogley thought. *One courtroom, even a makeshift one, looks pretty much like another.* He'd done trials in some other colony worlds in his time and found that each colony somehow didn't believe that crime would happen on it, so didn't build a courtroom. Then, after a time, when they learned they needed one, they had to make do with whatever they could scramble together. Cogley didn't want to appear rude, however, so he did look around the room. It was as he expected: a large room with a table at the front to serve as the judge's bench and two tables in front of that for the prosecution and defense. Against the far wall were two rows of chairs that would serve as the jury box. More rows of chairs in the back for what would be the spectators gallery—nowhere near enough chairs to seat everyone on Aneher II who would want to watch this trial.

Cogley made a mental note to subpoena every witness he might conceivably require in the trial, so that he could be sure they would have seats. He realized that would mean he and Ms. Shaw were issuing subpoenas to some of the same people, but it was always better to operate with an overabundance of caution in these matters. That way he would be sure the witnesses he needed would be there without having to rely on the prosecution's case.

"I imagine you want to be shown your rooms," Nemov said. "Judge Carabatsos and Ms. Shaw, Helen Latham has graciously invited you to stay at her house. It is the best house in Serenity. Mr. Cogley, we have arranged rooms for you and your staff at Ellington's Boardinghouse."

"I'm afraid that won't do. Won't do at all," Judge Carabatsos said, his voice booming out to fill the room, as if he were already presiding over the trial.

"I beg your pardon?" Nemov said.

Areel said, "While Judge Carabatsos and I appreciate the offer of hospitality, we can't stay at the Latham house. How would it look for the judge and prosecuting attorney at a murder trial to be staying with the victim's wife?"

"Quite inappropriate," Carabatsos agreed.

"Yes, I see. Stupid of us not to have realized," Nemov said. "We will find other rooms for you, of course." Nemov turned to Cogley as he added, "Trouble is, there is no more room at Ellington's, and it is the nicest in the colony."

"I have no objections to finding other rooms," Cogley said. Then he looked at Carabatsos and added, "That is, as long as no one will accuse me of bribing a judge."

"It *is* somewhat irregular," Carabatsos said then he looked back at Cogley and gave him a slight, almost unnoticeable, smile. "But I suppose we can overlook it in this one instance."

The judge's answer and especially his smile told Cogley what he had been trying to learn. Yes, like many judges Carabatsos could be formal and stuffy when required. Some, however, liked to keep up the attitude when it wasn't required. In addition, some judges tended to be "prosecutors' judges," who would almost automatically rule in favor of every prosecution motion and objection. Cogley suspected that the Federation would not have sent such a judge to this trial. Everything would have to be fair and aboveboard for the Klingons and the Organians. Carabatsos's smile told Cogley that not only was he here to get to the truth, wherever it might be found, he was actually looking forward to experiencing firsthand Cogley's famed tactics. Carabatsos would be fair, but he wouldn't throw unnecessary barricades in front of the defense case.

"Good. It is settled," Nemov said, and Cogley noted that he looked relieved that his faux pas had been straightened out so easily. "Then I will take Ms. Shaw and Judge Carabatsos to Ellington's." Nemov looked at Cogley. "Mr. Alexander will show you to your rooms. Lou, I believe the Morton's have some extra rooms."

The formalities over, Cogley, Jackie, and Lawrence went with Alexander to their boardinghouse. Lawrence had asked whether Serenity had any hotels, and Lawrence explained that Daniel Latham had decided boardinghouses or bed-and-breakfasts would work better than hotels. The colony didn't get many visitors so there weren't many guest rooms, and the planet was inhospitable enough as it was. Having only rooming houses and boardinghouses might make a visitor's stay a little more pleasant.

As they walked, Cogley noted that what he had suspected even in the air-conditioned courtroom was true. The heat on Aneher was every bit as pervasive as the briefings the Federation gave them about the planet indicated. Probably more. Simply walking down Main Street toward the boardinghouse soon made his clothes drenched with sweat.

But it was more than the sun's heat that Cogley noted. As they walked, he could feel the stares of every colonist they passed. Even through the protective goggles that everyone, himself included, was wearing, Cogley could feel the heat of their hatred in their stares just as easily as he felt the heat of Aneher's sun. These people knew who Cogley was and why he was here—to defend the Klingon accused of killing their leader—and they did not seem to appreciate Cogley's presence.

"I suppose you'll be wanting to see your client, soon as you're settled in," Alexander said as he led the defense team to their rooms.

"Actually, no. I'd rather see Mrs. Latham. My associates and I don't seem to be too popular. I think our first official act should be one of condolence."

14. "Quite an eclectic little town out there," Peter Lawrence said as he looked out the window of Cogley's room in Morton's Room and Board and down the length of Serenity's Main Street. Outside a surprising number of Serenity's citizens had actually braved the midday sun and were standing in the street with a purpose. Everyone who was out in the sweltering heat was looking up at the windows of the guest rooms at Morton's. Parents pointed out the boardinghouse to their children. Those who didn't have children whispered to each other or pointed to the boardinghouse windows anyway. Others simply stared. But, it seemed, all eyes were on the rooms where Samuel T. Cogley and his party were staying. Even as he looked back at the people looking at him, Lawrence continued his thought. "This place looks like a cross between an old mining town and an army barracks. And that's probably being insulting to army barracks."

"I know," Cogley said, joining Lawrence at the window. *Might as well give them a glimpse of what they came to see,* he thought. "I've seen some pretty barren and undeveloped colonies before, but Serenity looks like everybody just gave up on it. Like they decided it was a place to go to and mine, get rich, then get out of as quickly as possible. From what I read of Daniel Latham on our trip here, that attitude must have been particularly galling to him."

"So what's our first move after we unpack? We really going to interview Helen Latham?"

"We are," Cogley said, "but not first. A little more background wouldn't hurt, and I know how we might be able to get it. Louis Alexander's investigation reports were very thorough, but they were rather . . ."

"Sterile?" Jackie said, finishing Cogley's thoughts as he trailed off.

"Exactly," Cogley said, grateful once again that his years of working with her had given them a distinct rapport. She not only knew what he thought about those reports, she also knew that he was asking her whether she agreed with his assessment.

Lawrence had seen this type of communication between the two many times. At one time it had astonished him. Then one day after he had worked with Cogley for several months, he found that he could do it, too. Maybe not as well as Jackie, but Lawrence had reached the point where he, too, could anticipate what Cogley was going to say or ask, and say it for him.

"And you want *me* to go see if that old bond between Starfleet security buddies will get Lou to open up a little bit more?"

Cogley and Jackie said nothing. They simply looked at each other, both of them smiling the type of contented smile that parents share when a child has learned a lesson particularly well.

Lawrence found Louis Alexander sitting behind his desk in his City Hall office. He wasn't doing anything. Not pushing papers or readying some report. He was waiting for Lawrence.

"I figured you'd come calling, Pete," Alexander said, and gestured to a wooden chair that was in front of his desk. Lawrence took in the office as he crossed it to the chair. If Sam had been there, he might have called the office "sterile," although Lawrence would have used the word "utilitarian." Rather like one of the sheriff's offices in the westerns he and Sam enjoyed. It was furnished with a wooden desk, some file cabinets, a couple of chairs, and some shelves. No personal touches or individuality. There was one surprise Lawrence found as he sat in the chair: for a straight-backed, round wood chair, it was surprisingly comfortable.

"Yeah," Lawrence said, as if to answer Alexander's comment that he was expected, "I realized that I didn't remember how long ago it was since we've seen each other, so I came to ask you."

Alexander smiled. *Polite small talk first*, he thought. *Well, that's fine with me. No rush. I can chat with the best of them*. He rubbed his chin, emulating a gesture of deep thought, then said, "It's gotta be seven, eight years now. Guess we kind of lost track of each other when we went our separate ways. You retired from Starfleet and went to work for Cogley. A few years later, I retired myself. Only I got bored so I started hunting around for something to do. That's how I ended up on this hellspawn of a planet.

"So tell me, Pete, how was it exactly that you did end up working for . . ."

"A nut like Cogley?" Lawrence said, realizing that he had anticipated the ultimate direction of Alexander's sentence as well as he had Cogley's a few minutes earlier.

"Yeah. I wasn't going to word it that way, but that was the gist of it."

"Don't worry. Enough other people have asked the question, wording it exactly that way, that I'm used to it by now. As for how, it's a long story, I wouldn't want to bore you with it right now. Maybe later."

It was the same answer Lawrence gave most people who asked him, because he didn't intend the matter to go further; he never really meant that maybe later he would give them the details. There was never going to be a later. Because it was a story Lawrence could never tell.

It had happened several years ago, a few months before Lawrence had reached his twentieth anniversary as a Starfleet security guard, just before his pension would fully vest and he'd be able to retire. The problem was, he was pretty sure he didn't want to retire. Certain, in fact. He'd talked to enough friends who had served and gone the retirement route to be sure that "retirement" was just "death" with more syllables to it.

The thing was, he didn't know what there was left for him in Starfleet. He'd been promoted as high as he was likely to go, because he'd also determined long ago that the sedentary lifestyle of a desk job was out of the question for him. A few years—hell, a few months—of inactive desk duty and he'd be ready for an extended stay at the asylum on Elba II. In fact, he'd probably commit himself voluntarily. At the same time, riding shotgun on a starship—waiting around through days of inactivity for those rare moments when he and a few other security officers would go planetside with phasers in hand so that they could play backup to some captain or first officer who had gone adventuring and happened to stub his or her toe— had become as boring as he feared retirement would be.

What he hadn't known at the time was that there was a third choice that presented itself, because, as a man with a long and honored career in Starfleet security but now looking for a change, he was exactly the sort of officer that a little-known organization called Section 31 was looking for.

When they contacted him, Section 31 told Lawrence that they had almost always existed, had been established under the Federation charter to do the jobs that Starfleet itself felt was too dirty for it. There were those in Starfleet who had known early on that as Earth went into space, there would not only be overt threats such as one posed by the Klingons, but also hidden threats from beings that might plot and plan for years, decades, or even centuries before attacking. Experiences with the Suliban and the Xindi only proved that these people were right to take some paranoid precautions.

But the Federation didn't want to launch Starfleet's grand missions of exploration and friendship under a cloud of paranoia. So it chartered Section 31 to be paranoid for it. It set up a covert organization of secret operatives who would surreptitiously seek out and identify the extraordinary threats so that the Federation would know what menaces were out there and how it should deal with them.

Section 31 had investigated Lawrence just as thoroughly and as covertly as it performed all of its missions. And it decided he was exactly what they were looking for. So, at a time when Lawrence was trying to decide which of two slow and boring deaths better suited him, Section 31 offered him a new occupation for which he was suited: covert investigations and operations.

He served in Section 31 for several months and found that he excelled at investigative work. But even as he excelled, with every day that he served, things around him in

Section 31 made him increasingly uncomfortable. The paranoia that was the underpinning of Section 31's charter started to become more than just some precautionary worries that justified the organization. It started to seep through every level of Section 31, touching every operative and every operation until paranoia wasn't the backdrop of the organization, it was the foundation.

Section 31 changed its own charter. It no longer regarded its function as merely seeking out and identifying threats; its mission now was to deal with the threats. Preemptively, if possible, and in ways what were quiet, covert, and frequently extralegal.

Things came to a philosophical head for Lawrence when Section 31 assigned him to investigate Samuel T. Cogley. The old lawyer was making quite a name for himself representing clients whose ideals were frequently in opposition to what Section 31 believed to be the best interests of Starfleet. It knew there had to be more to this old lawyer than eccentricity—some secret agenda that put him at odds with Starfleet so often. Section 31 wanted to learn what Cogley's agenda was, so that it could deal with him. So Section 31 assigned Peter Lawrence to investigate Cogley.

Which Lawrence did. As thoroughly and efficiently and professionally as he performed any of the investigations Section 31 assigned to him. But this time, and for the first time, Lawrence discovered that there was nothing more to Section 31's fears than an unhealthy paranoia.

Cogley had no secret agenda. He had no agenda at all. He had nothing more than a firm conviction that all beings were entitled to the best possible defense. And when no one else would offer that defense, Samuel T. Cogley would.

After several weeks spent investigating Cogley, Peter Lawrence was convinced of two things: Cogley was the single most honorable person Lawrence had ever met, and Lawrence wanted—no, needed—to work for him.

So he walked away from Section 31 and into Samuel Cogley's employ. Officially, all he did was to tender his resignation from Starfleet. Just another twenty-year man cashing in his pension so that he could enjoy the fishing on new worlds.

Unofficially, it hadn't been that easy. Leaving the Section 31s of the universe never was. How he had been able to leave with his reputation and his life intact was another story, and it was one that no one would ever know. Not Louis Alexander. Not Samuel Cogley. Not anyone. *Ever.*

Alexander noticed that Lawrence seemed to be lost in thought. It made him uncomfortable. "Can I offer you a cuppa coffee?" he asked, nodding his head at a coffeemaker that sat on a wall-mounted shelf beside his desk. "It's fresh brewed."

Lawrence shook his head, then looked over at the wall and regarded the coffeemaker with astonishment. "*Coffee*? In *this* heat?"

"You'd be surprised, old buddy. I actually find hot beverages make me feel cooler."

"No, thanks. Think I'll pass," Lawrence said, a slight hint of disdain in his voice.

"Suit yourself," Alexander said, standing up and crossing over to the coffeemaker. "But you don't mind if I indulge, do you?"

"It's your funeral," Lawrence said, waving his hand dismissively at his friend.

band's death to show any sorrow, why should I offer her any of mine? he thought. Then he finished his sentence by saying, ". . . I'm sorry we had to meet under these circumstances."

"Yes, it is horrible," Helen Latham said, but the smile she had fixed to her face never disappeared. "Still, no matter what the circumstances, you're welcome in my house."

Cogley noticed that as she said this last part, she spread her arms slightly, as if she were showcasing the living room for her visitors. Cogley was, in fact, sure that was exactly what she was doing. He decided to put his theory to the test and said, "Thank you. It's lovely." The way the smile on Helen Latham's face broadened and more of her perfect white teeth showed through her painted lips, made Cogley even more positive of his assessment. Which is why he decided to try to throw her off her stride. "Kretassan, isn't it?"

"Why, yes . . ." Helen said, and a look of surprise washed over her face. But she quickly regained control of herself, refixed the smile to her face, and added, "Yes, it is. But I must confess, I didn't think a man of your . . . ah . . . particular tastes would recognize Kretassan furniture."

"Oh, I get around quite a bit," Cogley said, and he smiled himself, not because he found the pleasantries the two of them were engaging in to be in any way pleasant, but because his reputation had, again, preceded him. He used that, as well as the preconceptions it engendered in people. It made people think they knew what they could expect from him. Which only made it all the easier for him to surprise them.

"I'm sure you had a long and hot walk over here from Norton's," Helen said after Cogley had introduced Jackie

Alexander took one of the cups that was sitting beside the coffeemaker and poured coffee into it. He gave every indication that he was concentrating all his efforts on a relatively simple task, hoping that this act of apparent normalcy might signify that a groundwork of pleasantries had been laid and that it was time for Lawrence to move on in his agenda.

He got his wish. "So how are things in Serenity?" Lawrence asked. "Is it a nice place to live?"

"Nice? Pete, you've been outside. It's hotter'n Vulcan out there. As for the people, they're nice enough. But, you know people. Heat like this can make any of us short-tempered. Look, Pete, why don't you get out of impulse drive and jump her on up to warp power? What you want to know is, could any of my people have killed Dan Latham?"

"Unfortunately, yes," Lawrence answered, putting a slight pause between the two words to show Alexander that he regretted their meeting again under these conditions and that he had to ask the questions he was going to ask. "I want to know that and more."

"Well, I can tell you the answer to your question is yes. One of us could have killed Dan. He'd made a few enemies in this colony."

"You hinted at some of it in your report. Disagreements with the senior staff on how to run the colony. Problems with his wife. But we need more than hints in court. What can you tell me, Lou?"

"Well, I don't know all the details on any of it. But I can give you the highlights." Then Alexander stopped when he realized that Lawrence was just sitting in his chair listening, but not doing anything else. "Don't you need a tricorder or something to take this down?"

"Nope. You wondered why Sam Cogley would hire me. One of the main reasons is my memory. I can remember conversations exactly and repeat them for him word for word. Usually with all the inflections intact. Sam likes it because it's one more way he doesn't have to rely on machines."

"He's that serious about hating machines?"

"Hate may be a little strong, but, yes, he's that serious. Still, he likes my little memory tricks for another reason, too. They're the same thing a character in an old book could do."

"So, should we start with Helen Latham?"

"Let's end with her. You'll see why when I get there. Let's start with Chiaki Iino, our resident computer god. You might say he and Dan got off on the wrong foot—no pun intended, that's Homero's specialty—when Chiaki's was hurt working in the Klingon dilithium mine . . ."

" 'So after all that, Dan sent me a comm telling me what Helen had done and that he wanted every phaser in the colony confiscated, starting with the one Helen had pulled on him, which was in the wastebasket back in his study at home, and the one in his office, which he was going to leave out on his desk waiting for me.' "

It had taken Louis Alexander a little over forty minutes to give Peter Lawrence the background on who in Serenity might have had reason to kill Daniel Latham. It had taken Lawrence about half again as long to recount the conversation word for word to Cogley, because Cogley would stop him and ask him to repeat portions. When they finished, they watched a copy of the comm message Alexander had

received from Latham after his last argument wife.

"So what do you think, Sam?" Jackie asked af ley had digested all the information.

"Same thing as I did before. We should start by a call on Helen Latham."

15. Cogley had referred to it as a "condolence c

meant it. He fully intended to tell Helen Latham was sorry for her loss. He didn't care that the phra seem strange coming from not only a man she h met before but also the man who was represer Klingon accused of causing that loss. When Co Helen Latham, however, he knew that he couldn' any condolences.

She didn't so much greet them in the livin her house as she presented herself to them in he She stood statuesque in the showplace of her ho ing an elegant gown that had just enough blac sign to show that she remembered she was sup in mourning. Cogley realized that she migh have brought a black dress to the colony wo was sure she must have had something simple have worn, something that hinted she was cerned with grieving for her dead husband th she looked.

"Mrs. Latham . . ." Cogley began, and that whatever his intentions had been when this house, he couldn't bring himself to condolences. *If she doesn't care enough a*

LaSalle and explained that his other associate was arranging other interviews. "Would you like to sit down?"

"Yes, I would, but not here, if you don't mind."

"I'm afraid I don't understand."

"I am, as you saw, familiar with Kretassan furniture, and I find its most salient point is that while it looks elegant, it's not at all comfortable."

Helen looked around her, then dropped her voice to a near whisper, "You know, I agree with you. It really *isn't* very comfortable. Shall we go to another room?"

"I'd really like to see your husband's study. Shall we continue this in there?"

"Why . . . yes, I guess so."

Cogley noted the slight hesitation in her voice as she tried to decide how she wanted to answer. He had struck successfully a second time. She didn't really want to go into the study, but she didn't really have a reason not to, either.

Jacqueline LaSalle saw the look on Cogley's face—the same look she had once seen on her late husband's face when he was shown the initial plans for Memory Alpha—and said, "Mrs. Latham, I believe my boss has died and gone to heaven."

"Whatever do you mean?" Helen asked, then looked at Cogley herself. He was standing in the middle of the study, just looking at the books. The collection of books may not have been as big as Cogley's own back on Earth, but it was impressive in its own right. Several bookshelves lined the walls of Daniel Latham's study, each one filled to overflowing with books. Cogley walked from shelf to shelf, studying the books' spines and noting the authors. There were the works of Shakespeare, Hawthorne, Poe, Hemingway, Harris, King, and others. So many others.

Cogley reached out for one of the books, then turned back to Mrs. Latham. "May I?" he asked.

"Go ahead," Helen said with a tone of indifference.

Cogley pulled out the book and leafed through its pages gently, treating it as if it were a newborn baby. "Look at them, Jackie. Not a cracked spine or dog-ear in the collection."

"Dog-ear?" Helen asked.

"It's a way of marking one's place in a book while reading it," Cogley explained. "The corner of the page is folded down at the page the reader wants to mark. It's not recommended, though, and can decrease a book's value."

"Oh, well, then you definitely won't find a dog-ear in this room. Daniel certainly loved his books," Helen said. Cogley noted that the tone of indifference that had once floated in her voice had been replaced by one of petulance.

"Sam, look at this matched set of Dickens," Jackie said while taking in the books on the shelf directly behind Latham's desk.

"Yes, that was Daniel's pride and joy. I've never quite understood that set myself. As you can plainly see, the volumes are all bound and numbered, but the order's all wrong. See, it starts with *The Pickwick Papers* as one, then goes to *Oliver Twist* for two, then *Nicholas Nickleby,* and so on. The last one is seventeen, *The Mystery of Edwin Drood*. They're not in alphabetical order at all."

"The numbering's in chronological order. *The Pickwick Papers* was Dickens's first book, *Oliver Twist* his second. *The Mystery of Edwin Drood* was his last novel. In fact, he never finished it. He died while writing *Edwin Drood*. That's been one of the great unsolved mysteries of literature: Who killed Edwin Drood?"

Cogley started to cross to the books Jackie was looking at, but stopped suddenly. Out of the corner of his eye, he could see Helen Latham standing in the middle of the room and looking at him with the same anger in her eyes that he had seen coming from the colonists on Main Street. Then he realized that Helen wasn't looking at him with those angry eyes. She was looking at the books.

"I see you didn't approve of your husband's books, Mrs. Latham."

Helen laughed briefly, a quick little chuckle meant to offset tension, then said, "Oh I wouldn't say that. It was more like jealousy. At first, Daniel's love of books was endearing, actually. In fact, he used to write me love letters on actual paper. He still does—did—write that way: everything on paper. He'd only transfer it to the computer when he was finished with it.

"But over the years he spent so much time with his books they almost became like another woman. Anytime I couldn't find him, I knew he'd be here in his study reading. Some nights he didn't even come to bed, he'd stay up all night reading and rereading the same books he'd read time and again.

"Sometimes he'd try to hide the fact that he was reading them—put them in a drawer or slip them back on the bookshelf when he heard me coming. But I always knew. I can't begin to tell you the number of times I'd come in here and find him reading one of his books or making notes in them. You'd swear he was almost caressing them. Oh, he'd put them back on the shelf quick enough and devote his attention to me when I came in, but you could see what was important to him."

"You say he'd write in his books? You mean he kept a journal?"

"Why, yes, he did that, too."

"Would you mind if I saw it?"

"Not at all."

Helen opened the top left drawer of her late husband's desk, pulled out a book, and handed it to Cogley. He opened it and flipped through the pages, glancing at page after page of handwritten notations.

"May I take this to read overnight? It should help me get to know your husband better."

Helen shook her head and made a gesture with her hand to indicate that she did not care about the book. "Take it."

"Thank you. Jackie, be sure and tell Ms. Shaw that we have this and that she's welcome to look at it anytime she wants."

"Oh, I doubt she'll want it," Helen said. "I already told her about Daniel's journals, and Areel didn't seem to care about them in the least. *She* knows what's important in this matter."

"No doubt," Cogley said. He continued to study the books on the shelves while he asked her offhandedly, "Mrs. Latham, I'm reluctant to ask this, but my initial investigations have revealed some, well, rumors about your marriage. How were things between your husband and yourself?"

"That's what you get for listening to rumors, Mr. Cogley," Helen said, a tone of glacial ice quite noticeable in her voice. "Oh, you know, Daniel and I had our little squabbles, but for the most part things between us were fine."

Alexander took one of the cups that was sitting beside the coffeemaker and poured coffee into it. He gave every indication that he was concentrating all his efforts on a relatively simple task, hoping that this act of apparent normalcy might signify that a groundwork of pleasantries had been laid and that it was time for Lawrence to move on in his agenda.

He got his wish. "So how are things in Serenity?" Lawrence asked. "Is it a nice place to live?"

"Nice? Pete, you've been outside. It's hotter'n Vulcan out there. As for the people, they're nice enough. But, you know people. Heat like this can make any of us short-tempered. Look, Pete, why don't you get out of impulse drive and jump her on up to warp power? What you want to know is, could any of my people have killed Dan Latham?"

"Unfortunately, yes," Lawrence answered, putting a slight pause between the two words to show Alexander that he regretted their meeting again under these conditions and that he had to ask the questions he was going to ask. "I want to know that and more."

"Well, I can tell you the answer to your question is yes. One of us could have killed Dan. He'd made a few enemies in this colony."

"You hinted at some of it in your report. Disagreements with the senior staff on how to run the colony. Problems with his wife. But we need more than hints in court. What can you tell me, Lou?"

"Well, I don't know all the details on any of it. But I can give you the highlights." Then Alexander stopped when he realized that Lawrence was just sitting in his chair listening, but not doing anything else. "Don't you need a tricorder or something to take this down?"

"Nope. You wondered why Sam Cogley would hire me. One of the main reasons is my memory. I can remember conversations exactly and repeat them for him word for word. Usually with all the inflections intact. Sam likes it because it's one more way he doesn't have to rely on machines."

"He's that serious about hating machines?"

"Hate may be a little strong, but, yes, he's that serious. Still, he likes my little memory tricks for another reason, too. They're the same thing a character in an old book could do."

"So, should we start with Helen Latham?"

"Let's end with her. You'll see why when I get there. Let's start with Chiaki Iino, our resident computer god. You might say he and Dan got off on the wrong foot— no pun intended, that's Homero's specialty—when Chiaki's was hurt working in the Klingon dilithium mine . . ."

" 'So after all that, Dan sent me a comm telling me what Helen had done and that he wanted every phaser in the colony confiscated, starting with the one Helen had pulled on him, which was in the wastebasket back in his study at home, and the one in his office, which he was going to leave out on his desk waiting for me.' "

It had taken Louis Alexander a little over forty minutes to give Peter Lawrence the background on who in Serenity might have had reason to kill Daniel Latham. It had taken Lawrence about half again as long to recount the conversation word for word to Cogley, because Cogley would stop him and ask him to repeat portions. When they finished, they watched a copy of the comm message Alexander had received from Latham after his last argument with his wife.

"So what do you think, Sam?" Jackie asked after Cogley had digested all the information.

"Same thing as I did before. We should start by paying a call on Helen Latham."

15. **Cogley had referred to it as a "condolence call," and** meant it. He fully intended to tell Helen Latham that he was sorry for her loss. He didn't care that the phrase would seem strange coming from not only a man she had never met before but also the man who was representing the Klingon accused of causing that loss. When Cogley saw Helen Latham, however, he knew that he couldn't offer her any condolences.

She didn't so much greet them in the living room of her house as she presented herself to them in her domain. She stood statuesque in the showplace of her house, wearing an elegant gown that had just enough black in its design to show that she remembered she was supposed to be in mourning. Cogley realized that she might not even have brought a black dress to the colony world. But he was sure she must have had something simpler she could have worn, something that hinted she was more concerned with grieving for her dead husband than with how she looked.

"Mrs. Latham . . ." Cogley began, and then realized that whatever his intentions had been when he came to this house, he couldn't bring himself to offer her any condolences. *If she doesn't care enough about her hus-*

band's death to show any sorrow, why should I offer her any of mine? he thought. Then he finished his sentence by saying, ". . . I'm sorry we had to meet under these circumstances."

"Yes, it is horrible," Helen Latham said, but the smile she had fixed to her face never disappeared. "Still, no matter what the circumstances, you're welcome in my house."

Cogley noticed that as she said this last part, she spread her arms slightly, as if she were showcasing the living room for her visitors. Cogley was, in fact, sure that was exactly what she was doing. He decided to put his theory to the test and said, "Thank you. It's lovely." The way the smile on Helen Latham's face broadened and more of her perfect white teeth showed through her painted lips, made Cogley even more positive of his assessment. Which is why he decided to try to throw her off her stride. "Kretassan, isn't it?"

"Why, yes . . ." Helen said, and a look of surprise washed over her face. But she quickly regained control of herself, refixed the smile to her face, and added, "Yes, it is. But I must confess, I didn't think a man of your . . . ah . . . particular tastes would recognize Kretassan furniture."

"Oh, I get around quite a bit," Cogley said, and he smiled himself, not because he found the pleasantries the two of them were engaging in to be in any way pleasant, but because his reputation had, again, preceded him. He liked that, as well as the preconceptions it engendered in people. It made people think they knew what they could expect from him. Which only made it all the easier for him to surprise them.

"I'm sure you had a long and hot walk over here from Morton's," Helen said after Cogley had introduced Jackie

LaSalle and explained that his other associate was arranging other interviews. "Would you like to sit down?"

"Yes, I would, but not here, if you don't mind."

"I'm afraid I don't understand."

"I am, as you saw, familiar with Kretassan furniture, and I find its most salient point is that while it looks elegant, it's not at all comfortable."

Helen looked around her, then dropped her voice to a near whisper, "You know, I agree with you. It really *isn't* very comfortable. Shall we go to another room?"

"I'd really like to see your husband's study. Shall we continue this in there?"

"Why . . . yes, I guess so."

Cogley noted the slight hesitation in her voice as she tried to decide how she wanted to answer. He had struck successfully a second time. She didn't really want to go into the study, but she didn't really have a reason not to, either.

Jacqueline LaSalle saw the look on Cogley's face—the same look she had once seen on her late husband's face when he was shown the initial plans for Memory Alpha— and said, "Mrs. Latham, I believe my boss has died and gone to heaven."

"Whatever do you mean?" Helen asked, then looked at Cogley herself. He was standing in the middle of the study, just looking at the books. The collection of books may not have been as big as Cogley's own back on Earth, but it was impressive in its own right. Several bookshelves lined the walls of Daniel Latham's study, each one filled to overflowing with books. Cogley walked from shelf to shelf, studying the books' spines and noting the authors. There were the works of Shakespeare, Hawthorne, Poe, Hemingway, Harris, King, and others. So many others.

Cogley reached out for one of the books, then turned back to Mrs. Latham. "May I?" he asked.

"Go ahead," Helen said with a tone of indifference.

Cogley pulled out the book and leafed through its pages gently, treating it as if it were a newborn baby. "Look at them, Jackie. Not a cracked spine or dog-ear in the collection."

"Dog-ear?" Helen asked.

"It's a way of marking one's place in a book while reading it," Cogley explained. "The corner of the page is folded down at the page the reader wants to mark. It's not recommended, though, and can decrease a book's value."

"Oh, well, then you definitely won't find a dog-ear in this room. Daniel certainly loved his books," Helen said. Cogley noted that the tone of indifference that had once floated in her voice had been replaced by one of petulance.

"Sam, look at this matched set of Dickens," Jackie said while taking in the books on the shelf directly behind Latham's desk.

"Yes, that was Daniel's pride and joy. I've never quite understood that set myself. As you can plainly see, the volumes are all bound and numbered, but the order's all wrong. See, it starts with *The Pickwick Papers* as one, then goes to *Oliver Twist* for two, then *Nicholas Nickleby,* and so on. The last one is seventeen, *The Mystery of Edwin Drood.* They're not in alphabetical order at all."

"The numbering's in chronological order. *The Pickwick Papers* was Dickens's first book, *Oliver Twist* his second. *The Mystery of Edwin Drood* was his last novel. In fact, he never finished it. He died while writing *Edwin Drood*. That's been one of the great unsolved mysteries of literature: Who killed Edwin Drood?"

Cogley started to cross to the books Jackie was looking at, but stopped suddenly. Out of the corner of his eye, he could see Helen Latham standing in the middle of the room and looking at him with the same anger in her eyes that he had seen coming from the colonists on Main Street. Then he realized that Helen wasn't looking at him with those angry eyes. She was looking at the books.

"I see you didn't approve of your husband's books, Mrs. Latham."

Helen laughed briefly, a quick little chuckle meant to offset tension, then said, "Oh I wouldn't say that. It was more like jealousy. At first, Daniel's love of books was endearing, actually. In fact, he used to write me love letters on actual paper. He still does—did—write that way: everything on paper. He'd only transfer it to the computer when he was finished with it.

"But over the years he spent so much time with his books they almost became like another woman. Anytime I couldn't find him, I knew he'd be here in his study reading. Some nights he didn't even come to bed, he'd stay up all night reading and rereading the same books he'd read time and again.

"Sometimes he'd try to hide the fact that he was reading them—put them in a drawer or slip them back on the bookshelf when he heard me coming. But I always knew. I can't begin to tell you the number of times I'd come in here and find him reading one of his books or making notes in them. You'd swear he was almost caressing them. Oh, he'd put them back on the shelf quick enough and devote his attention to me when I came in, but you could see what was important to him."

"You say he'd write in his books? You mean he kept a journal?"

"Why, yes, he did that, too."

"Would you mind if I saw it?"

"Not at all."

Helen opened the top left drawer of her late husband's desk, pulled out a book, and handed it to Cogley. He opened it and flipped through the pages, glancing at page after page of handwritten notations.

"May I take this to read overnight? It should help me get to know your husband better."

Helen shook her head and made a gesture with her hand to indicate that she did not care about the book. "Take it."

"Thank you. Jackie, be sure and tell Ms. Shaw that we have this and that she's welcome to look at it anytime she wants."

"Oh, I doubt she'll want it," Helen said. "I already told her about Daniel's journals, and Areel didn't seem to care about them in the least. *She* knows what's important in this matter."

"No doubt," Cogley said. He continued to study the books on the shelves while he asked her offhandedly, "Mrs. Latham, I'm reluctant to ask this, but my initial investigations have revealed some, well, rumors about your marriage. How were things between your husband and yourself?"

"That's what you get for listening to rumors, Mr. Cogley," Helen said, a tone of glacial ice quite noticeable in her voice. "Oh, you know, Daniel and I had our little squabbles, but for the most part things between us were fine."

"No major fights or arguments recently?"

"Nothing out of the ordinary, no."

Cogley turned from the bookshelves and looked at Helen with a disarming smile. "So you never pulled a phaser on him?"

Helen froze. The icy chill that had been in her voice only moments before was in her entire being now. It had spread quickly through her body like the iceberg-filled waters of the North Atlantic. The way she stood and glared with narrowed eyes at Cogley—frozen and hostile—was every bit as chilling as her voice. *"Certainly not."*

"No, I didn't think so." Cogley smiled quickly at Helen, then moved his glance away from her and down to Latham's desk. "As you said, one shouldn't listen to rumors," Cogley added, not even looking at Helen but at the top of Latham's desk. The desk was empty but for a lamp and the two pictures that were on it. Not liquid crystal frames that would hold whatever digital images were programmed into them, but actual photographs printed on paper. One picture sat in an ornate metal frame. It was of Latham, Helen, and a young girl. The other picture was housed in a beautiful teak frame and showed the same girl, a little older, and a dog.

Helen noticed what Cogley was looking at and used the opportunity to change the subject quickly. "Yes, Daniel kept photographs, too. He said he wanted his memories to age and fade along with him."

She saw that Cogley was looking at the photo of the young girl and dog. "That one is our daughter, Katherine."

"I didn't realize you had a daughter."

The smile that Helen Latham had forced onto her face so often during the afternoon disappeared, this time to be replaced not by an icy or hostile expression but by the sort of sadness one might expect to see from a woman who was supposed to be in mourning. Helen picked up the picture of Katherine and the dog, looked at it for a moment, and ran her right hand over the glass covering the picture.

"She . . . died. There was an accident on one of the other colonies we were spearheading. It happened not too long after this photograph was taken. I guess that's why it's my favorite photo of her. It's how I always remember her."

"I'm sorry," Cogley said, suddenly aware that the condolences he wasn't able to offer earlier now seemed the easiest thing in the world. "She was a beautiful young girl."

Cogley nodded to Jackie, and the two of them started to move toward the door of Latham's study. Helen didn't even seem to notice they were going.

"We'll see ourselves out, Mrs. Latham. And I am sorry if I've awakened unpleasant memories."

This time, he meant every word.

16. Mak'Tor sat at his side of the table in the interview room, staring at Cogley.

The Klingon had already been brought from his cell in the Serenity jail to the makeshift interview room Louis Alexander had set up and was waiting when Alexander showed Cogley, Jackie, and Lawrence into the room. Mak'Tor was sitting in his chair, straight and stiff, with his back pressed against the chair back and his arms crossed in a posture anyone versed in body language would rate as very hostile. Mak'Tor didn't move when the others entered the room and sat down at the other side of the table. When Cogley greeted him and held out his right hand, Mak'Tor still didn't move. When Cogley introduced his colleagues, Mak'Tor didn't respond. When Cogley asked him how he was doing, Mak'Tor did not change his behavior. He sat in the chair and, because Cogley had chosen to sit directly opposite him, stared directly into Cogley's face without blinking.

Cogley, in turn, stared back at Mak'Tor, although Cogley *did* blink. And he also moved. He shifted his weight in his chair, leaned back in it, and did other things to make himself more comfortable. But he never took his eyes off Mak'Tor's. He smiled. He even chuckled. But he kept staring at Mak'Tor.

The two of them remained eye-to-eye for several minutes before Cogley finally sighed and said, "You know, I was the runt of the litter where I grew up in Montana. So I never was much good at playing chicken. Guess this round is yours."

Although Mak'Tor was puzzled by Cogley's words, his expression and posture did not change. He continued to sit up straight and stare at Cogley. He did this as Cogley opened his briefcase, pulled out the journal he had borrowed from Helen Latham, then sat back in his chair again and started to read it.

The two of them—attorney and client—sat in silence for several more minutes, Cogley reading and Mak'Tor staring, before the Klingon finally spoke. "It is obvious I do not wish to speak with you. Why are you still here?" he asked in a bellowing voice that filled the room.

Cogley kept reading.

"I said, 'Why are you still here?' " Mak'Tor repeated in an even louder voice. At the same time, he reached his right hand forward, put it on top of Cogley's book and pushed it down hard onto the table.

"Oh, are you talking to me?" Cogley asked with his best look of innocence.

"I want to know why you're still here."

"Because I'm your lawyer."

"I didn't ask for an advocate."

"You get one anyway. I understand they do the same thing in trials back on your homeworld: assign the defendants counsel."

"On my world, we seek justice with honor in our trials."

"Many years ago there was a famous advocate on Qo'noS named Kolos who didn't exactly share that position."

"You know of Kolos?" Mak'Tor asked. For the first time since Cogley entered the room, Mak'Tor's expression changed. He no longer stared at Cogley in sullen defiance. Instead his eyes were wide with surprise.

"Of course I do. I could hardly choose to represent a Klingon without learning as much as I could about your culture and history, especially your courtroom history. Besides, I'm the first human to represent a Klingon in a trial, it stands to reason that I'd learn about the first Klingon to represent a human. Which brings us back to my first question, how are you doing?"

Mak'Tor stared at Cogley again, but this time not in defiance but in puzzlement and wonder. "I don't understand the question. I've been accused of killing a man. I am in a jail. How I am 'doing' should be obvious."

Cogley had been in this same position—sitting in a jail interview room talking to a prisoner—often enough to recognize when the person he was interviewing was venting. So he didn't respond to Mak'Tor. Instead, he continued to look the Klingon directly in the eye. It wasn't a look of defiance. Instead, he had a pleasant and expectant expression on his face, one that seemed to say, *It's still your turn to say something.*

"I didn't kill Latham," Mak'Tor said finally, when he couldn't take being looked at any longer.

"I didn't think that you did," Cogley replied.

"Why not? Isn't that the immediate reaction of you Earthers? That the Klingon killed your leader?"

Cogley looked at Lawrence and moved his head almost imperceptibly. Lawrence, who was looking for the gesture, saw it, but anyone else would have missed it. In response, Lawrence walked over and stood beside Mak'Tor, then stared down at him.

"As I said earlier, this is Peter Lawrence." As Cogley was speaking, Mak'Tor didn't look at him but looked up into the face of Lawrence. Lawrence loomed over the seated Klingon and just stood there looking down at him without saying a word. "He does my investigative work," Cogley continued. "He's very good at his job. Intelligent, quick-witted, has a hell of a memory, and one more thing . . ."

Cogley stopped speaking.

For a few moments, the room was silent. Cogley simply sat and looked at Mak'Tor. Lawrence stood and looked down at Mak'Tor. Mak'Tor, in turn, continued to look up at Lawrence. With each passing second, Mak'Tor's anger welled up inside him like a pressure cooker whose release valves had been closed. When he couldn't tolerate Lawrence lowering down at him any longer, Mak'Tor stood up and looked Lawrence directly in the eye.

That's when two things happened simultaneously.

"He throws a mean right hook," Cogley said, finishing his sentence.

And Lawrence threw a mean right hook at Mak'Tor's jaw.

Mak'Tor wasn't expecting Lawrence's punch at all. Not even his Klingon battle training had prepared him to anticipate the possibility of an attack in this setting or under these circumstances. Still, even though he wasn't expecting the blow and was thrown off balance when he had to shift his weight to his bad leg without being able to prepare himself properly for the maneuver, he almost managed to avoid the punch. As it was, Lawrence's right fist connected in a glancing blow to Mak'Tor's jaw.

It didn't knock Mak'Tor down, only staggered him. Slightly. In less than two seconds, however, he had regained his balance, even as he lost his temper.

He whirled around—both his hands locked into fists and his right arm coiled in readiness to deliver a blow—and moved toward Cogley. "Do you have a death wish, Earther?" he demanded, even as he cocked his right arm back even farther, readying his fist to strike Cogley's face.

Cogley did nothing.

Mak'Tor looked down at Cogley, towering over him, still ready to pummel him given half an opportunity, but Cogley didn't move. Didn't ready a defense. Didn't scramble, trying to evade the attack that he must surely have believed would follow. Cogley simply looked up at Mak'Tor, smiled wryly, and said:

"That's why not."

And Mak'Tor laughed.

His arms fell to his side. His fists unclenched. And he laughed long and loud and from deep within his soul.

"Well played, human," Mak'Tor said as he sat down, still laughing. "I . . . like you. And I've only been able to say that about one other of your kind."

"Daniel Latham?" Cogley asked.

"Yes, Latham. Like you, Latham didn't back down. He stood up for what he believed. He was a man of honor.

"Him, on the other hand . . ." Mak'Tor inclined his head toward Lawrence as Lawrence resumed his position behind Cogley. Although the way Mak'Tor let his sentence trail off made it sound like a threat, the broad smile on his face indicated something entirely different. "Still, I suppose I can forgive him this one time. He was, after all, only following orders."

Mak'Tor turned back to face Cogley again, looking eye-to-eye, the broad smile still on his face. "Ask your questions."

"I really only have one: What happened that night?"

"I came to Latham's office that night at the appointed time."

"You had an appointment?"

"Yes. He had sent me a message earlier that day and told me we had many things to discuss."

"Did he tell you what he wanted to discuss?"

"Not everything. His communication did indicate that he believed a member of his senior staff was supplying sensitive information to someone in my colony."

"A spy?"

"Yes. Although for some reason, Latham's comm didn't refer to him as a spy but as 'our mutual friend.' "

Cogley laughed briefly, then said, "A little joke on Latham's part. *Our Mutual Friend* is the name of a famous book back on our home planet."

"Yes, I should have suspected. Latham and his books . . ."

"What happened after you arrived at Latham's office?"

"Nothing. I entered Latham's office and found it as it was, in a state of disarray as if there had been a fight. Latham was lying on the floor with what appeared to be a phaser blast in his chest. So I went to him."

"You thought he had been attacked?"

"Yes."

"Did you draw your own weapon?"

"No. I wasn't wearing it. Out of respect to Latham, I did not wear my disruptor when I visited him in his office."

"What did you do next?"

"I knelt down beside Latham to examine him. I was checking him for a pulse when—"

"Where were you checking for the pulse?" Cogley interrupted him.

"Here," Mak'Tor answered, and lifted the first two fingers of his right hand up to the carotid artery in his own neck.

"Thank you. Sorry for the interruption. Go on."

"There is nothing more to say. I was checking Latham for a pulse when three men came into the office. I turned to look at them, to explain what I had found, but they didn't give me the opportunity. They shot me with their phasers before I could say anything.

"Then I woke up here in this jail and learned that I was to stand trial for Latham's murder." Mak'Tor paused for a moment, looked at all three of the humans in the room with him as if measuring them, then continued. "The idea that I would have wanted to kill Latham is laughable. He is probably the only human in this misbegotten colony that I *wouldn't* have wanted to kill."

"Yes, well, we'll probably do better if you *don't* say that during the trial," Cogley said. He put his hand to his chin, then looked up at the wall above and behind Mak'-Tor, staring at it with a blank expression for several seconds. Then he returned his gaze to Mak'Tor.

"Anything else you can remember?"

"No."

Cogley looked back over his shoulder. "Peter, Mak'Tor said something about a spy here in Serenity."

"Already noted, Sam. I'll get right on it."

"Then you think this spy is important?" Mak'Tor asked. "You think he's the murderer?"

"I don't know if he, or she, is the murderer, but yes, he's important. It's always easier to convince the jury there's a reasonable doubt when you can give them a choice of one from Column A or one from Column B."

17. "I was wondering when you'd get around to this," Louis Alexander said as he unlocked the door to Daniel Latham's office. "Mind you, I'm not saying you were wrong in seeing Helen and your client first, but this *is* just a colony world. We don't have all the latest police security equipment out here. I understand they're working on a miniature force field generator you can put inside a room you want to seal, to keep people out. But here, well, I did what I could. Locked the doors and windows, and kept the keys. Personally locked the coordinates of the office out of the transporter controls, so no one could beam in here unless they put in my override code. But I can't guarantee you that no one has been in the room since the murder."

"I'm sure you did what you could, Mr. Alexander," Cogley said. In his many years as an attorney, he'd had to give many such reassuring talks, and he used everything he had ever learned about making his voice sound comforting. "I realize this hasn't been an easy time for any of you. I couldn't get here earlier. I'm sure Ms. Shaw wanted to look over the murder scene without my prying eyes around."

Alexander grinned. "Yeah, it was something like that. Shouldn't that be *Lieutenant* Shaw, though? She *is* a Starfleet JAG officer, after all."

"This is a trial in a civilian court," Cogley explained. "Ms. Shaw requested that the JAG office lend her to the Federation, because Serenity doesn't have any prosecutors of its own that could handle a case like this. Ordinarily there wouldn't be any problems with this, but the Klingon Empire is upset enough about the trial as it is. Neither Starfleet nor the Federation wanted to give the appearance that Starfleet was involved in the prosecution, so they gave Ms. Shaw temporary leave of absence to prosecute the case. For the duration, she's as much a civilian as you or I. And we're all supposed to remember not to call her Lieutenant."

"Well, civilian or JAG, she's through in here now," Alexander said, indicating Latham's office. "She wanted me to tell you that you were free to look around. Speaking of which, I've got something for you."

Cogley turned back to Alexander with a puzzled look on his face. Alexander reached into his pocket and pulled out a small book bound in leather and identical to the book Helen Latham had given Cogley earlier that day.

"It was the journal book Dan had in his desk here. I know Helen gave you one, but it was older. This is the most recent one, the one Dan was keeping when he died. I've read it. Believe me, if Helen had read this one, she would *never* have given it to you."

Cogley reached out his hand and took the journal. For a moment he ran his hand along the exquisite leather binding in an admiring way. He realized that Latham must have had a matched set of these journal books made so that he could keep them, as he kept the other matched sets in his study back in his house. Then Cogley opened the journal and was going to flip through the pages when he saw that someone had placed a bookmark near the middle of the book. He opened the book to those pages and read.

Personal Journal of Daniel Latham: December 13, 2267

>*It's over.*

>*Twenty-two years now over, sloughed away like the skin of a Bastrikian coiler, dead and unwanted.*

>*I find so many thoughts and conflicting emotions coursing through me, but mostly anger and surprise. Not anger at learning that Helen and Grig have betrayed me like some latter-day Lancelot and Guenevere. I've more than suspected what they were doing—been sure of it—for far too long to be surprised by their infidelities. So long, in fact, that the first emotion I had after Helen practically admitted what she had done was relief. My anger and sur-*

prise are at myself, at what I wanted to do in the aftermath of our last argument, not at what Helen did.

When Helen hit me, I felt anger. Rage. Hatred. I wanted to hit her. And when she pulled the phaser on me, I actually called her a "bitch." I don't know who the man in my study was tonight, but it wasn't me. I don't swear, there are far too many better ways to express yourself than common curse words.

I'll never be able to forgive Helen for what she did tonight. Ultimately, it wasn't her unfaithfulness or her shrewish behavior or self-centered indulgences that drove her away from me. It wasn't even that she hit me. But after she hit me, she filled me with so much rage I wanted to hit her back. No, I can never forgive Helen for the fact that she made me want to hit another person.

A beat passed after Cogley had finished reading the journal entry before he did anything other than to look down at the handwritten words. In that time, he absorbed what he had read: five disjointed paragraphs, written in anger, which somehow seemed to capture a man's entire life. Cogley felt strangely conflicted. He loved books, lived for the written word, loved both the broad strokes they could paint and the subtleties they could communicate. So he was thankful for Latham's journal. After reading that one entry, he thought he knew the man better than he would have from all the interviews he could have conducted with Serenity's senior staff. At the same time, however, reading the journal entry made him feel uncomfortable, almost like he was prying. What those words communicated was pain. Cogley didn't think he had ever seen a soul bared so fully, made so open and vulnerable before. And, for the first time in his life, he was almost sorry that he could read.

Cogley shut the book and looked at Alexander. "I went through Dan's office and took that out when I found it. Like I said, I couldn't guarantee I'd be able to keep everyone out of there, no matter what I did. And I thought it was important that you and Ms. Shaw get that, not anyone else."

"I can understand Ms. Shaw. But why me?"

"Dan was my friend. Not enough people in Serenity could make that claim, or make it stick, anyway. I'm not interested in convicting Mak'Tor, unless he did it. What I want is the truth, no matter what it is. I figure if both you and Ms. Shaw have that, it only increases the chances that we'll get it."

"So has Areel seen it?"

"Yeah. She's got it, too. There's a little trick someone showed me you can do with transporters. Beam something into the pattern buffer and with a little manipulation you hold it there long enough to make two beam-outs. *Voila!* Instant copy. I heard the Federation's looking into using the same idea to create something called replicators. Actually, it's *Ms. Shaw* who's got the copy. I figured *you* being the big book lover, you should get the original."

Alexander opened the door to Latham's office and stepped aside, making an "after you" gesture with his arm. Cogley entered the office, stopping by the doorway in the dark room.

"Computer, lights," Alexander said. The room immediately brightened.

"Are you finished in there?" Cogley asked, inclining his head toward Latham's office.

"Yeah. I've gone through it. Ms. Shaw's gone through it. We're done with it. You can do what you want in there now."

"I was supposed to meet Homero Galdamiz here. He must be running late."

"Naw. I told Homero *you* were running late. I wanted to be sure we were alone when I gave you that book. He should be along any time now. And I've got to get back to my office. Ms. Shaw wants to go over my testimony with me."

Cogley held up Latham's book. "Thank you for this," he said, smiling.

"You want to thank me? Just find out who killed Dan."

As Alexander walked back to his own office, Cogley put the journal in his pocket, then began to walk around Latham's office. As he did, he moved his head slowly from left to right, sweeping the room with his eyes, taking in every detail. There weren't many. Latham had kept his office bare, so there was not a lot that could have spilled onto the floor during the fight everyone believed happened in the office. Some papers, which had been on Latham's desk, were lying on the floor, scattered about like the late-October leaves Cogley used to see in Butte. A pen lay next to the desk in the middle of the room. The desk was off center, sitting on a slight bias, as if two people had bumped into it while fighting. It appeared for all the world to be a perfectly typical aftermath of a fight. Almost too perfect, Cogley realized.

When Cogley was through looking at the office, he finally turned his attention to the far wall. Below it he could see the outline on the floor that Alexander had placed around Latham's body, when the body had been there.

They had, of course, moved Latham days ago. It would never have done to leave the corpse out in the Aneher heat for too long. So now, all that was left of a human being was a crude black outline drawn onto cheap, bare flooring.

It was while Cogley was looking at the stark black outline that he noticed something shining on the floor under Latham's desk. He walked over and picked up a photograph of Helen Latham. It was obviously a picture taken at an earlier time, a time when Latham would have wanted to show off his wife to the world. But now it lay on the ground, its teak frame chipped and its glass broken. One more piece of debris from what had once been a man's life. One more shard of yesterday.

"Sorry I'm late, Mr. Cogley," Galdamiz said. "Lou Alexander told me that you were runnin' behind an' that I could take my time gettin' here."

Cogley looked up from the picture and put it on the desk. "Think nothing of it," he said. "I finished my other errands a little earlier than I thought I would, so I came over here." Cogley didn't enjoy lying. The endless jokes that had been around for as long as his profession had existed to the contrary, lying was not something Cogley had ever felt comfortable doing. But Alexander seemed to think it was important that the others not know he had Latham's journal, and everything Cogley could tell about Alexander so far told him to trust the man's instincts.

"Well, you asked for this meetin', Mr. Cogley. What can I do for you?"

"I just wanted to clear up a couple of points. I've read the interviews you gave Louis Alexander." As he spoke, Cogley opened his briefcase and pulled out a comm unit. He thumbed a couple of controls and called up the video that Alexander had made with Iino, Nemov, and Galdamiz re-creating what happened when they found Mak'Tor. "This is what you told him happened that night."

Cogley played the video for them. When it had finished, Cogley asked, "Is that how you remember it?"

"Well, Chiaki's no Anton Karidian, but what do Iino know about actin'? Yeah, that's pretty much how it was. If you got any doubts, you can Latham to rest."

Cogley walked over to the doorway. As he did, he rolled his eyes up in their sockets. He could understand why Alexander had warned him about Galdamiz's alleged sense of humor. "You were standing where?" he asked, when he reached the doorway.

Galdamiz came over and stood next to him. "I was about here. Grig was right where you're standin' and Chiaki was to your right."

"Can you show me where Mak'Tor was?"

Galdamiz crossed the room to where the outline had been drawn on the floor and kneeled in front of it, his back to Cogley. "He was right here, like this," Galdamiz said.

"From where I am, I can't see the face of the person lying on the floor."

"Neither could I. Mak'Tor was in the way."

"Then how did you know it was Latham?"

"He was in Latham's office and wearin' Latham's clothes. I didn't figure it was Yuri Gagarin."

"You didn't like Daniel Latham much, did you?"

"Naw, I liked him okay."

"But you argued with him about how to run the colony's mines."

"So we didn't see eye-to-eye about that. Doesn't mean I

didn't like him. I used to argue with my brother all the time, but I liked him."

"Then, if you liked him, why did witnesses say that you attacked Latham in the street the day before the murder?"

"That? Didn't mean nothin'. It was hot. I was mad 'cause I'd just lost a good worker to one of those damned jurisdictional hearings. And I'm not proud to admit it, but I'd had a little too much to drink that day at lunch."

"I see. Thank you," was all Cogley said in reply. But he remembered that the fight occurred in the morning, long before Galdamiz would have been drinking his lunch. Cogley realized that Galdamiz apparently didn't feel the same discomfort about lying that he did, but that he should have, considering how poorly he did it.

"Yes. That is the way I remember it happening," Grigoriy Nemov said, after Cogley had shown him Iino's re-creation. "But I've already been over that with Louis and Ms. Shaw."

"I appreciate that, Mr. Nemov. But it doesn't hurt to go over these things more than once. Sometimes you remember a little detail that you may have forgotten before."

"There are no such details. That is exactly how it happened."

Nemov had been working on his computer, when Cogley came in. Even as Cogley asked his questions and Nemov watched the re-creation, he kept looking back at his computer in irritation. "Is this almost over? I'm in charge of this colony now, rather unexpectedly. There is much work I must do."

"Then I won't take up much more of your time," Cogley said. Nemov smiled at that and turned his attention back to his computer. "I was just wondering," Cogley persisted. "You have a computer here on your desk. There was a computer on Daniel Latham's desk, but it's not there now. Do you know where it is?"

"Ms. Shaw took it. She said she wanted to study its memory core before trial."

"That is unfortunate. Areel will play by the rules of discovery and let me see the computer. Eventually. But I was hoping I might be able to see it a little earlier than that. She didn't tell you how long she thought she'd need it, did she?"

"No. But if it will get you out of my office sooner, Chiaki Iino may be of help in this."

"Yes, he might, at that. Thank you for your time."

Cogley started to walk toward the door. As he did, he looked at Nemov's office more carefully than he had when he entered it. The office was almost the exact opposite of Latham's. Where Latham kept his office bare, Nemov filled his with expensive furniture, reproductions of famous paintings, and personal items. There were even, Cogley recognized, some re-creations of some prehistoric statues found in an archaeological dig on Vulcan.

"I know you look busy," Cogley said, turning back to Nemov, "but Daniel Latham's death actually came at a pretty convenient time for you, didn't it?"

Nemov looked up at him but said nothing.

"I mean, Latham was about to divorce his wife because of you. And maybe she'd get nothing, which wouldn't make her too attractive to a man like you, would it?"

"I think you should leave," Nemov said, containing his anger so that his voice conveyed only a hint of the threat he might have liked to communicate.

"Now you get all the perks of running this colony. Soon you might even be moving into that big, fancy house at the end of the street. Yup, timing couldn't have been better."

Nemov rose from his chair and looked as if he were about to come toward Cogley. Cogley simply smiled and pulled a piece of paper from his coat pocket. He lay it on the fancy chair that sat beside the door. "It's a subpoena, Mr. Nemov. I'll see you in court."

"Yes, Mr. Cogley," Iino said. "What I did in the reenactment for Louis is exactly how I remember that night."

Cogley noted that all three men—Galdamiz, Nemov, and Iino—still agreed about what had happened in Latham's office when they found Mak'Tor in it. Either it was the truth as they remembered it, or, in the days after the murder, the three had been able to confer enough to get their story straight. Or both.

"Let me ask you another thing. I wanted to go over the files in Latham's computers, to see if there was anything of use there."

"I thought you didn't like computers."

"Yes, but not everyone feels that way. Most people like them. I know Daniel Latham used one when he had to, because everyone else in Serenity used one. So I want to see what's on his. There might be something important there. Anyway, that's why I need your help, *you* like computers.

"Trouble is, Ms. Shaw has taken Latham's computer from his office. But Mr. Nemov said you might be able to help me. That is, if you don't mind helping the man defending the person accused of killing Daniel Latham."

"I'll be honest with you, Mr. Cogley, I really don't care

what happens on this colony any longer. You know about Ron Sayger and me?"

"Yes."

"Ron has a week to go on his sentence. We've both already put in for transfers off Aneher. As soon as this whole trial is over, the Federation should approve my transfer. So, even if the Federation hadn't ordered us to cooperate with you fully to keep the Klingons from claiming Mak'-Tor didn't receive a fair trial, I'd be willing to help you. The faster you get this over with, the faster I can get off this sinkhole."

Iino turned back to the computer that was on his desk. It was large, much bigger than any of the others Cogley had seen in Serenity.

"I've got the main server for the colony right here. And, you'll be glad to know, I cloned the memory core of Latham's computer in it."

"Cloned? How do you clone a machine?"

"Sorry. Technobabble. On an outer colony like this, computers get used and reused. Each time they are, the memory is wiped so that the new user will have a clean computer. But SOP says that before the memory is wiped, we're supposed to store an exact copy of the memory core—a clone, if you will—on the colony's server. That way if there was something important, it's not lost.

"I had already cloned Latham's memory core before Ms. Shaw took the computer. So whatever you want to see, I have a copy of it right here."

"Fine. Let's start with the night of the murder. Is there any computer activity from that night?"

Iino was about to order the computer to display the activity of Daniel Latham's computer from the night of the murder, when he looked up at Latham and apologized. "Sorry. This is going to take a little longer than I thought. The computer's just started its daily systemwide diagnostic scan."

"How did it do that? I didn't see you order it."

"I've instructed the computer to do it every day at this time. Don't worry, it doesn't mean that I won't be able to get what you want. It just means the computer will be a little slower."

Iino ordered the computer to display the requested activity.

"There's not much here. Not surprising. Latham didn't use his computer a lot. He sent a file to his computer by comm link. Looks like he did some work on that file. He sent a message to his wife's computer about twenty minutes before he died. He sent out a notice to the entire senior staff that he wanted a meeting with us the next morning. We never did find out what we were supposed to be meeting over. And that's about it."

"Can you tell me what file he was working on?"

"Just a second and I'll—" Then Chiaki looked up from his computer monitor, puzzled. "That's odd. According to this, the file Latham was working on was deleted from his computer. But only about a minute before we came into the room."

"A minute?" Cogley said. "Latham was probably dead by then. That would mean . . ." he said, thinking out loud.

"That the murderer deleted the file after he killed Latham. There was something in it that bastard Klingon didn't want us to see."

"But we *do* want to see it. Can you retrieve the file?" Cogley asked.

"It'll take some doing, but I should be able to get it."

"If you need any help, my associate Jacqueline LaSalle used to work for the Daystrom Institute."

"With all due respect to Ms. LaSalle's past accomplishments, these computers are old. I don't think anyone's as familiar with them as I am. I doubt even Richard Daystrom himself could get the files faster than I could."

"Then I'll leave you to it. But one more thing. Why did you threaten Daniel Latham the morning of the murder?"

"I had just seen Ron get sentenced to the same Klingon mines that crippled me. I was mad and I vented some plasma at Latham. Yes, I threatened him. But that doesn't mean I killed him."

No. No, it doesn't, Cogley thought as he left Iino's office. *On the other hand, it doesn't mean that you* didn't *kill him either.*

18.

"You're meeting Khogo *where?*" Louis Alexander asked, when Cogley stopped in to discuss the details of his night's agenda.

"The *'Iw Taj,*" Cogley answered, his pronunciation of the Klingon name almost flawless.

"And do you happen to know what *'Iw Taj* means?" Alexander asked, stumbling over the Klingon words but giving them the best phonetic approximation his tongue could manage.

"It doesn't have an exact translation, because the Klingon language doesn't have adjectives as such," Jackie said. At one point in her career at the Daystrom Institute, her duties included giving indoctrination lectures to the new hires. She was still able to adopt a decided pedagogical tone in her voice, when she thought she needed it, "Its closest English approximation would be 'The Bloody Dagger.' "

Alexander looked at Jackie in surprise. Not because she knew the translation of the phrase, but because the fact that she knew it probably meant . . .

"Please don't tell me that you're gonna let *her* go, too?" he demanded, pointing his index finger at Jackie.

Lawrence, who had been standing right next to Alexander, took a couple of steps away from him, turned his back to his old friend, and whistled softly. Lawrence said nothing, but his actions clearly warned, "You're on your own on this one, pal."

Jackie didn't say a word, at first. She simply walked up to Alexander, smiling all the time. When she reached him, she stood directly in front of him, narrowed her eyes, and stared directly into his. The look would have withered cypress trees in a swamp. "The question, Mr. Alexander, isn't whether Sam's going to 'let me go,' to use your antediluvian phrase. The question is, who's going to stop me?" Jackie leaned toward Alexander, so that her face was only inches from his and their noses almost touched. "You?"

The tone in Jackie's voice was one that had always astonished Cogley. He'd heard her use it before, in similar situations, including once—and only once—with Peter Lawrence. There was just enough of a hint of derision in the way Jackie voiced that "You?" to let Alexander know two things: As far as Jackie was concerned, he was welcome to try and stop her. And what the odds of success were, if he did. At the same time, there was just enough hint of friendliness in her voice to blunt the edge from the situation and give everyone a graceful way out of it.

Alexander knew when he was beaten and took that graceful way out. "Uh. No, ma'am. I don't figure I got enough backup. Not even with all those extra people the *Enterprise* sent down. But look, I can't just let you three go waltzing in there like it was a stroll in Central Park."

"Nor did we intend to, Mr. Alexander."

"Lou."

"Only if you call me Sam."

"Sam it is. But if you didn't intend to go strolling in there, what did you have in mind?"

"Lou, that's exactly what we came here to discuss."

"Sam, are you *sure* you know what we're doing?" Peter Lawrence asked, as he, Cogley, and Jackie walked along the Neutral Zone toward the *'Iw Taj*. After they had passed through the weapons checkpoint and had both a Klingon warrior and one of the Serenity security officers verify that they had no weapons on them, they moved down the dirt street that ran through the center of the Neutral Zone. They walked past that part of the Neutral Zone where those colonists from Serenity who ventured into the area chose to congregate and continued into the section of the Neutral Zone that was closer to the Klingon colony. As Lawrence spoke, he looked around him and saw almost nothing but Klingon faces.

"No." Cogley said. "But when have I ever let that stop me?"

Lawrence didn't even have to stop to think about the answer. He couldn't remember a time when Cogley didn't actually know what he was doing. But he also knew that it wouldn't stop Cogley, even if he didn't know. If Cogley thought it was the right thing to do, he would do it, even if everyone else in the Federation—hell, everyone else in the galaxy—thought it was the worst idea since World War III.

"At least evening's coming and it's cooling down some. Made the walk more pleasant," Cogley said. They reached the door of the *'Iw Taj* and paused outside of it. Cogley looked at the swinging door of the Klingon bar and smiled that wry smile of his that Lawrence found both endearing and annoying, depending on what Cogley was about to do to him.

"Well," Cogley said, and Lawrence realized, to his surprise, that at that moment he found the smile endearing, "in for a penny, in for a pound."

"How much is a penny worth in Federation credits?" Lawrence asked.

"You don't want to know," Cogley said.

"Why? Afraid I'll find out how cheaply you're willing to sell my life?"

"Something like that," Cogley replied. Then Cogley pushed open the door of the *'Iw Taj* and entered.

The *'Iw Taj*, like all Klingon bars, was dark. Dark was a condition that was hardly limited to their bars. As a race, the Klingons tended to keep everything underilluminated and drab. Cogley had read the reports that Jonathan Archer, the first captain of the first warp ship to bear the name *Enterprise*, had filed about his time as a prisoner of the Klingon Empire and its justice system. Archer had said, ironically enough, that about the only time during his weeks of captivity that he ever saw anything bright was when he was in the ice fields of the Klingon prison Rura Penthe.

The three humans looked around and saw that the bar was full. In almost the exact center of the bar, there was one table that had only one Klingon sitting at it, even though there were two more chairs at the table. In addition, as if by arrangement, the other tables in *'Iw Taj* had been pulled away from the table in the middle of the room, as if to create a buffer zone around it.

"I think we're expected," Lawrence said.

Cogley walked directly over to the table, pulled out one of the empty chairs, sat down, and said, "Mr. Khogo, I presume."

"I am Khogo, *toDSaH*!"

"Sorry. A little ice breaker."

If a face could snarl, then Khogo's face was a caged and abused lion, but Cogley could see a look of puzzlement pass over Khogo's face, then quickly be replaced by the snarl. "Sorry, not familiar with our Earth expressions, are you?"

"No. Mak'Tor may have wanted to have dealings with you Earthers. I do not. I limit my contact to your contamination only on those occasions that Mak'Tor requires it of me. Which is the only reason I am here now. Had you not arranged for Mak'Tor to communicate with me and order my presence, I would be as far away from you as possible." Khogo grunted as he said the words, as if to show his distaste of what he was doing. "But let us not prolong the unpleasantness of this evening any more than is necessary."

"Fine. These are the associates I told you would be coming with me. Jacqueline LaSalle," Cogley said, and gestured toward Jackie, who was sitting in the third chair at the table. "And this is . . ." Cogley continued turning to where Lawrence should have been sitting. "Oh dear, he's not— Jackie, where *is* Peter?"

"I think he's finding a chair," Jackie said, and looked over at one of the nearby tables, which had two Klingons sitting at it and four empty chairs around it. "Khogo must have forgotten to get enough for all of us."

"Hi," Peter Lawrence said to the two Klingons sitting at that table. "My friends and I are having a meeting with your boss there and it looks like he miscounted the chairs. An oversight, I'm sure." Lawrence looked back at Khogo. "I don't think he meant to insult me by not having a chair for me. You don't mind, do you?" Lawrence picked up one of the empty chairs to move it to Khogo's table.

"Yes I do, Earther," one of the Klingons said. "We *both* mind."

"Really," Lawrence to them, and smiled broadly. "*Both* of you. Well, sorry, but you do have more than you need."

Lawrence walked away from the table, carrying the chair. Even as the two Klingons rose from where they were sitting, Lawrence moved to Khogo's table, set his chair down, next to Cogley's, sat down, and said, "Did I miss anything?"

Which is when the bigger of the two Klingons from the next table placed his large hand on Lawrence's shoulder and lifted him up.

"I said we *did* mind if you took our chair, *petaQ!*"

The Klingon spun Lawrence around and encircled the human's chest with his large arms in a tight bear hug, pinning his arms to his sides. Immediately the second Klingon, who was the smaller of the two by the slightest of margins, advanced on Lawrence, forming his massive hands into fists. The hatred that erupted from his eyes told anyone who looked into them that he intended to beat Lawrence to within an inch of his life, if not a foot or two more.

"This should be entertaining," Khogo said, and his smile showcased a set of badly yellowed and decaying teeth.

"It should, indeed," Cogley said in response, and flashed Khogo a smile of his own.

Even as Cogley and Khogo spoke, Lawrence moved. He picked up his right foot and drove it down hard on the foot of the Klingon who held him, mashing the specially built metal heel on his shoe into the Klingon's instep. At the same time, he drove the back of his head into the bridge of the Klingon's nose, breaking it with a crunching sound that Lawrence found most satisfying.

The Klingon screamed in pain and loosened his grip. Lawrence quickly slid down out of the Klingon's arms and went into a crouch. Then he sprang and launched himself at the second Klingon, who was now only a foot away from him. Lawrence moved his right arm up, combining the force of his leap with the force of his blow, and caught the Klingon with an open-handed smash to the chin. The Klingon's head snapped back. Lawrence was then on the Klingon. He drove his knee into the Klingon's stomach, causing him to double over, then locked his fingers together behind the Klingon's neck and pulled his head down, driving the Klingon's face into his knee.

When the second Klingon lay unconscious on the floor, Lawrence turned just in time to confront the first Klingon, who was running at him, blood streaming from his broken nose and staining the dark leather tunic of his uniform. Lawrence sidestepped the Klingon like a matador would a charging bull, and as the Klingon flew past him, Lawrence drove his left elbow into the crook of the Klingon's neck. This Klingon, too, hit the floor in a crumpled, unconscious heap.

Lawrence turned back to face Khogo, who was standing and walking toward Lawrence, getting ready to join the battle.

"*Qovpatlh!* I could kill you now and say it was a tragic accident. There would be none to dispute my word."

"You could," Lawrence said, standing his ground. "And as much as I'd hate to spoil your fun, or that of any of your friends here," Lawrence added, pointing in the direction of several other patrons of the *'Iw Taj* who were getting out of their chairs and preparing to join the fight, "do it and you'll lose Aneher."

"The planet is *ours!*" Khogo snapped, but he held up his hand to signal to the others that they should stay any attack they planned.

"Smart choice," Lawrence said.

"You see, Khogo, it's like this," Cogley said, and the acting head of the Klingon colony turned back to look down at the lawyer.

Cogley still sat in his chair. He looked up at Khogo and spoke in a pleasant, conversational tone, as if the two were talking about the weather or some even more enjoyable subject. "You may think you have the better claim to the planet. But kill us and the Federation will file a formal complaint with the Organians. Under the terms of the treaty, after such an unprovoked murder, the Klingon Empire would forfeit all claim to the planet. I'm sure the High Council would reserve a special place in *Gre'thor* for you if you caused that."

"As I said before, I could claim your death was an accident and there would be none to doubt me.

"However," he added as he gestured for the other Klingons in the bar to sit, "we shall abstain from any actions at this moment. It will only make our ultimate victory over you on this planet all the sweeter. After all, isn't it you Earthers who say, 'Abstinence makes the heart grow fonder?'"

"Actually, it's—" Lawrence started to say, but a quick, subtle look from Cogley stopped him, even as Cogley surreptitiously reached into his pocket and pressed a button on a communicator he had there.

"You have shown what is, for you, remarkable common sense, Khogo," said a voice that definitely was not Cogley's, even though it came from Cogley.

Every eye in the 'Iw Taj turned to look at Cogley, and when they did, another Klingon suddenly appeared in the 'Iw Taj inside the shimmering aura of a transporter beam. The voice resonated in the memories of every Klingon in the bar. Everyone looked at him and immediately recognized him, even before he had materialized fully.

"Is *this* how you obey my direct commands?" the Klingon asked. His voice, filled with the booming resonance of one used to issuing commands, drowned out all other noise in the bar.

"Mak'Tor!" Khogo said in surprise. "Have . . . you . . . returned?"

Mak'Tor ignored Khogo's question and continued his commands. "These two men and woman are my personal envoys. My *advocates*. You are to treat them as you would me. If any—and I mean *any*—harm should befall them, I personally guarantee that every man, woman, and child in this colony will end their lives not in battle but as requisition clerks."

"See?" Cogley said to Khogo in a stage whisper, then pulled out and held up the Federation communicator that Mak'Tor had been using to monitor the meeting. "It wouldn't have been just your word."

Khogo said nothing, but he looked at Cogley with a fury that would have dwarfed a supernova.

"And you!" Mak'Tor said, pointing at Khogo. Khogo turned back to face Mak'Tor, and he slumped a little, like an errant child being scolded by his parent. "To answer your question before you soil yourself, no, I have not returned. I still await trial in the human colony. But they have shown me more honor than you have with your miserable plotting. The humans allowed me to participate with my advocates in this meeting so that your pathetic trap would fail. I have given them my warrior's oath that I would return to them, and I will.

"But remember my words, all of you.

"And, Khogo, unless you want to find yourself slopping the *targs,* you will give my advocate every cooperation. And that includes answering his questions."

When he finished his speech, Mak'Tor activated the Federation communicator he was carrying, then disappeared in the same sparkling aura of a transporter beam that had earlier presaged his arrival.

"You have questions for me, Earther?" Khogo said without turning to face Cogley but staring at the spot where Mak'Tor had been with an expression that would have melted a warp baffle plate.

"Only one. You'd like to see me lose this trial and have Mak'Tor convicted of Daniel Latham's murder, wouldn't you?"

"Yes. Your Daniel Latham and his insistence that our two colonies cooperate is already dead. With Mak'Tor gone and his *dishonorable*"—Khogo practically spat the word out—"insistence that we placate you Earthers forgotten, we could treat you as we should. The way a Klingon warrior would treat *any* invader on Klingon land.

"Yes, I want to see Mak'Tor lose this pitiful excuse for a 'fair trial,' so that *I* will be in charge of this planet, and we will be able to expel you from our world."

"I thank you for your honesty," Cogley said.

Cogley and Jackie stood and were preparing to leave, but Khogo held out an arm to block their path.

"A moment. I answered your question. I request the same favor."

"Ask away."

"Do you truly believe you can secure an acquittal for a Klingon from an Earther jury?"

Cogley reached into his pocket, pulled out a piece of paper, and handed it to Khogo.

"That's a subpoena requesting your testimony at the trial. I call it a request, but consider it an order from Mak'-Tor. So why don't you come watch the trial and find out."

"And you," Khogo said, pointing to Lawrence. "You showed a warrior's heart. But what would you have done if I had not told my people to refrain from any attack?"

"Well, you got me there," Lawrence said with the sheepish expression of a boy who was caught with his hand in a cookie jar. "All I know is . . ."

Lawrence moved his hand quickly and suddenly a type-1 phaser simply appeared in it, pointed directly at Khogo's chest. Then Lawrence shifted his arm to the left, pointed his phaser at the chair he had taken from the other table, and fired it. The chair simply disappeared, vaporized in the phaser's blue-green light.

". . . I wouldn't have been the *first* to die."

"But . . . How did. . . ? The weapons checkpoints . . ." Khogo stammered and then broke out into loud, uncontrolled laughter. Cogley wasn't sure, but he could have sworn he could hear a trace of admiration in that laugh.

Cogley, Lawrence, and Jackie took the opportunity afforded by Khogo's laughter to leave the *'Iw Taj* and walk back to Serenity.

"You played your part well, Peter."

"Thanks. Just so you don't expect too many repeat performances."

"Tell me, how *did* you get that phaser past the checkpoints?"

Lawrence looked at Cogley and grinned. "You know what they say about magicians, Sam. What would happen to my reputation, if I were to show you the mirrors?"

Cogley laughed, which caused Lawrence to laugh in return. The three humans walked down the main road of the Neutral Zone back toward the Federation section, the two men laughing all the time. When Jackie finally decided that they had been insufferably pleased with themselves long enough, she said, "Sam, I'm always happy for the chance to make some new friends, but exactly what did that accomplish?"

"Well, we know that Khogo would love to eliminate Mak'Tor as the head of this colony. But I doubt he's got the connections within the High Council to pull that off. I wanted to find out if he was devious enough to kill Latham and frame Mak'Tor to get rid of both of the people who stood in his way. I think the little trap he set for us proved he is."

"Okay, so he would have wanted to kill Latham. But could he have done it?"

"Mak'Tor told us he ordered Khogo to program their transporters so that he could beam over to Latham's office for their meeting. All Khogo had to do was beam himself to Latham's office a few minutes before the meeting, kill Latham, stage the fight, and beam back before Mak'Tor arrived."

"But why did he use a phaser?" Jackie asked.

"He probably planned to beat Latham to death," Lawrence said, and Cogley nodded his agreement. "He couldn't use a disruptor, because Mak'Tor didn't take his disruptor to Latham's office. So, he planned to beat Latham to death and make it look like it happened in a fight."

Lawrence snapped his fingers, "Hey! I'll bet Khogo's been behind all those things like the spy in Serenity. Stir up enough trouble to make it seem natural that Mak'Tor and Latham would be arguing, then plan the frame-up so that it looked like it happened in a fight."

He looked at Cogley and could tell from Cogley's smile that the lawyer agreed with his reasoning. "Anyway, when Khogo saw Latham's phaser lying on the desk, he picked it up and used it. It was quicker and quieter. And how better to frame Mak'Tor than to use the weapon that was lying in the room that Mak'Tor would be in a few minutes later? Presto, Latham's dead. Mak'Tor's accused of the murder, and Khogo has the two people who he thought were standing in his way *out* of his way."

"But *did* he do it?" Jackie asked.

Cogley shook his head, not to say no, but to show his frustration over the case. Something was eluding him, and he didn't know what it was.

"I wish I knew," he sighed. "I wish I knew."

19.   "Mr. Cogley, do I understand you correctly? You say you *don't* want a separation of witnesses?"

Cogley stood up behind the defense table and said, "No, Your Honor. We have every confidence in the integrity of the prosecution's witnesses."

Judge Carabatsos shrugged his shoulders and turned his attention to Areel Shaw. "Ms. Shaw, you may call your first witness."

"Thank you, Your Honor. The prosecution calls Dr. Cary Mankiewicz."

As Areel Shaw guided Dr. Mankiewicz through his testimony—yes, he's a doctor; yes, he examined the body of Daniel Latham; yes, based on the wounds, in his expert medical opinion, Daniel Latham died as the result of being shot at close range with a type-2 phaser set on kill—Mak'-Tor turned to Jacqueline LaSalle and asked, "What is a separation of witnesses?"

Jackie caught the quick but stern look from Judge Carabatsos, reminded their client that he needed to speak in a voice that was much softer than what Klingons thought of as a whisper. Then she answered his question. "A separation of witnesses is an order forbidding people who are going to be witnesses from watching the actual trial. It's done so that they don't hear the other testimony and shape their own to conform to what they've heard."

"And Samuel Cogley does not wish to do this for what reason?"

"Sam claims they had an old saying back in Montana where he grew up, 'Don't show blood to the pecking order.' " Jackie answered the unasked question hanging in Mak'Tor's puzzled look. "It means, 'Don't show your enemies your weakness.' The prosecution's witnesses had several days to confer and coordinate their testimony before we even arrived on Aneher. So asking for a separation of witnesses probably wouldn't have accomplished anything. But if we *don't* ask for one, we're telling the prosecution that it doesn't matter to us whether their witnesses are coordinating their testimony, we're just not afraid of what they're going to say."

"Ah, I understand. Have I ever told you that Samuel Cogley would make a good Klingon?"

"No, but I'll be sure and pass on the compliment."

Jackie didn't get the chance, because at that moment Areel Shaw turned to the defense table and said, "Your witness, Mr. Cogley."

Cogley could feel all eyes in the courtroom turn to him expectantly. It seemed that this—not the actual trial itself, not the guilt or innocence of Mak'Tor—was what everyone had come for. The performance of Samuel T. Cogley, noted defense attorney famous for his courtroom theatrics. Cogley smiled, as if to acknowledge the eyes that were fixed on him. While still sitting down he asked in a calm voice, "Doctor, how many settings does a standard type-2 phaser have?"

Although Cogley had remained seated, Areel Shaw did rise. "Objection, Your Honor. The question is irrelevant and calls for knowledge outside of the doctor's field of expertise."

"Well, that didn't take long," Cogley said to no one in particular.

"Mr. Cogley, you will address any comments to the court," Judge Carabatsos admonished him.

"My apologies, Your Honor. As to Ms. Shaw's relevancy argument, the rules of evidence say that evidence is relevant if it tends to confirm or deny a fact at issue in the trial. I could outline any number of scenarios in which this information could shed light on the question of who fired that phaser. As for Ms. Shaw's other objection, I can rephrase. Doctor, how many settings does a standard type-2 phaser have, if you know?"

Cogley turned toward Areel and repeated the last phrase he had said, "If you know."

"Four. Heat, stun, disrupt, and dematerialize. Disrupt is commonly called the kill setting."

"And you testified that the phaser that killed Daniel Latham was set on disrupt, the so-called kill setting, correct?"

"Yes."

"Well, I guess we know the phaser wasn't set on stun, because Daniel Latham wasn't stunned. But how do you know it wasn't set on dematerialize instead of disrupt?"

Areel Shaw was about to stand and object again, but she caught a confident look on Dr. Mankiewicz's face and thought better of it.

"Because if it had been set on dematerialize, the body would have been vaporized," Mankiewicz said, a smug smile on his face. "There wouldn't have been a body."

"Yes, I guess that would explain things, wouldn't it? No more questions."

"Ms. Shaw, please call your next witness," Carabatsos said.

"I call Khogo, son of Moag, to the stand."

Khogo had looked like a grizzly in a bear trap while he sat in the back of the courtroom watching the proceedings: surly, practically snarling, and like he wanted to bite everyone in the neck. As he walked to the witness stand, he looked at Mak'Tor with an expression that said if he hadn't been required to surrender his *d'k tahg* before entering the room, the knife would be buried in Mak'Tor's neck now.

"Your Honor, Khogo has been ordered to cooperate with us by the Klingon High Council, so he is not here willingly. I request the privilege of treating him as a hostile witness."

"Mr. Cogley?" Carabatsos asked.

"No objection, Your Honor," Cogley said, "provided I'm accorded the same privilege."

"Khogo, do you remember the night Daniel Latham was killed?"

"A Klingon's memory is not to be questioned."

"That would be a 'yes'?"

Khogo didn't answer, he just sat and stared at Areel, the same hate in his eyes for her that he had flashed toward Mak'Tor earlier.

"Well, I won't push it. On that night, when was the last time you saw Mak'Tor?"

"Mak'Tor called me into his office. He told me that he had a meeting with Daniel Latham scheduled for that night."

"Did he say what time?"

"No. I knew it was to be late, sometime during your colony's so-called Landing Day celebration, but I didn't know the exact time."

"How did you know it was to be during the celebration?"

"Because Mak'Tor ordered me to program the transporters to send him directly to Latham's office. He said he didn't want to be walking through the streets when they would be full of drunken celebrants."

Areel sneaked a quick peek at Cogley, waiting for the objection, but there was none forthcoming.

"What did you do then?"

"What I was ordered to do. I programmed the transporters as directed. Then I went back to my office."

"Did you see Mak'Tor any more that night?"

"No."

"Your witness, Mr. Cogley."

Cogley stood up and walked up to the witness stand. He smiled at Khogo, waiting for Khogo to glare back at him. When he got the reaction he wanted, he said, "You don't like Mak'Tor, do you?"

"He is my commanding officer. It is not my place to have a personal opinion of him."

"You'd hardly be the first soldier to have an opinion of his commanding officer."

"It is not the Klingon way."

"Ah well, so much for that Klingon memory you were so proud of."

"What do you mean?" Khogo demanded, spitting the words out.

"Didn't you tell me only yesterday how you wanted Mak'Tor to be convicted so you could run your colony the way you thought it should be run?"

As he had with Areel, Khogo sat and stared rather than answered.

"You do recognize this voice, don't you?" Cogley asked. As Cogley spoke, Jackie was already keying her comm unit, timing the function perfectly so that as soon as Cogley finished his question, the unit played a recorded voice in the courtroom, *"Yes, I want to see Mak'Tor lose this pitiful excuse for a 'fair trial,' so that I will be in charge of this planet, and we will be able to expel you from our world."*

"That is your voice, isn't it?"

Again Khogo didn't answer.

"I'll move on," Cogley said. "You don't really like humans either, do you?"

"No."

"Don't want to have anything to do with them?"

"No."

"In fact, you told me only yesterday, did you not, that you limit your contact with humans to those times when Mak'Tor orders you to have contact with them?"

"Yes."

"So, if you don't like humans and you have little contact with humans, how is it that yesterday when I interviewed you, you used the decidedly human phrase, 'Absence makes the heart grow fonder'?"

"I didn't."

"You didn't?"

"No."

"You didn't say that to me yesterday?"

"You are trying to trap me by intentionally misquoting the phrase," Khogo said with a smug smile on his face. He gestured toward Jackie with a wave of his right arm. "If you check your recording device, you will see that the correct phrase is 'Abstinence makes the heart grow fonder,' and *that* is what I said yesterday."

As if on cue, the unit in Jackie's hand played a recording of Khogo from the day before saying, *"After all, isn't it you Earthers who say, 'Abstinence makes the heart grow fonder'?"*

"Why, so you did," Cogley said, the same smile on his face that he'd had when he started his cross-examination. "No further questions."

"Ms. Shaw?" Carabatsos said, indicating Areel should call her next witness.

Areel Shaw stood up and faced the judge. "One moment, Your Honor," she said. She turned and faced the gallery in the back of the courtroom, surveying all of the witnesses who were waiting there to testify.

"Ms. Shaw, we're waiting."

"Sorry, Your Honor. To be honest, I'm a little taken aback by the progress we've made so far. I was expecting a more vigorous jury selection process by Mr. Cogley and a longer cross-examination of my witnesses. Your Honor, it will be time for the morning recess soon, but I'd just as soon not have the testimony of any of my witnesses interrupted. Would it be all right to take our break now?"

"Mr. Cogley?" Carabatsos asked.

"No objection."

After the courtroom recessed, Peter Lawrence walked from the spectators' gallery up to Cogley.

"Well?" Cogley asked him. "Were you watching?"

"Yup. And it happened exactly as you predicted it would. You were right." Then he added with a smile, "Which always saves me a lot of work."

"But what does it mean for our case?" Jackie asked. "What's our next step?"

"I don't know," Cogley said. He didn't have the smile

he'd worn earlier on his face anymore. Now his jaw was locked and he had a grim and determined look on his face.

Jackie recognized that look. "Sam, what's wrong?" she asked.

"The case isn't coming together right," Cogley said. "Something's wrong. I'm missing something. I'm still trying to figure out what it is. The thing is, if I don't figure it out, I think Mak'Tor will be convicted."

20. "I call Helen Latham to the stand," Areel Shaw said, when the court came out of recess.

At this announcement, Cogley doffed his mental hat to Areel. *Perfect timing,* he thought. Calling the wife of the victim was a standard prosecution tactic in a murder case. Even if the wife didn't really have any firsthand knowledge about the murder, as Helen Latham didn't, there was always a certain sympathy factor to be won with the jury by displaying the grieving widow for them. But Cogley also knew that in this case, Helen Latham would be one of the more problematic witnesses for the prosecution, especially when the details of her final argument with Latham were revealed. By calling Helen now, Areel could lead off with testimony about her life with Daniel, so that the first thing the jury heard would be the sympathetic details. Oh, the jury would hear the not-so-good eventually, but only after the good had been laid out for all to see. And by having Helen testify about that final argument in direct examination, it wouldn't look like they were hiding anything from the jury. Then Areel could quickly follow Helen's testimony with other testimony, something damning that would make the jury forget the later parts of Helen's testimony. It's what he would have done if he were in Areel's place.

Cogley was surprised as Helen walked to the witness stand. *I'll be damned,* he thought, *she* does *have a black dress, after all.*

As he listened to Helen Latham relate the early years of her marriage to Daniel, the tragedy of their daughter, Katherine's, death and how their marriage had gone through some "bumpy patches" after Katherine, Cogley had to give Helen credit, too. Her performance was flawless, her timing and delivery impeccable. Even the slight antebellum air she adopted, the same one she had used yesterday when Cogley spoke with her, worked. She had the jury believing that she was every inch the grieving widow.

"Mrs. Latham, can you tell us about the last time you saw your husband, Daniel, alive?"

Cogley knew this was the key moment in her testimony this morning, and she hit it in stride. She said a simple, "Oh," looked away from Areel and the jury, let an expression of chagrin come over her, and peered down at the floor in contrition. "I'm afraid that's not very pleasant. Almost as unpleasant as knowing that Daniel is dead."

"I'm sorry if I'm causing you any pain, but the jury does have to know, Mrs. Latham."

She didn't oversell it. She never went to the extreme of taking out a handkerchief or daubing her tear-filled eyes. Instead, she simply talked in a quiet voice that broke only occasionally.

"Daniel and I had an argument that night."

"About what?"

"It was a silly thing. He was working on something, some colony business. I came in to remind him that he had other duties to the colony and that he should be out as part of the Landing Day festivities. Whatever he was working on, he hadn't finished it yet, because he was writing in that book of his when I came in. He put the book away as soon as I entered, closed it up, and slipped it onto the bookshelf right behind him, but I'm afraid I just lost my temper with him. Told him he was being selfish and that he owed it to the colony to join in the celebration.

"Well, one thing led to another. We started arguing louder and louder, and I . . . well, I'm afraid that I slapped him."

"What did your husband do when you slapped him?"

"He got a funny look on his face. I don't think I ever saw him as mad as he was right then. And he started coming toward me. And I panicked. I just panicked."

"What do you mean, 'panicked'?"

"I . . . well . . . that is . . . I thought he was going to hit me, so I . . . Daniel had a phaser in his desk and I'm afraid I pulled it out on him."

There was an audible gasp from the courtroom as the good citizens of Serenity learned this fact for the first time.

"Order," Judge Carabatsos said, rapping his gavel on the table that served as a judge's bench.

When the murmur that had run through the spectators quieted down, Areel Shaw turned back to Helen Latham. "Go on, Mrs. Latham. You said you pulled out your husband's phaser. Now, we've heard testimony that a phaser has several settings. Do you know what setting your husband's phaser was on?"

"I didn't at the time. I've learned since that it was on

kill. But I swear I didn't know that. I don't even know how to change the setting."

"Why would your husband keep his phaser on kill? If you know, Mrs. Latham." Areel turned toward Cogley. "If you know."

"I know it wasn't charged. Daniel told me that when he took it from me. I guess he didn't care what setting it was on, considering it wasn't charged."

At this testimony Judge Carabatsos looked down at Cogley, ready to sustain the defense objection for speculation. But Cogley said nothing.

"What happened then?"

"Daniel took the phaser from me and told me I should leave. Forever."

A softer murmur went through the spectators at this testimony, which Carabatsos quieted with a softer rap of the gavel.

"Did you?"

"Leave? Yes. But not forever. I intended to come back the next day and talk things out with him, but I thought at that time it would be better to leave, let us both cool down. If I had only known what was going to happen to him that night, I would never have left. As it is, the final memory I have of my dear husband is my pointing a phaser at him."

It was a masterful performance. Cogley would have stood and applauded it, were it not a definite breach of decorum. So he had to content himself with saying, ever so softly, "Bravo, my dear. An excellent performance."

Then he stood to cross-examine. "Mrs. Latham, did it surprise you to learn that your husband had been shot with a phaser?"

"Well, of course. Wouldn't *any* wife be surprised to learn that her husband had been murdered?"

"I'm sorry, my mistake, I didn't make my question clear. Did it surprise you to learn that your husband had been shot with a phaser and not a Klingon disruptor?"

"I don't understand how that matters."

Cogley turned to Carabatsos and said, "Your Honor?"

"The witness is instructed to answer the question."

"Yes, I think I did ask Louis Alexander why Mak'Tor would have used a phaser and not his own disruptor."

"So despite your claim that you know so little about weapons that you couldn't change the setting on a standard-issue phaser, you are familiar enough with them to know the difference between a phaser and a disruptor?"

Cogley turned and went back to his chair before Helen could even answer the question. How she answered the question didn't really matter. The point of the question had been the question itself, not the answer.

21. "I call Grigoriy Nemov to the stand," Areel said immediately.

After Nemov took the stand, Areel led him quickly through the preliminary matters of his testimony: his background, his duties on Serenity, his working relationship with both Daniel Latham and Mak'Tor. In other cases, she might have spent more time on such matters, but Serenity was a small colony. Everyone on the jury knew Nemov and what he did. As a result, she was soon able to get to the substance of Nemov's testimony.

"Mr. Nemov, what happened on the night of the Landing Day celebration?"

"I ran into Homero Galdamiz and Chiaki Iino in the streets. We talked about some things, and Chiaki mentioned that Daniel was meeting with Mak'Tor that night. Homero said he didn't think that was proper. He said that Daniel should be celebrating with the colony. We agreed, and we decided to do something about it."

"What did you decide to do?"

"We decided to go to Daniel's office to talk some sense into him. I believe Homero wanted to drag him out of there, if necessary."

"Did the three of you go to Daniel Latham's office?"

"Yes."

"What did you find when you got there?"

"We opened the door. Office was a mess. It looked like someone had been fighting in it. Then we saw Daniel lying on the floor dead."

"Interrupting you for a moment, did you know he was dead at the time?"

"No, but he *looked* dead."

"What else did you see?"

"We saw a Klingon kneeling over Daniel's body with a phaser in his hand."

"Did you recognize the Klingon you saw kneeling over Daniel Latham's body with a phaser in his hand?"

"Yes. I have seen him many times."

"Is that Klingon in this room?"

"Yes. He is the Klingon sitting at the table to my left. The one sitting next to Mr. Cogley."

"May the record reflect that the witness has identified the defendant?" Areel asked.

"So noted," Judge Carabatsos said.

"What did you do then?"

"I warned the others that the defendant had a phaser, and we shot him."

"All three of you?"

"Yes."

"What did the defendant do?"

"He tried to stand up, then fell unconscious."

After this, Areel led Nemov through more testimony. Nemov described how Galdamiz went to look for Louis Alexander, and he sent Iino to find Helen Latham. He described what he and Alexander did in Latham's office after Alexander arrived and what happened when they went to tell Helen Latham of Daniel's death.

"Mr. Nemov, let's go back some. On the day Daniel Latham died, what did you do in the morning?"

"We had a jurisdictional hearing over the bar fight from the night before."

"And after that, did you meet with Daniel Latham?"

"Yes."

"What did you talk about?"

"I told him I believed there was a spy in our colony."

"What do you mean, 'spy'?"

"I mean someone from Serenity, probably someone on the senior staff, was supplying sensitive information to Mak'Tor."

"Why did you believe that?"

Nemov outlined for the court the same things he had shown Daniel Latham a few days earlier, the mistake in the crop yield reports, how it was corrected, and how Mak'Tor was using the corrected crop yield information even before the Federation had it and before the Klingon High Council should have had it.

"What did Daniel Latham think of your report?"

"He agreed that there was probably a spy on the senior staff. Although Daniel said he didn't think Mak'Tor was responsible for the spy, he thought it was the work of Khogo."

"That's a lie!" Khogo shouted, and stood up to point an accusing finger at Nemov.

"Order! Order!" Judge Carabatsos ordered, slamming his gavel down on the bench. "I remind the representative of the Klingon Empire of where he is. Such outbursts may be routine in a Klingon tribunal, but they will not be tolerated in my court. You will control yourself, or I will order you detained in one of Serenity's cells for contempt of court."

Khogo glared at Carabatsos with the same hatred he had shown Cogley and Mak'Tor earlier. He was about to say something more, when he saw that Mak'Tor was looking at him with an expression that mixed disapproval with a large amount of threat. Khogo sat down with surprising meekness.

"Your Honor," Mak'Tor said to Judge Carabatsos, "I realize it is unusual for the accused to address the court. I wish to apologize for my second's outburst. He has forgotten that it is the desire of the Klingon Empire to learn the truth in this matter. We will show both the Organians and your Federation that we have nothing to hide and nothing to fear."

"It's rather unusual to say this to the defendant in a trial, but thank you, Mak'Tor," Carabatsos said, meaning every word, because Mak'Tor had restored order in the court. "You may proceed, Ms. Shaw."

"Mr. Nemov, you were saying that Daniel Latham believed Khogo, not Mak'Tor, was responsible for the spy. Did you agree with him?"

"No. Daniel had a very high opinion of Mak'Tor, but I think recent events have shown it was misplaced."

"Objection."

"Sustained. The jury will disregard the last remark of the witness."

"What did Daniel Latham do after you showed him this information?"

"He said he would meet with Mak'Tor that night to discuss the matter."

"That night? Are you sure he meant that night?"

"Yes. I even reminded Daniel that it was Landing Day, but he insisted that the meeting be that night."

"So that night Daniel Latham and Mak'Tor met to discuss the spy in—"

"Objection."

Areel Shaw snapped her head back to look at Cogley.

"Your Honor," Cogley said, "this assumes facts not in evidence."

"Please, Mr. Cogley, what facts not in evidence could it possibly assume?" Areel demanded.

"That there was a meeting, for one. Or what was discussed at that meeting, if there even was one."

"Your Honor, the defendant and Daniel Latham scheduled a meeting for that night. We have several witnesses who have established that. We also know that Daniel Latham said he was going to discuss the matter of the spy with Mak'Tor. Finally, the defendant was found in Daniel Latham's office.

How Mr. Cogley can say we haven't proven there was a meeting is beyond me."

"I can say it for a simple reason, Your Honor. Ms. Shaw *hasn't* proven there was a meeting. She's offered no testimony, no evidence from anyone who saw or heard any meeting between Daniel Latham and Mak'Tor that night. Yes, Mak'Tor was found in Daniel Latham's office. But by the time Mr. Nemov and the others found Mak'Tor there, Daniel Latham was dead. Ms. Shaw's evidence doesn't exclude the possibility Daniel Latham was already dead when Mak'Tor arrived in the office and that there was no meeting."

"Your Honor—"

"No, Ms. Shaw, Mr. Cogley is correct. You haven't proven there was any meeting. His objection is sustained."

"Let's review, then, Mr. Nemov. Daniel Latham agreed with you that there was a spy in Serenity?"

"Yes."

"He said he was going to meet with Mak'Tor that night, even though you reminded him it was the Landing Day celebration?"

"Yes."

"And he said that he was going to discuss the matter of the spy with Mak'Tor?"

"Yes."

"Mr. Nemov, if we assume that Daniel Latham and Mak'Tor did meet that night and we further assume that they did discuss the matter of the spy, what, hypothetically, do you think Mak'Tor's reaction would have been?"

"Objection."

"Overruled."

"He would have been very upset. Angry."

"Angry enough to have started a fight with Daniel Latham?"

"Yes."

"Angry enough to pick up Daniel Latham's phaser and shoot him with it?"

"Objection. That goes to the ultimate issue, Your Honor. It's for the jury, not Mr. Nemov, to decide."

"Sustained."

Even though Cogley's objection had been sustained, Areel Shaw smiled as she sat down and said, "Your witness." Much like Cogley's question earlier, the point of the question was to let the jury hear the question itself and not the answer.

"Mr. Nemov, you said that you found Mak'Tor kneeling over Daniel Latham's body and that you saw a phaser in his hand?"

"Yes.

"Are you sure about what you saw?"

"Quite sure."

"You sure he was kneeling?"

"Yes."

"Do you know the difference between kneeling and crouching?"

"Yes."

"With the permission of the court, could you please come off the witness stand and demonstrate that difference?"

"Your Honor, this is preposterous." Areel Shaw said, standing quickly as she spoke.

"I assume there was an objection there somewhere, Your Honor, so let me just respond that Mr. Nemov has testified about what he claimed he saw that evening. Am

I not to be allowed to test the witness's powers of observation?"

"The objection is overruled. But, Mr. Cogley, remember we are in court. Some decorum, please."

"Thank you, Your Honor. Mr. Nemov."

Nemov came down from the witness stand and stood in front of Cogley.

"Now then, Mr. Nemov, would you please show the jury what a kneeling position is."

Nemov knelt on the ground.

"And that's what you saw Mak'Tor doing that night?"

"Yes."

"Would you please stand up."

Nemov stood up.

"I notice it took you a little effort to do that. You had to move one of your legs and plant your foot on the ground. Then you had to shift your weight to that foot and push off the ground. So it took you a little time to stand up. And *you* hadn't even been shot by a phaser, had you?"

Judge Carabatsos rapped his gavel on the bench to silence the slight laughter that ran through the courtroom. "Mr. Cogley, remember what I said about decorum."

"My apologies, Your Honor," Cogley said. Then he turned back to Nemov. "Now then, Mr. Nemov, would you please demonstrate a crouch?"

Nemov bent down and got into a crouch.

"Now stand up."

Nemov stood up.

"There, Mr. Nemov, did you see how much quicker you were able to stand up from the crouch than you were from the kneel? It took practically no effort at all, and certainly no adjustment of your position first. Are you asking this jury to believe that Mak'Tor—a Klingon warrior—would have been kneeling over Daniel Latham's body and not crouching? Are you asking this jury to believe a man who has just murdered another person, who knows he could be discovered at any moment, would kneel and not crouch? Would make it more difficult for himself to stand up?"

Areel Shaw was on her feet even more quickly than if she had been crouching. "Objection!"

Before Judge Carabatsos could rule, however, Nemov said, firmly, "I am asking the jury to believe the truth. The Klingon was kneeling."

"Moving on then, Mr. Nemov, did you see any meeting between Mak'Tor and Daniel Latham?" Cogley asked.

"No."

"Did you hear one?"

"No."

"Did either Daniel Latham or Mak'Tor tell you they had one?"

"No."

"Did you talk to anyone else who saw or heard this alleged meeting?"

"No."

"So, for all you know, there never was any such meeting?"

"I know that Klingon bastard was found kneeling over Daniel's body at the time the meeting was scheduled to take place."

"You will refrain from such characterizations, Mr. Nemov," Judge Carabatsos said, anticipating Cogley's objection.

"Mr. Nemov, you testified that Daniel Latham told you

he didn't believe Mak'Tor was responsible for the spy you believed was in your colony."

"Yes."

"But you didn't agree with him, did you?"

"No."

"You believed there was a spy and that Mak'Tor had arranged for that spy, correct?"

"Yes."

"So, if there had been a meeting and Daniel Latham accused Mak'Tor of planting a spy, Mak'Tor would have known the accusation was true?"

"Yes."

"Then why would Mak'Tor have gotten angry, angry enough to commit murder?"

"I don't understand the question."

"*If* Daniel Latham had confronted Mak'Tor about planting a spy, wouldn't it have made more sense for Mak'Tor simply to deny the allegation, then secretly deactivate the spy?"

"I don't know."

"This whole story you're asking the jury to believe—the meeting you can't verify ever happened, Mak'Tor's kneeling instead of crouching, Mak'Tor's getting angry enough to fight and kill Daniel Latham over this trifling matter instead of silently withdrawing the spy so no one could prove the spy ever existed—isn't all of this nothing but wishful thinking on your part? Isn't it you telling the jury what you *wish* were true instead of what is *actually* true?"

Cogley was waiting for a loud objection from Areel Shaw, but it didn't come. Even as Nemov answered the question, "No," Cogley turned and looked at Areel. She wasn't paying attention to the trial. Instead she was talking rather animatedly with Chiaki Iino.

"No further questions, Your Honor," Cogley said.

"Your Honor, I need to present some new evidence that has only just come to my attention."

"New evidence, Ms. Shaw?" Cogley asked. "Isn't that just a little stale?"

Areel ignored Cogley's barb. "I assure this court that I didn't know about this evidence before now. Mr. Iino only just brought it to me. I've just had Mr. Iino comm a copy to Mr. Cogley." Areel looked to Iino, who nodded his confirmation, then looked at Jackie and saw that she was reading the information. "I assure you that I wasn't trying to conceal anything from Mr. Cogley. He got the information as soon as I did. But it is of vital importance to this case, and I must be allowed to introduce it."

"Your Honor, I object. In this day and age, trial by ambush should not be allowed," Cogley said.

"I will respect Ms. Shaw's representation that she did not know anything about this evidence before now. Objection overruled."

Areel Shaw smiled. The smile broadened when she saw Jackie's face. Jackie was experienced enough to be sure that her back was to the jury, so that they could not see her face, but Areel Shaw could. Jacqueline LaSalle didn't speak, but her expression was shouting, "Oh no!"

22. Areel Shaw had to wait before her moment could begin.

For the best effect, Iino's testimony required that one of the colony's large viewscreens be brought into the court. That way he could link to the screen and the whole courtroom would be able to see what he had found. Areel didn't mind the wait, however. She spent it looking at Cogley and barely containing a smug smile.

She had to give Cogley credit, though. He didn't react. When she was in law school taking trial advocacy cases, she had learned an axiom about what to do in front of a jury. "Never let them see you sweat," or so the old saying went. As the axiom had its origins centuries ago in the field of live theater, she assumed Cogley had heard it too. But whether he had or not, he was living by it now. Whatever thoughts and concerns were going through his head, he didn't let the jury see what he was thinking.

When the viewscreen was set up and Iino had taken the stand, Areel moved up by the jury box so that when he talked to her, he would be talking directly toward the jury.

"Please state your name and occupation for the record."

"Chiaki Iino. Computer systems and network administrator for Serenity."

"Mr. Iino, where did you get your training?"

"I interned at the Daystrom Institute in . . ."

"If it please the court, the defense is more than willing to stipulate to Mr. Iino's background and that he's an expert witness in the area of computers."

"Ms. Shaw?" Carabatsos asked.

Areel glanced at the jury. Offering to stipulate to an expert witness's credentials was a standard trial tactic. If she agreed to stipulate to Iino's credentials, the jury wouldn't get to hear them, so they couldn't be impressed by the degree of his expert training. For that reason, she usually refused such proffered stipulations. She *wanted* the jury to hear her experts' background and training and be impressed by them. These jurors, however, had lived with

Iino for almost a year, and knew what he did. They had probably gone to Iino when their own computers had gone down.

And Areel *really* wanted to get to the heart of this matter.

"Very well, Your Honor, we accept the stipulation. Mr. Iino," she said, turning back to the witness stand, "the jury has heard me say that you've brought me new evidence. How did you happen to come by this evidence?"

"We have Mr. Cogley to thank for that," Iino said, and nodded toward the defense table.

"Mr. Cogley? Really," Areel said, and smiled directly at Cogley. "How so?"

"Mr. Cogley came to my office yesterday. He had wanted to see what was on the memory core of Daniel Latham's computer."

"Why didn't he just look at the computer?"

"You had the computer so that you could go over its memory core yourself. Mr. Cogley came to me and asked whether I could help him recover the information."

"Were you able to help him?"

"Yes." Iino explained how he cloned the memory of Latham's computer into the colony's server and went over it with Cogley to see what activity there had been on Latham's computer the night he died.

"What did you find?"

"There wasn't much activity. Daniel didn't use his computer very often. He sent a message to his wife's computer twenty minutes before he died. A little after that, he sent out a notice to the entire senior staff that he wanted a meeting with us the next morning. The most significant activity was that earlier that day he sent a file from his personal comm unit to his office computer. Then he did some work on that file."

"By office computer, do you mean the one in his home?"

"No. Daniel always referred to his office at home as his study. His office computer was the one he had in his office at City Hall."

"In other words, the computer in the room where he was killed?"

"Yes."

"Go on."

"Mr. Cogley told me he wanted to see that file. When I checked on it, I discovered that it had been deleted from the memory, maybe one minute before we found him dead."

"Who is 'we'?"

"Grig, Homero, and me. We went to Daniel's office to get him out of that damn meeting with Mak'Tor and get him to come out to the celebration. When we came in, we saw Daniel lying on the floor dead and the defendant kneeling over him."

"A moment. Did you say *kneeling*?"

"Yes."

"Not crouching?"

"No."

"And you know the difference between kneeling and crouching?"

"Yes."

"And the defendant was definitely kneeling, not crouching?"

"Objection. Leading."

"Sustained."

"Was the defendant kneeling or crouching?"

"Kneeling."

"You're sure?"

"I'm positive."

"Thank you. Go on."

"Grig warned us that the defendant had a phaser, so we all shot him. And then we—"

"Mr. Nemov has already told the jury what you all did after you found the defendant *kneeling* over Daniel Latham's body. Let's go on with the file."

"As I said, I determined that the file Mr. Cogley wanted to see had been deleted from the memory one minute before we entered the office and found the defendant."

"So the defendant was in Daniel Latham's office when the file was deleted?"

"Objection."

"Sustained."

"Who was in the office when the file was deleted?"

"Objection."

"Sustained."

Areel looked up and smiled at Cogley again. Of course the objections had been sustained, but the jurors would still conjecture about what the answers probably were and draw their own conclusion. That was only human nature.

"What did Mr. Cogley do when he learned that this file had been deleted by someone in the office—"

"Objection."

"I'll rephrase. What did Mr. Cogley do when he learned that this file had been deleted only one minute before you found the defendant *kneeling* over Daniel Latham's body?"

"He told me that he wanted me to retrieve that file. He seemed quite insistent on it. He even offered me the assistance of Ms. LaSalle."

"Were you able to recover the file?"

"Yes. I told you what I wanted, and you gave me Daniel's computer. Most people don't know this, but when a file is deleted from the memory of the computer, it isn't physically removed. It's made inactive, so it can't be accessed and other files can overwrite it. Eventually, it may become irretrievable, if enough other files overwrite it. But there wasn't any activity on Latham's computer, so there wasn't any overwriting done to this file."

"Which means what?"

"It means the file was still in the memory core and was basically intact. All I had to do was find it physically."

"Where is that file now?"

"Well, it's in the memory of Daniel's computer, which you have. It's in the cloned memory on the server in my office. And I've downloaded a copy onto my unit here."

Iino manipulated the touchpad of his unit, and the file appeared on the plasma screen in the courtroom.

"Mr. Iino, is this a fair and accurate copy of the file you retrieved from Daniel Latham's computer?"

"Yes."

"Can you display it so that the jury can read it all?"

"Yes."

Iino again pressed the touchpad, and both pages of the file appeared on the screen in a type large enough that the jury could see it from across the room.

"Could you please read it?"

Iino read . . .

December 13, 2267

FROM: DANIEL LATHAM SERENITY COLONY ANE-HER II

TO: WILLIAM THOM DIVISION OF COLONIZA-TION TAU SECTOR UNITED FEDERATION OF PLAN-ETS

Bill:

This will be short. It's late and I never wanted to write anything like this.

First the good news. Crop and mining yields are up again. I've attached the yield reports from both divisions. I know they aren't the type of spectacular improvements you people in the Federation are looking for, but Serenity shows steady improvement. I have, for the most part, good people working here. As they get more acclimated to the harsh conditions here on Aneher, they're able to work longer hours and the yields show steady improvement.

I believe this justifies my insistence that the conventional mining techniques continue to be employed and that Mr. Galdamiz's recommendations be rejected.

Now for the bad news. Grigoriy Nemov has come to me with evidence that Mak'Tor and Khogo have planted a spy in Serenity. I've also attached his data. We're looking into this from our end, but we need to know how you want us to proceed.

Even more disturbing is the final report that I'm attaching. It's the culmination of several weeks' investigation undertaken by us into the mining techniques that Mak'Tor and Khogo are using in their colony.

The bastards are cheating.

We became suspicious of what the Klingons were doing

when they didn't seem to be affected by the heat and sun at all. That and the frequent supply sleds that would come to their colony. Those sleds are supposed to be unmanned. They aren't. The Klingons have been smuggling in new [columnists] to replace those miners who had expended themselves working in Aneher's extremes. That way, the Klingons always had fresh workers and their mines looked far more efficient than they actually were.

Shipping people wearing environmental suits in the holds of transports that lack controls and life-support systems like so much cargo isn't just wrong it [courts] murder. Look at the file, Bill. You need to get Federation and Starfleet security on this ASAP. We've got to stop the bastards before someone dies!

Jackie had been watching the jurors, as they listened to Iino read the report or read it for themselves. She was studying their faces, gauging whether they fully understood what it meant. And she could tell by their faces that they did.

She was sure that Areel Shaw would call another witness to drive the point home even further, but it wasn't necessary. The jurors understood.

The one thing that had been missing from Areel Shaw's case, the one argument Sam had been able to make was motive; Areel didn't really have a strong motive to ascribe to Mak'Tor.

Until now. This report handed her motive on the proverbial silver platter.

23. "That is another of your damned Federation lies! You arrest our leader! Accuse him falsely!"

Everyone in the courtroom looked back at Khogo, who was standing and shouting his protest. Everyone except Cogley. He looked at Mak'Tor, and his client's expression told him everything he wanted to know. For all Khogo's protestations—and it did seem to Cogley that he was protesting too much—the report was true.

"Order! Order!" Carabatsos was shouting, trying to be heard over Khogo, but to no avail.

"You dare to put him on trial in this sham court! Present lies and fabrications as evidence. Your souls will rot in *Gre'thor* for these lies. *Fek'lhr* will gnaw on your bones. You will—"

Khogo disappeared in the twinkling sparkle of a transporter beam.

"Sorry, Your Honor," Louis Alexander said. "Took us a little longer to lock in on him than we thought."

"Quite all right, Mr. Alexander," Judge Carabatsos said. "Where is Khogo?"

"We transported him directly to one of our cells right now. I assumed you were going to find him in contempt of court."

"Thank you, Mr. Alexander. And you're quite correct. I'd like to let Khogo spend a few hours in a cell to calm down, but won't the Klingon Empire complain that its representative was excluded from the trial?"

"We thought there might be trouble with Khogo, Your Honor," Alexander said, "so we had prepared a special cell for him. It has a viewscreen just outside it that will show him the trial."

"Most efficient, Mr. Alexander. I commend your thoroughness. Let him spend the rest of the day in your jail. You can beam Khogo back to his colony as soon as court has adjourned for the day."

"Your Honor," Cogley said to the court, "I move for a mistrial."

Carabatsos smiled. He had been expecting this motion.

"Sorry, Mr. Cogley, *you* were the one who didn't want a separation of witnesses. Motion denied. Ms. Shaw?"

"I'm through with the witness, Your Honor."

"Mr. Cogley, any cross?"

Cogley stood up and walked to the viewscreen. He pointed to it and asked, "Mr. Iino, what's that?"

"It's the report I retrieved from Daniel Latham's computer."

"No, I meant the item in the report I'm pointing to. What's that?"

"It appears to be a comma."

" 'Appears to be,' but it isn't. Study it more carefully. It isn't a comma. Can you see what it is?"

"Yes, it's a subscripted number one."

"So it is. And so is this. And this. And this. And this. In fact, *every* comma in this document isn't a comma at all, but a subscripted number one. It would appear that there was some overwriting and data corruption in this file, after all. So how can we be sure *any* of it's accurate?"

"That isn't data corruption, Mr. Cogley, it's a scanning transcription error."

"A what?"

"Daniel Latham wrote everything out longhand. Usually, when he finished writing, he'd dictate the document directly into the computer. Sometimes, when he was pressed for time, he'd scan the document into his computer. Trouble was, Daniel didn't have the best handwriting and the character recognition program couldn't always make out what he had written. I tried to tweak the program as best I could to compensate for Daniel's writing, but no matter what I did, there were always some of these transcription errors."

"And is that why those two words, 'columnists' and 'courts,' are in brackets? Transcription error?"

"When the program can't recognize a word, it substitutes a word from its dictionary that appears to be closest to what was written. It highlights the approximations with brackets."

"So 'columnists' would be some program's best guess as to what Daniel Latham meant?"

"Yes."

"And this guess wasn't very good, was it? I mean the word should obviously be 'colonists,' not 'columnists,' correct?"

"Objection."

"He's *their* computer expert, Your Honor."

"Overruled."

"It would appear so, yes."

"So we really can't trust this document at all, can we? No further questions."

Areel Shaw looked up at Iino from her chair and didn't bother standing for the questions she had to ask on redirect. "Mr. Iino, as Mr. Cogley has acknowledged that you're an expert, would you please give your expert opinion as to how accurately the program translated the original document?"

"Objection, Mr. Iino has never seen the original document."

"But he does know the program he designed and tweaked, Your Honor."

"Overruled."

Areel could barely contain her glee as Iino said, "I would say it was more than ninety-eight percent accurate. The subscripted one error is negligible, and of the two words the program didn't recognize, it got one correct."

"Thank you, Mr. Iino. I call Homero Galdamiz."

After Galdamiz took the stand, Areel wasn't as willing to accept Cogley's offer to stipulate to his qualifications as an expert. She didn't think the jury would have been as familiar with him or what he did. So Galdamiz ran through his background and training in xenogeology and mining techniques. When he finished, Areel turned to the bench and said, "Your Honor, I move that Mr. Galdamiz be accepted as an expert on mining and mining techniques."

"No objection."

"It is so ordered," Carabatsos said.

"Mr. Galdamiz, you heard the report from Daniel Latham which Mr. Iino read into the record?"

"Yeah."

"And have you also had a chance to read it yourself?"

"Yeah."

"Based on your years of experience in mining and mining techniques, do you have an opinion as to what effect this report would have had on the Klingons' efforts to colonize Aneher II?"

"Objection. The witness is being asked to speculate what affect this report might have on the evaluations of the Organians, a race of aliens I doubt any of us in this court-room has had any contact with."

"Overruled."

"You may answer, Mr. Galdamiz," Areel said.

"I think it would have killed them."

"Killed them?"

"Well, killed their chances, I mean. Look, I really don't know the Klingons all that well, but this makes it look like they were desperate."

"How so?"

"Both the Klingons and the Federation are tryin' to prove to the Organians that we can colonize this planet better than the other side. Now, accordin' to this report, we're doin' okay here in Serenity. Maybe not as good as everyone would like, but okay. But the Klingons are smug-glin' in replacement miners and makin' their mines look better than they actually are.

"Maybe I don't know the Organians either, but I don't care who's lookin' at this report, they're gonna see that the Klingons are runnin' scared. They don't think they can compete with us head-to-head, so they're cheatin'. Klin-gon to that last hope—"

"Order," Carabatsos said, as the gallery started to laugh and groan at Galdamiz's pun. "Mr. Galdamiz, just say what you have to say."

"Sorry, Your Honor. What I was sayin' is that the Klingons were hopin' to fool everyone, includin' the Organians, as to how well they were doin'. For a while it was workin'. But now we can see it was never workin' at all. I think once the Organians got ahold of this report, they would have ruled in the Federation's favor."

"Mr. Galdamiz, how do you think Mak'Tor would have responded, if he learned of this report?"

"One moment, Your Honor," Cogley said, standing up and moving out from behind the defense table. "May we approach the bench?"

Carabatsos motioned that Areel and Cogley should approach the bench. Areel looked strangely at Jackie when Cogley's associate also came to the bench, but she didn't say anything.

"What is it, Mr. Cogley?"

"Your Honor, this witness has already testified that he doesn't know the Klingons all that well. I think I should be allowed a voir dire on his expertise, if any, with the Klingons, before he's allowed to offer any opinion as to what a Klingon might do."

Carabatsos looked at Cogley. Then he looked at Areel. Then he looked at the jury. Then he sat in silence for a moment and thought.

"I'm reluctant to send the jury out of the room for the purpose of this voir dire, Mr. Cogley. Too much of that can become disruptive."

"Oh, I have no objection to the jury's being in the courtroom during the voir dire, Your Honor. All they'll be hearing is whether Mr. Galdamiz is an expert; they won't be hearing his opinion as yet."

"Very well. But please keep it as brief as possible."

"Two questions, Your Honor," Cogley said as he walked to his place in front of the witness stand for his examination. Then he looked back at the bench, shrugged his shoulders, and said, "Maybe three."

"Mr. Galdamiz, I just wanted to ask you a few questions as a matter of foundation before we go on. You don't mind, do you?"

"Naw."

"Do you meet with the Klingons?"

"Whaddya mean?"

"I mean, do any part of your duties as the head of the mines in Serenity require you to meet with the Klingons?"

"Oh. No. I leave—or left—havin' to deal with them to Daniel and Grig."

"So you have no interaction with the Klingons?"

"Naw."

"Not even socially?"

"Socially? What, you mean like at parties and things? Mr. Cogley, you ever seen a Klingon at a party?"

"I think the more important question is, Mr. Galdamiz, have you?"

"Naw. I couldn't Kahless if I never saw another Klingon in my life."

"I'm sorry, Ms. Shaw, but Mr. Cogley's point would seem to be in order."

"Then may I have permission to call another witness at this time, Your Honor? One who *is* an expert on Klingons."

"Mr. Cogley, you have the right to cross-examine this witness before Ms. Shaw calls this new witness she's suggesting. Do you wish to do so?" Carabatsos said, turning to Cogley.

Cogley gave a benign and accommodating smile. "Oh, I have no objection to Ms. Shaw's calling another witness, Your Honor," he said. Areel turned to face the gallery, preparing to call her next witness. Before she could do so, however, Cogley quickly added, "Provided I'm permitted to cross-examine Mr. Galdamiz immediately after the testimony of this witness."

"That's fine, Your Honor," Areel said, not even turning back to face Cogley. "I recall Grigoriy Nemov to the stand."

"Mr. Nemov, you're still under oath," Carabatsos reminded Nemov as the man climbed back into the witness stand.

"Mr. Nemov, you've already testified as to your duties and responsibilities in the colony. How often did these duties require you to interact with the Klingon colony?"

"Daily. There wasn't a day I didn't meet with or talk with them."

"With whom did you meet most often?"

"Mak'Tor and Khogo."

"Do you think you know Mak'Tor well?"

"As well as anybody in Serenity. Probably better." Nemov glared down at Mak'Tor and said, "It would appear, even better than Daniel did."

"Mr. Nemov, you also heard the report that Mr. Iino read into the record."

"Yes."

"And have you read it for yourself?"

"Yes."

"How do you think Mak'Tor would have responded, if he had learned of this report?"

"He would have been furious. Violent."

"How violent?"

"I think he would have been capable of killing."

"Do you have any doubt?"

"None. I think if Mak'Tor had learned of this report during his meeting with Daniel, he would have killed Daniel in a fit of rage."

"Would he have used Daniel Latham's phaser?"

"Possibly. Daniel's phaser was lying on the desk. It would not be beyond Mak'Tor to have taken it and shot Daniel in a fit of rage."

"And what of that computer file, the report Daniel Latham was writing?"

"Mak'Tor would have tried to destroy it, delete the file from the computer. His only mistake was not realizing the file would remain in the memory core. Or getting out of the office before we came in."

"No further questions, Your Honor." Areel was standing by the jury box facing the witness stand. She turned her head to look over her shoulder at the clock that hung over the rear door of the courtroom. "Your Honor, it's now just after noon. Perhaps this would be a good time to break for lunch."

"Mr. Cogley?"

Cogley did not answer Carabatsos. Or move. He just sat behind the defense table as if stunned, staring directly ahead of him.

24. "Sam? *Sam?*" Jacqueline LaSalle said to Cogley and nudged him gently in the side.

" 'Hadn't finished writing it yet,' " Cogley whispered to Jackie. "That's what she said, isn't it?"

"What?" Jackie whispered back.

"Never mind," Cogley whispered in response. He turned from the defense table to look into the courtroom. "One moment, Your Honor. Ms. Shaw is being precipitous. I was promised I could cross-examine Homero Galdamiz before we broke for lunch."

"Mr. Cogley, we're all hungry. What difference could waiting until after lunch make?" Areel asked.

"Mr. Galdamiz offered some very damning testimony, Your Honor. I want the opportunity to challenge it now."

"Very well, Mr. Cogley." Carabatsos said. Then he turned toward Areel, "You did agree to this, Ms. Shaw."

"Mr. Galdamiz, I remind you, you're still under oath," Judge Carabatsos said to Galdamiz as the miner returned to the witness chair. "Your witness, Mr. Cogley."

"One moment, Your Honor," Cogley said. Then he leaned over and whispered to Jackie, "Where's Peter?"

"I don't know. He hasn't reported in yet," Jackie whispered in response.

"Comm him," Cogley whispered, with some urgency in his voice. "I can vamp for time, but we need Peter's report *now!* If he hasn't finished, tell him to send up what he has."

Cogley approached the witness stand, smiling. "Mr. Galdamiz, you testified that you didn't have much contact with the Klingons, is that correct?"

"I said I didn't have *any*."

"Does that include Khogo?"

"Who?" Galdamiz said.

"The second-in-command of the Klingon colony. The man who Mr. Alexander transported out of here not too long ago."

"Oh yeah, him."

"Well, *did* you have any contact with Khogo?"

Galdamiz paused for a moment, then said, "No."

"Your Honor, where is this leading?" Areel asked.

"Ms. Shaw has a point, Mr. Cogley. Can I assume your questions do also?"

Cogley was about to answer when he noticed some movement out of the corner of his eye, movement he had seen many times in his career. He turned his head and looked at the defense table. Yes, Jackie had moved his pen off his pad and put it directly on the table. Peter *had* reported in.

"If I may have a moment, Your Honor." Cogley walked back to the defense table and talked briefly with Jackie as she showed him something on her comm unit. *Bless you, Peter*, Cogley thought. Then he turned to the bench with a broad smile on his face and said, "Oh, they do, Your Honor. As for where they're leading, Ms. Shaw," he said, and shared his smile with her, "they're leading to the truth." He looked toward Jackie, who held up her unit, then he added, "Oh, and I wanted to thank you for bringing in that viewscreen. It should prove quite handy."

Cogley whirled and faced Galdamiz with a ferocity that reminded Jackie of a lion advancing on its prey, and for good reason.

"Mr. Galdamiz, let's talk about your qualifications as a mining expert. Do you recognize this?"

Without a word or signal from Cogley, Jackie had already played her fingers across the touch screen of her comm unit, and a new document appeared on the viewscreen.

Galdamiz looked at it for a moment, puzzled.

"Yes, I do, but how'd you get it?"

"What is it, Mr. Galdamiz?"

"It's my résumé. But how did *you* get it?"

"The résumé that, as an independent contractor hired by the United Federation of Planets, you filed with their Division of Colonization?"

"Oh," Galdamiz said, realizing the answer to his question. "Yeah, that résumé."

"And quite an impressive résumé it is. BS in xenogeology from the Prohaska School at Datanides University on Centauri. Then we have a Lynch Fellowship in mining technique from Weston. But you sell yourself short."

"Whadda ya mean?"

"Well, for example, nowhere does your résumé include this."

Another document appeared on the screen, and Galdamiz's face bleached as white as the grubs he ground underfoot in his sunless mines.

It was a diploma.

"This appears to be a degree in computer science from the Marshall Institute on Styris IV with your name on it, Mr. Galdamiz. Why isn't it on your résumé? Or this?"

A new document appeared on the screen. "This is one of the reports from the former head of a Federation colony on Epcir Prime. It mentions you quite prominently. It's especially complimentary of your skills with computers. That *is* you in those documents, isn't it?"

"Yeah," Galdamiz replied softly.

"You're quite the multifaceted wonder, Mr. Galdamiz. But why don't you list your computer skills on your résumé?"

"I prefer workin' in mines. I don't put my computer skills down so I don't end up in the computer section," Galdamiz said.

"Understandable," Cogley said, nodding his agreement. "By the way, how are things going for you back home?"

"Objection. Relevance."

"Overruled," Carabatsos said. He had no idea where Cogley was going with his line of questioning, but he was sure that the lawyer knew, and Carabatsos was very interested in arriving at that destination.

"I don't understand."

"Well, do you recognize this?" Cogley asked as another document appeared on the screen. It was a dunning letter from a credit agency that threatened legal action if a payment on the account was not made soon.

"Or this?" Cogley asked as another dunning letter from a second credit agency appeared on the screen.

"Or *this?*" Cogley asked a third time, as a third dunning letter from yet another institution appeared on the screen.

"How are you gettin' these?"

"I take it from that answer you *do* recognize them. They are all letters from various credit agencies and banks seeking past-due payments, aren't they?"

"Yeah."

"So things aren't exactly rosy at home, are they? In fact, wouldn't it be accurate to say that you're in rather a significant amount of debt?"

"Yes," Galdamiz said, almost whimpering his response.

"You're facing the prospect of losing your house, your furniture, and several investment properties, would *that* be correct?"

"Yeah."

"So a little extra money wouldn't just be convenient for you right now. It would be practically essential?"

"Everyone needs extra money, Mr. Cogley."

"I guess that's a fair statement. I know I do. Books are so expensive, don't you know?" Cogley narrowed his eyes and locked them on Galdamiz's eyes. "What's important is how they earn it. I know how I earn *my* extra money, Mr. Galdamiz. How did you earn *yours?*"

"What . . . what extra money?"

"This money," Cogley said. As he did, the screen filled with a memo from the institution that had written the first dunning letter, indicating a payment of one thousand credits had been paid on the outstanding balance. "Or this money," he continued, as a thousand-credit payment memo from the second institution appeared on the screen. "And this money," Cogley said a third time, as a credit memo from the third institution appeared on the screen. "Where did that money come from, Mr. Galdamiz?"

"I dunno. Here and there. Odd jobs. I think we sold some stock."

"Stock sales are a matter of public record. If I were to subspace-radio your brokers, would I find any records of these sales?"

Cogley waited several seconds in silence, but Galdamiz didn't answer the question.

"Well maybe *I* can clear up this little mystery, Mr. Galdamiz. Do you remember testifying that you had no contact with the Klingons?"

"Yeah."

"Do you remember testifying that you didn't even know who Khogo was?"

"Yeah."

"By the way, Mr. Galdamiz, I notice you're being a little more reserved in your manner of speaking."

"Huh?"

"Your puns, Mr. Galdamiz, your puns. Where are those puns that you find so entertaining? You know, puns like 'Abstinence makes the heart grow fonder'?"

Galdamiz buried his face in his right hand.

"Oh, that's right, you didn't say that, did you? Khogo made that statement. But we all know the real saying isn't 'Abstinence makes the heart grow fonder.' The saying is '*Absence* makes the heart grow fonder,' isn't it?"

There was no answer.

"My problem is, 'Abstinence makes the heart grow fonder' is a marvelous pun, Mr. Galdamiz. One worthy of you at your best. But if you didn't have any contact with Khogo, and Khogo testified that he had as little contact with humans as possible, then where did Khogo hear the phrase 'Abstinence makes the heart grow fonder'? Can you tell me that, Mr. Galdamiz?"

"Objection!" Areel Shaw cried.

"Overruled."

Cogley went on. "Unless he heard it from you, and the two of you are lying. But why would you lie about having met Khogo?"

More silence filled the room.

"It's because you and Khogo met regularly, isn't it? Met when you supplied him with the information he needed and he gave you the money you so desperately needed. The money you used to make those payments. Isn't that the reason, Mr. Galdamiz? Aren't you the spy that Khogo hired to infiltrate Serenity for him?"

Shaw stood up. "Objection! Your honor, Mr. Cogley is badgering the witness."

Carabastos nodded in reply. "Sustained. Mr. Cogley, that's enough. Mr. Galdamiz, please answer Mr. Cogley's question."

Galdamiz looked up, and for the first time Cogley realized that the miner hadn't just buried his face into his hand, he had been crying.

As the tears streamed down Galdamiz's face, he stammered. "I decline . . . to answer . . . on the grounds it may incrim . . . incriminate me."

"Thank you, Mr. Galdamiz. I think you *have* answered my question," Cogley said. Then he turned to Carabatsos and added, "Your Honor, I have no objection to the lunch break now."

25. Then all hell broke loose.

It may have been the lunch hour, but few were eating. Based on information supplied to them by Peter Lawrence, Louis Alexander, Grigoriy Nemov, and Areel Shaw—with the able assistance of various operatives of Starfleet security from around the sector—were all busy checking on the activities of Homero Galdamiz. When court reconvened that afternoon, well after any normal lunch hour would have ended, a very embarrassed Areel Shaw addressed the court outside the presence of the jury.

"Your Honor, the United Federation of Planets wishes to congratulate and thank Mr. Cogley for the service he performed this morning. During our recess, agencies throughout the Federation, as well as Mr. Alexander's forces here on Aneher, have looked into the recent activities of Homero Galdamiz. Ms. LaSalle and Mr. Iino located several backdoor programs in the colony's computer system, which they traced back to Mr. Galdamiz. And Federation operatives have found both suspicious deposits into Mr. Galdamiz's financial accounts and numerous other irregularities.

"Mr. Galdamiz was arrested an hour ago. He has confessed to being a spy for the Klingons but refuses to say anything more until his lawyer can work out a deal for him. He wanted to know if *you* would represent him, Mr. Cogley."

Cogley laughed. Galdamiz had moxie, Cogley had to give him that. But it was all Cogley would be giving him. "No," he answered, and no one was surprised by the answer. "There's a little matter of a conflict of interests and a bigger matter of *lack* of interest."

"Anyway, that's the current situation, Your Honor. Obviously, the jury will need to be examined to determine whether this turn of events will have any effect—"

"I disagree, Your Honor. Questioning the jury at this time is pointless. Continuing with this trial at this time is pointless."

"What?" Areel Shaw practically screamed the question. It was the first time Cogley could ever remember seeing her that close to losing control.

"We've already had two witnesses in the trial—Homero Galdamiz and Khogo—perjure themselves. That's enough to taint this trial. But there's an even bigger taint. Mr. Galdamiz's actions raise a more serious problem. He must have feared Daniel Latham was getting close to him, so he killed Latham and framed Mak'Tor."

"If he did that, why would he leave a file identifying a Klingon spy on Latham's computer?"

"He didn't. He deleted it, just as you thought Mak'Tor had."

"How could he have deleted it? Chiaki Iino testified that the file was deleted only one minute before the three of them entered Latham's office. When the file was deleted, Galdamiz was with Iino and Nemov. He *couldn't* have deleted it."

"I don't know much about computers, Ms. Shaw, but even I know how to give a computer a delayed command, tell it to do something a minute or an hour from now. Mr. Iino has such a command built into the Serenity computers to do a daily diagnostic scan. All Mr. Galdamiz needed to do was tell the computer to delete the file at a time when he knew he'd be with someone else and Mak'-Tor would be in the office, giving him an alibi and framing my client."

"Your Honor, that's just speculation."

"The same might be said for your circumstantial case, Ms. Shaw."

"Nevertheless, Mr. Cogley," Carabatsos said, "I'm not inclined to grant your motion. We will examine the jury to make sure that it hasn't been tainted by today's events. And you may certainly make your argument to the jury at the proper time, but I think the prosecution's case should go forward."

"Thank you, Your Honor."

"Then, in the alternative, Your Honor, I move to strike the report that Daniel Latham allegedly wrote."

"What?" Areel said again, coming even closer to losing her composure.

"The thing is full of transcription errors and was stored on a computer whose memory core was corrupted by backdoor spy programs. There's no telling who may have learned about the back door and used it to access that file. Hell, the entire thing could have been planted in Latham's computer to make it look like Mak'Tor had a motive for killing Daniel Latham."

"Your Honor, that is the most ridiculous argument I've ever heard," Areel said in response.

"Ridiculous? How so? It's not as if you have an expert witness who can testify that it was written in Daniel Latham's style."

Areel Shaw's face brightened as a broad smile spread over it.

"As a matter of fact, Mr. Cogley, I do."

"Ladies and gentlemen of the jury, I apologize that we were late in reconvening this afternoon," Judge Carabatsos said to both the jury and the spectators in the back of the courtroom. "As you might have gathered from the questions we asked you, it's been an event-filled afternoon. I thank you for the honesty of your answers and apologize for any inconvenience or discomfort it may have caused you.

"As you can see, however, we're ready to proceed now, and Ms. Shaw's first witness is already on the witness stand." Carabatsos turned to the witness and said, "Mrs. Latham, I remind you you're still under oath."

"Mrs. Latham, how long did you know Daniel Latham?" Areel asked her witness.

"We were married for twenty-two years. I met him three years before that. So twenty-five years."

"Twenty-five years. And in those twenty-five years, did you have occasion to read things Daniel Latham had read?"

"Many, many occasions. Even before we were married, Daniel sent me handwritten love letters. After that, I used to proofread his speeches and reports. I read almost everything that he wrote."

"Would you consider yourself an expert on Daniel Latham's writing style?"

Areel knew she was taking a shortcut laying the foundation she needed to qualify Helen Latham as an expert. But she wanted this pointless exercise to end. Maybe this was enough to satisfy the court. To her delight, Cogley did not object to the question.

"Yes."

"Your Honor, I move that Mrs. Latham be recognized as an expert on the matter of Daniel Latham's writing style."

"No objection."

Areel looked back at Cogley. She wasn't sure what he was up to, but it was too late to turn back now.

"You were in court when Mr. Iino read the report that is purported to have been written by your late husband, and during the break I gave you a copy of the same report. Did you read it?"

"Yes, the one accusing the Klingons of smuggling replacement miners and notifying the Federation that Serenity had a spy. I just can't believe Homero would do that."

"Mrs. Latham, in your expert opinion, did Daniel Latham write that report?"

"Yes."

"Is there any doubt in your mind that your late husband wrote that report?"

"None whatsoever. It has Daniel in every word."

"No further questions."

Cogley rose and started to question her while he was still behind the defense table, making it look as if this were a trivial matter, one not even worth approaching the jury over.

"Mrs. Latham, you claim to be an expert on the writing style of Daniel Latham?"

"Yes."

"When was the last time you actually read anything written by your husband?"

"I read Daniel's writings almost every day."

"So you'd recognize other things your husband wrote and would be able to identify them?"

"Yes."

"Let's see." Cogley nodded to Jackie, and one of the journal entries from the book Helen Latham had given Cogley appeared on the screen. Cogley walked over to the screen and pointed to the document.

"Read that, Mrs Latham, and tell me, in your expert opinion, whether Daniel Latham wrote it."

Helen Latham read the viewscreen.

"Yes. I believe he did."

"Then how about this?" Cogley asked as another entry Cogley had chosen from the same journal book appeared on the screen.

"Again, yes."

"And this one?"

A third document appeared on the screen, one Cogley himself had written in a close approximation of Latham's style.

"No. Daniel didn't write that. It reads more like something you might have written, Mr. Cogley."

Cogley waited for the current of laughter that ran through the courtroom to die down. "And this one? Did Daniel Latham write this document?"

Helen Latham read over the document:

Personal Journal of Daniel Latham: December 13, 2267

It's over.

Twenty-two years now over, sloughed away like the skin of a Bastrikian coiler, dead and unwanted.

I find so many thoughts and conflicting emotions coursing through me, but mostly anger and surprise. Not anger at learning that Helen and Grig have betrayed me like some latter-day Lancelot and Guenevere. I've more than suspected what they were doing— been sure of it—for far too long to be surprised by their infidelities. So long, in fact, that the first emotion I had after Helen practically admitted what she had done was relief. My anger and surprise are at myself, at what I wanted in the aftermath of our last argument, not at what Helen did.

When Helen hit me, I felt anger. Rage. Hatred. I wanted to hit her. And when she pulled the phaser on me, I actually called her a "bitch." I don't know who the man in my study was tonight, but it wasn't me. I don't swear— there are far too many better ways to express yourself than common curse words.

I'll never be able to forgive Helen for what she did tonight. Ultimately, it wasn't her unfaithfulness or her shrewish behavior or self-centered indulgences that drove her away from me. It wasn't even that she hit me. But after she hit me, she filled me with so much rage I wanted to hit her back. No, I can never forgive Helen for the fact that she made me want *to hit another person.*

When she finished reading the journal entry, her face went white, then a look of hatred came over it, a look she launched at Cogley. But she was trapped. Daniel Latham had written it. She knew it and she knew that Cogley knew it. If she said no, he would be able to question her opinions. She knew she had to identify it.

"Yes, Daniel wrote that."

"What does it purport to be, Mrs. Latham?"

"Daniel kept a journal. This appears to be the final entry in his journal, written the night he died."

"And you're sure Daniel Latham wrote it?"

"Yes."

"According to this, you and Daniel Latham weren't very happy in those final days of your marriage. You appear to have quarreled violently, and he accused you of having an affair with Grigoriy Nemov."

"It isn't true. Grig and I weren't having an affair."

"No? Well, maybe your husband didn't know you as well as he thought he did. But the same might be said of you. How well did you know your husband?"

"As well as I know anyone."

"How is it that you could claim to know your husband well and yet know so little of his habits?"

"I don't know what you mean."

"Do you remember when I came to your house yesterday?"

"Yes."

"Do you remember my comment that your husband's books had no dog-ears or cracked spines?"

"Yes. I didn't know what a dog-ear was, so you explained it to me. A dog-ear is from folding the corner of a page down to mark your place. You told me no true book collector would ever do it."

"And after I explained it to you, do you remember

telling me that I wouldn't find a dog-ear in the whole collection, because your husband was very careful about his books?"

"Yes."

"But didn't you also tell me that your husband used to write in his books?"

"Yes, his journals," Helen said, and gestured toward the viewscreen.

"Not his journals, Mrs. Latham. He kept his journals in his desk drawers, didn't he?"

"Yes."

"Do you remember telling me that sometimes you'd find Daniel writing in a book that he'd put back on his book-shelf?"

"Yes."

"In fact, only this morning you testified as follows."

Jackie pressed her comm unit, and Helen Latham's voice came out of it. *"Whatever he was working on, he hadn't finished it yet, because he was writing in that book of his when I came in. He put the book away as soon as I entered, closed it up, and slipped it onto the bookshelf right behind him, but I'm afraid I just lost my temper with him."*

"Do you remember saying that, Mrs. Latham?"

"Yes."

"Your Honor, I object. This is going very far from direct examination."

"Overruled. You qualified Mrs. Latham as an expert, Ms. Shaw. Mr. Cogley should be allowed to test her expertise."

"Did you testify to that this morning?"

"Yes."

"So you, who claim to know your husband's habits well, maintain that he wrote things in a book he kept on the bookshelf directly behind his desk?"

"Yes."

"Do you remember my looking at the books on that shelf, Mrs. Latham, the ones you said your husband had been writing in?"

"Yes."

"Do you remember my telling you what the books were?"

"Yes. I believe it was a bound and numbered set of the works of Charles Dickens. A matched set."

"Exactly. Now, do you have any idea how much those books are worth?"

"No. I imagine you do."

"Would it surprise you to learn that set cost seven thousand credits?"

"No. Money was no object to Daniel when it came to his books."

"So you want this jury to believe that a man who didn't even dog-ear his books would write notes in a volume from a seven-thousand credit matched set of Dickens?"

"I can only tell you what I saw, Mr. Cogley. Daniel most definitely *did* write in one of those books."

"Yes, so *you* say."

"Objection."

"Withdrawn. Mrs. Latham, do you still claim that your husband wrote this document?" Cogley asked, pointing to the final journal entry still displayed on the viewscreen.

"Yes."

"And you're sure of that?"

"Yes."

"As sure as you are that he wrote *this* document?" The report Iino found on Latham's computer appeared on the viewscreen next to the journal entry.

"Yes."

"Do you see my problem, Mrs. Latham, why it's difficult to believe Daniel Latham wrote both? Do you see the line right there?" Cogley said pointing at a line in the journal entry.

"Yes."

"Please read it."

" 'And when she pulled the phaser on me, I actually called her a "bitch." I don't know who the man in my study was tonight, but it wasn't me. I don't swear—there are far too many better ways to express yourself than common curse words.' "

"Now read this line," Cogley said, pointing at the report.

" 'The bastards are cheating.' "

"Excellent, Mrs. Latham. Now please read this line," Cogley said, pointing to another line of the journal entry.

" 'You need to get Federation and Starfleet security on this ASAP. We've got to stop the bastards before someone dies!' "

"And you maintain that the same man who prided himself on not swearing wrote a report calling the Klingons 'bastards'?"

"Yes. I mean, who else could have written it?"

"How about someone who's an expert on her husband's writing style, such as yourself?"

"Why would *I* write such a report?"

"To frame Mak'Tor. To make it look as if he had a motive for killing your husband."

"That's ridiculous. I did no such thing."

"Can you prove you didn't write it, Mrs. Latham? Can you *prove* it?"

"How would I go about proving it?"

"That's not my concern. Although I suppose it's too bad for you that you can't find the first draft of that report?"

"First draft?"

"Yes. If your husband wrote it, he would have written the first draft by hand. It's a shame we can't find that first draft, in his own handwriting, so we could prove that he wrote it, isn't it?"

"I suppose."

"But we'll never find that draft, will we? Because it doesn't exist. Because your husband didn't write that report, you did."

"No."

"Mrs. Latham, didn't you hate your husband?"

"No."

"Didn't you blame him for the death of your daughter?"

"No."

"Didn't you hate the way he dragged you to these backward colony worlds and away from the high society you'd rather enjoy?"

"No."

"Isn't that why you had an affair with Grigoriy Nemov?"

"No."

"Isn't what why you killed your husband?"

"*What?* No. I didn't kill Daniel."

"But you did, Mrs. Latham, and I can prove it."

Cogley nodded to Jackie, who pressed her touchpad. On the viewscreen in the middle of the courtroom, a still from the recordings Louis Alexander had made with his tricorder appeared. A still of Daniel Latham's study.

"Do you recognize this, Mrs. Latham?" Cogley asked.

"It's my husband's study at home."

"And what's that object sitting on his desk" Cogley asked, pointing to the screen.

"It's a picture of our daughter, Katherine."

"*This* picture?" Cogley walked back to the defense table and pulled a teak-framed picture of Katherine Latham from his briefcase.

"Yes. Did you take that from my house?"

"Borrowed it," Cogley said, as he walked to the witness stand and placed the picture on the table next to it, where Helen could see it. "With the cooperation of Mr. Alexander and after Judge Carabatsos signed a search warrant. Is this the picture of your daughter you were talking about?"

"Yes."

Cogley walked back to the viewscreen and pointed to its display. "And it was sitting here on your husband's desk in your house?"

"Yes."

"Yesterday you told me it was your favorite picture of Katherine, didn't you?"

"Yes."

"Now then, Mrs. Latham, what's this?" Cogley asked, pointing to the viewscreen, which had changed its display to that of a different still from the scans Alexander had made. This one showed a different room.

"It's Daniel's office in City Hall."

"And what's this object?" Cogley asked, pointing to a dark square on the desk.

Helen Latham's eyes opened wide, and a look of worry came over her face. "It's . . . it's a picture of me, that Daniel had on his desk in his office."

"This picture?" Cogley asked after he walked back to the defense table and pulled the picture of Helen Latham from his briefcase. Even as Helen said, "Yes," softly, Cogley walked to the witness stand and put the second picture down next to the first. He turned the pictures on the table, so that they faced the jury box. Then he walked back to the viewscreen and pointed to it again. "And what is this object?" The screen had changed back to the display of Latham's home study, and Cogley pointed to another object that sat on the desk.

"A picture of Daniel, Katherine, and me."

"This picture?" Cogley said, walking back to the defense table and taking a third picture from his briefcase.

"Yes."

Cogley walked back to the witness stand and picked up the first two pictures, holding the one of Katherine in his right hand and the one of Helen in his left. "Now these two pictures, the one of you and the one of Katherine, match, don't they?" As he asked the question, he held the pictures up so that the jury could see what he was talking about.

"I don't know what you mean."

"Let me clarify for you, then. These two pictures are

the same size and are in matching teak frames, isn't that correct?"

"Yes."

"And isn't it a fact that your husband only kept *one* picture, the one of the three of you, on the desk in his study? And he kept these two matching pictures of you and Katherine on the desk in his office? Isn't that true?"

"I . . ." Helen hesitated, unsure of how to answer the question.

"Before you answer, I should point out that I have several witnesses who are prepared to swear under oath that that's exactly where your husband kept these pictures."

"Yes, it's true," she said finally.

"You went to your husband's office that night, didn't you?"

"No."

"You went there and fought again?"

"No."

"You fought and you saw the phaser lying on his desk."

"No."

"And just like you did during that earlier fight, you picked up that phaser, set it on kill, and fired. Only this time the phaser was charged, and you shot and killed your husband, didn't you?"

"No."

"Then if you didn't go to your husband's office, how do you explain this picture moving from his office to your house? How did it get to your house if *you* didn't put it in the pocket of your overcoat and move it?"

"All right, yes, I did go to Daniel's office that night. I was mad at him for throwing me out of the house. I wanted that picture of Katherine. It way my favorite, and Daniel didn't deserve it. He got my baby killed. So I took it and left. But Daniel wasn't in the office yet. When I was there, the office was empty."

"You expect this jury to believe that?"

"I expect the jury to believe the truth, Mr. Cogley," Helen Latham said, and suddenly the trace of antebellum had left her voice.

"The truth is, you killed your husband."

"Objection!"

"Sustained."

Cogley held up a hand. "I'll rephrase. *Did* you kill your husband?"

"No. After I left his office, I was with friends at the Landing Day celebration. I can give you their names and you can check with them. Chiaki testified that Daniel sent me a message twenty minutes before he died and that the report was deleted from his computer only a minute before he died. When those things happened, I was with friends. They can verify it."

"You could have written the message, planted it in your husband's computer, and ordered it to send the message at a later time. And you could have forged the report, planted it, and ordered the computer to delete it later to give yourself an alibi."

"No, I didn't, Mr. Cogley."

"Can you prove it? Can you provide us with that written first draft that would prove your husband and not you wrote that report?"

"Objection. The burden of proof here is not on the witness."

"Sustained. The witness doesn't have to answer."

Helen Latham sat up straight in the witness stand and

smiled a wide, satisfied smile. "It's all right, Your Honor. You see, I can prove it. I couldn't have written that report. Remember, there were transcription errors. You pointed them out yourself. The transcription errors. That proves the report was written by hand and scanned into Daniel's computer. Only Daniel could have written that report. And that happened after I joined my friends.

"I couldn't have deleted the file. Only your client could have."

Helen Latham rose from the witness stand and walked down the courtroom, a haughty and superior sway highlighting her step. Samuel Cogley slumped forward, looking to all the world like a man who had gone head-to-head with a grizzly and had come out much the worse for the experience.

And as Judge Carabatsos adjourned court for the day, Areel Shaw displayed a smile even wider and more satisfied than the one Helen Latham wore.

26. The study in Daniel Latham's house was dark. But not as dark as the figure, dressed in black from head to toe, that moved through the shadows in the room.

The figure crossed the room without turning on the lights and went directly to the bookshelf behind Latham's desk. Only when the figure reached the shelf did it activate a small light attached to a housing around its wrist.

A thin beam, almost as thin as one of Latham's pens, sprang from the light and fell on the books on the shelf, the bound and numbered matching set of Dickens.

The figure pulled the books from the shelf one by one,

flipped through the pages, and returned them to the shelf. Only when the figure pulled out the final book in the set, *The Mystery of Edwin Drood,* and flipped through its pages, did a smile cross its lips.

The first half of the novel was like all other books, filled with the preposterous printed words that Latham loved so much. But the second half of the book had blank pages, pages covered in Latham's thin, scratchy scrawl, a scrawl the figure had seen so many times before.

Yes, this was it. Latham's secret book, where he hid the writings he didn't want anyone to find. Writings too secret even for his damn journals. The figure skipped to the end of the book and started moving through the pages backward until it reached the last page with writing on it. It played the light down on the page and started to read.

The report was there, exactly as Latham had written it, the beginning almost the same as what the figure had left on Latham's computer so it could be found and read in court. The part about the spy and the Klingon smuggling replacement miners into their colony. The part that gave that bastard Mak'Tor a motive.

But the rest of the report, the part the figure couldn't allow anyone to see, the part the figure had edited out of the report before saving it, that was here too.

The figure dropped the book on the floor and stomped on it once as a wave of satisfaction rose up. Then the figure pointed a phaser pistol, set to vaporize, at the book and fired.

The book disappeared in a blue-green glow.

Even as the figure disappeared in the yellow twinkling glow of a transporter beam . . .

*   *   *

. . . And rematerialized in the brightly lit courtroom.

It took a moment for the figure's eyes to adjust to the light. And in that moment, it heard Louis Alexander's voice command, "Drop the phaser. Or, better yet, do me a favor. *Don't* drop it. I'm begging you to give me an excuse to shoot your sorry ass."

The figure looked around. Alexander and several of his security guards, as well as some of the guards sent down by the *Enterprise,* were in the room, and all with phasers pointing and ready.

That son of a bitch Cogley was also in the courtroom, along with his two assistants, Areel Shaw, and Judge Carabatsos.

The phaser pistol fell from the figure's hand and hit the floor with a loud thud.

Almost at the same time the phaser struck the floor, the viewscreen in the courtroom flickered and showed a video of the figure moving through Latham's study, finding the hidden book, and destroying it.

"You're not very photogenic, you know that?" Cogley asked. "But I think enough of you showed in that video to ensure a conviction for Ms. Shaw, now that she's got the right defendant. Oh, and about that book . . ."

Cogley reached into his briefcase and pulled out an exact duplicate of the book the figure had destroyed. "Afraid it was as much a forgery as that report you doctored. You see, yesterday Louis Alexander told me about a transporter trick someone showed him when he was in Starfleet. How you could use transporters to duplicate things. Make replicas. So I had him make a copy of that book to use as bait. You destroyed the copy." Cogley waved the book he was holding in a triumphant arc. "This is the original.

"But what was in this report that made you commit murder?" Cogley started to read the report. "Certainly not what we saw in court. You had no problems with that part of the report. In fact, you left it to be found. Although you really shouldn't have indulged yourself and added the word 'bastards.' That was a mistake. Daniel Latham would never have written that. No, it's these opening paragraphs you wanted to destroy. The part that goes:

" 'I hope you're sitting down when you read this, Bill, because what I'm about to write next is going to shock you. Serenity isn't working. Not as presently constituted.

" 'The Federation offered too many incentives. It attracted too many people looking to get rich quick on the colony. The senior staff I have is uncooperative and belligerent. They don't see me as the leader of this colony as much as the obstacle standing between them and those riches.

" 'Serenity will never succeed with the staff we have now. I must reluctantly recommend that the Federation recall the entire senior staff and replace it. Myself included.

" 'I was responsible for picking this team. I missed all the signs. I'm as much to blame for this failure as anyone else. Maybe Helen is right. Maybe it is time for me to stop planet hopping and settle down and retire. Because I sure made a mess of this one.

" 'I'll await word from you and the Federation about what you want to do.

" 'Let me move on, then, to the other part of this communiqué, the regular status reports. First the good news.'

"Yes, I imagine that's what did it. That report is why you killed Daniel Latham," Cogley said as he closed the book and handed it back to Alexander. "Thanks, Lou," he said. Then he turned back to the figure and said, "I imagine you were in City Hall outside Latham's office and overheard Latham reading his report aloud as he edited it on his computer. And you knew you had to kill him. Then after you killed him, you deleted the beginning paragraphs about removing the senior staff and left the rest of the report, the part about the spy and the part about the smuggling. The parts that you hoped would make everyone believe Mak'Tor had a motive for killing Daniel Latham."

Cogley shook his head. "You know what the sad part is? I should have known it was you right away. The case should never have gone to trial. But it wasn't until the trial, until I heard the report, that I started putting the pieces together. Once I heard the report, I realized who *couldn't* have killed Daniel Latham. Then, when Ms. Shaw looked over her shoulder at the clock, I realized something else, something that had been bothering me from the start. Something I should have remembered."

Cogley looked the figure directly in the eye and smiled. It was very big and very satisfying. "And that's when I knew *you* were the murderer."

From across the room, Grigoriy Nemov snarled at Cogley.

27. "Ultimately, Nemov showed less gumption than Galdamiz did," Louis Alexander said as he spooned another helping of jam onto his toast.

The celebration breakfast for Cogley, Jackie, Lawrence,

and Alexander was in full swing. They were celebrating both proving who had killed Daniel Latham and the offer that the Federation had made to Cogley. The Federation was a widespread organization, covering much of the galaxy. The Federation wanted to know whether Cogley would consider serving as a type of legal ombudsman, who the Federation could send to its many planets to handle legal affairs for its citizens. Cogley said that he might be interested, "as long as the cases, themselves, are interesting."

They had invited Mak'Tor to the breakfast, but he declined. He said he had too many duties as leader of the Klingon colony that needed his personal attention. "There may be cause for celebration," Mak'Tor had explained, "but I will be too busy correcting the mess that I am confident Khogo has left behind."

Areel Shaw also declined. She explained that she, too, was busy. She had to make arrangements with the Federation to prosecute Nemov. Arrangements that included bringing the new prosecutor on the case up to warp. She had begged off handling the new case, having had more than enough of Aneher II.

So it was Cogley, Jackie, Lawrence, and Alexander who were dining on Serenity's finest. It wasn't haute cuisine, but it tasted wonderful.

"Homero may have admitted he was the spy," Alexander continued, "but at least he's holding out some other details about how the Klingons worked things until he can make a deal with the Federation. Figures they might go lenient on him if he's able to give them some inside info on the Klingons. Or, at least, help them embarrass the Klingons with the Organians.

"Grig, on the other hand . . . One night in jail and he cracked like an egg," Alexander said, and tapped his knife against the shell of his soft-boiled egg as a demonstration. "Told Peter and me everything. You pretty much had it pegged, Sam."

"He never loved Helen Latham?" Cogley asked.

"He wouldn't come right out and admit that, but I don't think so, no. Figured he could sweep her off her feet and get her to leave Daniel for him. Then, once he got all he figured he could get from her, he'd leave her for someone else who had something to offer.

"Even if that didn't work," Alexander went on, "he thought he had it covered. He hoped, at the very least, his affair with Helen would make things so uncomfortable for Daniel that he'd leave Serenity. And that would leave Nemov in charge. He'd have exploited the planet. Let Homero strip mine, maybe even sell off the mining rights for a fortune. Whatever would turn the quickest profit for him."

"Then Latham made things complicated for him by throwing Helen out," Lawrence said, "and Nemov wasn't sure where he stood. So he went to Latham's office that night to have it out with him about Helen. But when he was outside the door, he heard Daniel working on that report of his, reading it into the computer while he made the corrections. And Nemov lost it."

"I can imagine," Cogley said. "If that report had gone through, there would be no strip mining. No fortune. Our Mr. Nemov would have been out in the cold. Ironic, considering the surroundings."

"According to Nemov, he started screaming at Latham," Alexander said, "and all Latham did in response was mock him. That only made him madder. He saw the phaser on the desk and shot Latham with it. I'll give him credit, though, he didn't panic."

"No," Cogley agreed. "He remembered Mak'Tor was coming for a meeting and immediately planned to frame him."

"Staged the fight, doctored the report, and ordered the computer to delete it at a time he knew Mak'Tor would be in the office. Then he went out, gathered up a few other people, and came back to the office, so he could 'find' Mak'Tor there with Daniel's body."

"He even caught a break there," Lawrence said. "Galdamiz told us that he came to Latham's office that night to have it out with him and found him dead. Must have gotten there just after Nemov left and before Mak'Tor arrived. He also remembered Mak'Tor was coming and had the same idea as Nemov. He went out to get some people to bring back to the office with him, where they could find Mak'Tor and Latham's body. So both Nemov and Galdamiz were trying to get the others to go back to Daniel's office, which made things much easier for the two of them."

"But what put you on to him, Sam?" Alexander asked.

"Jackie gave me my first clue."

"Jackie?"

"Yes. I referred to this as 'The Case of the Colonist's Corpse,' which got Sam to start thinking, why was there a corpse in the first place?"

"Why was there a corpse? Hell, when you have a murder, you have a corpse."

"Not necessarily, Lou," Cogley said. "That's what the problem was. Look, pretend you're Mak'Tor and you've just killed Daniel Latham with a phaser. What are you going to do? Would you, of all things, kneel over the body where both you and it could be found? Wouldn't it make more sense to set the phaser on dematerialize and vaporize the body? That way, if anyone came into the office, you could claim you were there to meet with Latham, but he never showed up. By the time anyone figured out what had happened, you could be safely back in the Klingon colony.

"No, the only way finding a body made sense was if someone *wanted* the body to be found. And *that* only made sense if someone was trying to frame Mak'Tor. So the fact that there even was a corpse made me sure Mak'-Tor wasn't the killer."

"I guess I retired from Starfleet too early," Alexander said. "I never thought of that."

"After that a couple of other things also convinced me that Mak'Tor was innocent. First, there was the fact that a phaser was used at all. A Klingon warrior gets into a fight with a fifty-eight-year-old man and shoots him with a phaser rather than just beating him to death? It didn't make sense. Then there was the fact that Mak'Tor was found kneeling over the body. A Klingon who's just shot a man to death would be expecting trouble at any second. He wouldn't kneel. He'd crouch, so that he could spring into an attack more easily. If Mak'Tor was kneeling, it's because he didn't shoot Latham and wasn't expecting trouble."

"Okay, then what about the report? You told Nemov that once you heard the report you knew who didn't kill Latham. How'd you work that little piece of magic?"

"Same principle, actually. Who would want the report

to be found? Not Mak'Tor. But if he didn't want that report found, wouldn't it make more sense to vaporize the computer with the phaser, rather than to delete that file and then leave the computer around so that someone might be able to recover the file?"

"Yeah."

"So, that meant the computer with the damning report was left behind to be found, because someone *wanted* it to be found. But again, who would want that report found? Khogo? No. Galdamiz? He might have left the report to be found, but he would have deleted all mention of the spy first. Iino was a possibility, but I didn't think so. He told me he and Ron Sayger were leaving Serenity as soon as Sayger was released, and I believed him. He wants to put the whole of Serenity behind him. I just didn't think he would have cared enough about any of it to kill Latham, arrange for the report to be found, and frame Mak'Tor. So that left only Helen Latham and Nemov."

"Why only them? Why not anyone else in the colony?"

"Because Khogo, Galdamiz, Iino, Helen Latham, and Nemov were the only people who knew Mak'Tor was going to be in Latham's office that night. You can't arrange to frame a person unless you know in advance that the person is going to be where you need him to be to make the frame work."

"Okay, so it was either Helen or Nemov. Why not Helen?"

"Helen didn't know that Mak'Tor wouldn't bring his disruptor to Latham's office. She wouldn't have planned a frame involving a phaser unless she knew Mak'Tor wouldn't have his disruptor, because it wouldn't make sense for Mak'Tor to use a phaser when he had his disruptor."

"So, what did you mean when you told Nemov you should have known it was him all along and it was Areel Shaw's looking at the clock that convinced you?"

"Ms. Shaw checked the clock by looking at it over her shoulder. She didn't turn toward it, she just looked over her shoulder at it."

"So?"

"So Nemov, Galdamiz, and Iino *all* said that when they came into Latham's office, Mak'Tor was kneeling over the body with his back to them. Then he looked over his shoulder at them and snarled. He didn't turn toward them, he looked over his shoulder at them."

"Right," Alexander said, starting to understand, "a Klingon who had a phaser in his hand would have turned his body toward them to aim the phaser at them."

"Exactly."

"And that meant Mak'Tor didn't have a phaser in his hand, so how did Nemov know he had a phaser to shout his warning?"

"Correct. But even if Mak'Tor did have the phaser in his hand, Nemov still couldn't have known it was there. Mak'Tor was kneeling in front of Latham's body with his back to the door where they were standing. Galdamiz told me from where they were standing, they couldn't see Latham's chest or face. And Mak'Tor told me he was checking Latham's neck for a pulse. So even if Mak'Tor did have the phaser in one hand and was checking the pulse with the other, his back would have blocked Nemov's line of sight. Nemov couldn't have seen the phaser in Mak'Tor's hand or the phaser wound in

Latham's chest, so he couldn't have known there was a phaser unless he put it there to frame Mak'Tor."

"But if he couldn't see the phaser, why did he say he could?"

"Because he knew it was there, where Mak'Tor could grab it and shoot. He wanted the others to shoot Mak'Tor before Mak'Tor had a chance to pick the phaser up and use it."

Areel Shaw sat in the empty room that had been the courtroom and stared sullenly at the floor. She had tuned out the world to be with her own thoughts, so she didn't hear the other person enter the room until he spoke.

"Brooding, Areel?"

Areel shook, startled by the voice. She turned and was even more surprised to see James Kirk standing in front of her.

"Jim! Are you here to take the others back to Earth?"

"Yes. But I understand you're not coming with us?"

"No. I have to stay here until the new prosecutor who's going to handle Nemov's trial arrives. I'm supposed to fill him in."

"You're not going to prosecute Nemov?"

"No, I just want to get off this dust ball as soon as possible."

"You seem bitter. An innocent man was saved. Justice was served."

"I know. But this was going to be the case where I beat Samuel Cogley. Where I finally silenced all the office jokes. Now I'm going to be known as the prosecutor who couldn't even get a Klingon found guilty. I just . . ."

Areel shook her head in frustration and walked out of

the room, leaving Kirk alone. He was reminded of the resentment and intensity he had sensed in Areel back on board the *Enterprise* and realized he sensed the same thing from her now. Only this time it was stronger, darker. Disturbing.

Cogley was in his room at the boardinghouse, packing up his law books, looking at each of them as he put them into the crate, studying their covers and wondering if it was all worthwhile. Yes, he had won his case. Justice had been served. The truth had come out. But at what cost for himself? Or for Helen Latham?

He wasn't proud of what he had done: browbeating Helen on the witness stand with accusations he knew were false. But it was the only thing he could think of to do. When he saw Areel look at the clock—when he realized Nemov was the murderer—it had opened his mental floodgates. Other things he should have realized earlier came rushing in.

Helen had said that she'd seen Latham writing in one of his matched Dickens books. But Latham wouldn't do that. No book collector would write in a priceless volume of a matched set. Not unless it wasn't a real Dickensian collector's item but a dummy volume with blank pages designed to be written in.

He wondered why Latham would make such a book. Why make a fake Dickens volume for writing in? That's when another thought occurred to him. What if Latham kept a secret journal as well as his more public one? A volume where he wrote those things he wanted to be sure no one else saw.

What better place than the blank pages of a book no one

else would realize didn't exist? And what better place to hide a book than among other books? Bind this secret journal so that it looked like the other books on the shelf. Cogley had seen a volume of Edgar Allan Poe on Latham's bookshelf. He figured the "Purloined Letter" gambit would have appealed to Latham.

Then Cogley remembered the report Latham had written by hand and scanned in so that he could transfer it to his computer later. Why scan it? Why not bring that first draft and read it into the computer? And where was the original draft of the report Latham had been writing? It wasn't in any of his journal books. It wasn't in any of his wastebaskets. But he had to have a first draft somewhere that he had scanned into the computer. If there was a secret journal, the elusive first draft was there.

But where in Latham's study was it? Which of the many books would be the dummy containing the secret journal? And Cogley remembered *The Mystery of Edwin Drood*, Dickens's famous unfinished novel. Why had it been a part of the matched set in Daniel Latham's library? Most sets didn't include it. And why was it as thick as the other volumes in the set? Cogley had read *Drood* and knew its partial manuscript was less than half as long as any of Dickens's other novels. Cogley was sure he knew where the journal could be found.

He verified his suspicion on the lunch break. While everyone else was tracking down proof of Galdamiz's espionage, Cogley went to Daniel Latham's study and checked the volume of *Edwin Drood*. The secret writings were there, including the original draft.

After he read it and knew the real reason why Nemov had killed Daniel Latham, Cogley also realized that

Nemov would be desperate to make sure the secret journal was never discovered. If it were, his whole reason for killing Latham ceased to be. All he had to do was to let Nemov know it existed. The idea of exploiting Helen Latham came to him fully formed.

Cross-examine her about Latham's writing. Ask her about the times she saw Latham writing in one of the Dickens books. Point out to her how unlikely that was, because a book lover such as Daniel Latham would never deface a book by writing in it. Drop suggestions that there must be a handwritten first draft of the report somewhere and hope Nemov picked up on the hints. He even accused Helen Latham falsely of murdering her husband, to put Nemov off his guard, make him think Cogley suspected someone else.

It was the best plan he could devise on such short notice. And it had worked. Justice had been served. But at what cost?

He made it up to her as best he could by offering to buy Daniel's library. She accepted when she saw that he was offering more than top dollar. Oh, there were some books there he wanted. That Dickens set, primarily. But acquisition wasn't his main reason for buying the books.

"Conscience money, Mr. Cogley?" Helen Latham asked him when he gave her the money and Cogley noticed the Southern belle air had returned. He didn't answer her. What could he say other than yes? Conscience money and the fact that money was the only thing she had left from her marriage to Daniel, the only thing she would remember him by. So he figured she might as well have as much of it as possible, so that at least her memories of a good man would be pleasant.

"Were you planning to leave without saying good-bye?" Mak'Tor asked when he finally tired of waiting in the doorway for Cogley to see him.

Cogley looked up and smiled at his client. Mak'Tor's freedom was the justice that had been served. Cogley hoped they all made the most of it.

"No. We're not leaving until tomorrow. I was going to look for you later."

"I thought you would like to know I've sent Khogo back to Qo'noS for his part in the spying and the smuggling. It was as you suggested. He was trying to create problems between Daniel Latham and me, hoping we would quarrel. He planned to use that as a sign of my ineffectiveness and have me replaced by himself.

"He has, instead, disgraced the Klingon Empire and dishonored himself. I sent him home, where he can wallow in that disgrace and dishonor."

Mak'Tor started to spit, to signify that he found even thinking of Khogo distasteful. Then he caught himself.

"I have resumed my duties as head of the Klingon colony," Mak'Tor said. "The task I have before me will not be easy. You and Daniel Latham have shown me that there are humans of honor, humans who could even be Klingons. I plan to honor Latham's memory by making Aneher II a place where humans and Klingons can live together. It may be hard to convince the High Council of this, but it is the right thing to do."

Mak'Tor walked to Cogley and held out his hand. "Good-bye, Samuel Cogley. If we meet again, let us hope it is under better circumstances."

Cogley took Mak'Tor's hand and returned the shake. "Good-bye."

"Will they prosecute Nemov for Daniel Latham's murder?" Mak'Tor asked.

"Yes."

"Good. I could have sought to have him tried in a Klingon court. His attempt to frame me was a violation of Klingon law. But I thought better of it. You have shown me that the aims of your people and of the Klingon Empire can be the same, justice with honor. Now I can show the Empire the same thing by showing them my trust in you and your system."

Cogley smiled. Perhaps they'd all make the most of it, at that.

STAR TREK
SECTION 31

BASHIR
Never heard of it.

SLOAN
We keep a low profile....
We search out and identify
potential dangers to the
Federation.

BASHIR
And Starfleet sanctions
what you're doing?

SLOAN
We're an autonomous
department.

BASHIR
Authorized by whom?

SLOAN
Section Thirty-One was
part of the original
Starfleet Charter.

BASHIR
That was two hundred years
ago. Are you telling me
you've been on your own
ever since? Without specific
orders? Accountable to
nobody but yourselves?

SLOAN
You make it sound so
ominous.

BASHIR
Isn't it?

No law. No conscience. No stopping them.

A four book series available wherever books are sold.

Excerpt adapted from *Star Trek:Deep Space Nine*® "Inquisition"
written by Bradley Thompson & David Weddle.

2161.01